Night of Tiny Suns

A novel

Night of Tiny Suns

Edward King

*Published in the UK in 2024 by Everything with Words Limited,
Fifth Floor, 30–31 Furnival Street, London EC4A 1JQ*

www.everythingwithwords.com

Text copyright © Edward King 2024
Cover © Holly Ovenden 2024

Edward King has asserted his right under the Copyright, Design and Patents Act 1988 to be identified as the author of this work.

This book is sold subject to the condition that it shall not, by way of trade or otherwise, be lent, resold, hired out, or otherwise circulated without the publisher's prior consent in any form of binding or cover other than that in which it is published and without a similar condition, including this condition, being imposed on the subsequent purchaser.

This novel is entirely a work of fiction. The names, characters, events are the work of the author's imagination. Any resemblance to actual persons, living or dead is entirely coincidental.

FSC
www.fsc.org
MIX
Paper | Supporting
responsible forestry
FSC® C171272

*Printed and bound in Great Britain by
CPI Group (UK) Ltd, Croydon CR0 4YY*

A CIP catalogue record for this book is available from the British Library.

ISBN 978-1-911427-42-1

They were the damned, the chosen, the infantry, looking down on the rest of the human race from their own unapproachable world.

      Alexander Baron, *From the City,*
           From the Plough

So this is how it is to be a man. Just him and his new brother. The sound of their dust-muffled footsteps under a low crescent moon. Allah's moon. Perhaps it will be a night like this when he takes a wife. Allah might reward him with just such a night.

In his hands were two old cooking oil containers packed with pungent powder. They tugged at his arms but the weight was reassuring, the gravity of their purpose. The Pakistani was a few paces ahead of him, encumbered only by a short-handled hoe and small sack. They shuffled up a narrow alley between high blank walls. It cut a dark furrow beneath a star-thronged sky, which loomed boldly above the familiar mud buildings. Within them were his many relations, asleep but soon to awaken. The sight of the unassuming dwellings, all he had known in his life, dulled his fear and sharpened his will. He was a man now. None of them knew this. Only his father, who had trusted him.

The alley opened onto a footpath running parallel to a deep ditch. They stopped to check their bearings. It had been cool when they set off and the boy regretted having wrapped the cotton shawl around his shoulders. His back was sweaty. The Pakistani had set a brisk pace. Crouching, he unwound it in one practised, fluid motion. Immediately the night air nipped at his damp neck. Sensing the Pakistani's indecision, he touched him lightly on the arm and indicated left across a small field – cousin Janan's field, neat rows of young wheat just visible against the grey soil. The Pakistani patted him in silent recognition and the boy flushed with pride.

They moved off again. Somewhere ahead a donkey brayed alarm. The hamlet beyond the next row of trees was in view of the foreigners' fort. Perhaps their night soldiers were waiting in the shadows. Their fat black glasses could see in the dark; at least that is what his brother Imran claimed. He had wanted to ask the Pakistani but was afraid to sound like a coward so he just lived with the burrowing uncertainty. Still in single file, they followed one of the narrow irrigation dykes across the field. The boy raised the two containers away from his body to keep his balance, feeling awkward in doing so. It was not the gait of a warrior.

The hamlet revealed itself through gaps between the trees, a pale uniform band of dried mud walls, twelve feet high. There was a footbridge made of logs and mud that led into it. This was their objective. The boy clicked his tongue lightly, pointing towards the bridge with his chin. He added emphasis by extending one of the containers. Stopping short by about fifty paces, they squatted down and waited, alert. The boy had explained to the Pakistani that maybe it was dangerous to venture into the hamlet because in the fort there was a camera perched atop its mast, vigilant like an eagle. If you can see the camera, the camera can see you. The Pakistani had been patient with him. 'Ah but it cannot see all directions all of the time young Mamur – and it will be dark.' Nevertheless, they did not pass beyond the trees.

Content they were alone, the Pakistani gestured and they moved off. Everybody knew that the foreigners no longer used the bridge. The children always laughed at them labouring through the stream, sodden and cursing, when there was a dry alternative so nearby. Sometimes the foreign soldiers placed ladders across and stepped gingerly from rung to rung, top heavy like donkeys en route to market with enormous sacks of maize balanced on their backs. One great pink oaf had crashed into the stream, scattering the gleeful children like startled birds, shrieking. The other soldiers had joined in the mirth, whooping and hollering in their strange tongue.

It was time to punish this habitual diversion either side of the bridge. Passing his sack and hoe to the boy, the Pakistani began feeling around to identify the fallen tree he had been told the soldiers used to clamber out. Half a pace further on was a slight hollow. The Pakistani took back the hoe and started digging. It was a precise and economical hole just big enough for one of the containers. The boy was impressed: clearly his companion was a veteran of many such forays. It reassured him. Reaching for the sack, the Pakistani noticed the boy's rapt attention.

'Don't look at me', he hissed, 'look out for the Americans.'

Shamed to have been upbraided by his mentor, the boy peered impotently into the gloom. He blunted the affront by imagining himself correcting the Pakistani: the foreigners here were British. Behind him the Pakistani laid an oblong piece of wood along the top of the container. It was wrapped in plastic and had two wires poking out from one end. One of these he connected dextrously to the container before sweeping the spoil back over the hole. Next he scraped a narrow channel with his fingers for one arm's length towards the field. The sound reminded the boy of his father's goats foraging around their compound in winter. Still he dared not look.

He wished he had a rifle. It would give his vigil some teeth. But the Pakistani had insisted it was pointless: 'better to blend with the farmers.' The boy had held his father's Kalashnikov a few times and knew how to operate it, even if he had never been allowed to fire it. When he proved himself, the Pakistani would take him over the mountains to Waziristan, to be trained. This was a promise. What tales he would tell of breaking bread among those wild, proud people who grew their hair long and kept their feuds even longer. There were Arab fighters there too. 'I will listen,' he vowed, 'like I did when serving tea to my grandfather.'

The battery was buried where the foreigners' metal detectors would not find it, a comfortable distance beyond the mine. But the Pakistani did not connect it yet. He clicked his tongue and the boy followed him a few paces along the stream to another obvious bypass. The process was repeated with slightly more haste. The Pakistani was more nervous than he appeared to the boy, knowing well the risks of working too long. From the pocket of his kameez he pulled out a small plastic torch and whispered for the boy to join him.

'We cannot get this wrong. Cup your hands around the light while I connect the batteries.'

They hunched over the second device, hearing one another breathe. The Pakistani's long hair tickled the boy's forehead. He could smell its grease.

Above them there was a sudden shrieking sound, like ripping canvas. They just had time to turn towards the sky.

'Bravo Zero Alpha, this is Banshee Three-Three. Two confirmed enemy KIA. Permission to terminate mission and return to base, over.'

The pilot's tinny voice clipped over the speaker. On the black and white screen above the major a pall of dust was drifting across the tree-line. Just visible on the thermal camera were the bright body parts of his victims. Sighing, he nodded to the ground controller who duly pressed the button on a transmitter and spoke into his headset.

'Roger, good work. Safe flight. Nice working with you. Out.'

Gul Khan opened his eyes as the thud reverberated up the valley. He had been dozing.

My boy Mamur!

The trapdoor opened in his stomach. He remained still, his wife slumbering immobile beside him under the blankets. Explosions were commonplace and this seemed distant. But he knew Mamur was with the Pakistani. Their bed was close to the packed earth floor of the mud dwelling: a thin mattress unrolled each night and covered with cushions. It was adjacent to a small fireplace burrowed into the floor, now just embers that cast a faint orange light across the interior, picking out the sequins on their wall hanging.

He stared at the cross-hatching of mud bricks in the arched ceiling. His mind was a bird in the orchard, flitting from branch to branch. If Mamur was placing mines then it was conceivable that one had been triggered accidentally. He knew this happened fairly often with inexperienced layers but the Pakistani was no novice. That didn't make sense. Most likely it was something entirely separate. The bang could have been a vehicle in the desert to the east; there were many mines on the dirt road to the city. It could be a large bomb much further north where he heard the Americans recently had launched a big incursion into the Movement's heartland. Maybe the British had trodden on another mine. They often patrolled at this time of night. He settled on that. Mamur had told him he would stay at the Wazirs' compound with the Pakistani. He had probably returned there hours ago. Yes, it must have been the British.

Gul Khan hid behind his eyelids for a time. Then a realisation: so why was there no helicopter? If the soldiers had trodden on a mine, the helicopter would arrive. They always came quickly. He could hear no helicopter. Maybe then they had found a mine and destroyed it. Deep down he knew he was behaving like the last panicked lamb driven to market: nosing every corner of the fold except the open gate.

The furious banging on his compound gates put an end to his delusion. His wife was roused ill-tempered and confused.

'What is it? What is that racket?'

'Nothing,' he lied, pulling on his kameez and stepping into worn plastic loafers at the door.

He was out before she could interrogate him further. Emerging from the fug of the room into the compound's courtyard, he paused while his eyesight adjusted. The moon had set below his high walls. He drew a shawl around himself and made straight for the tall metal gates. His animals were agitated, the dog most of all – a wolf-like beast straining on its thin rusty chain, baying with all its breath.

Gul Khan's younger cousin Janan was on the other side of the gates, breathless and clutching a torch.

'You must come Gul Khan; I think it is Mamur.'

'You think? What does that mean?'

Janan could not look at him, even in the darkness. Instead he led off, almost at a run. The weak torch beam flicked from side to side across a sandy track. Little puffs of dust occasionally reached forward into the pool of light, kicked up by Janan's hurried steps. On the horizon to their right, Gul Khan noticed that dawn had lifted night's blanket by a crack as if to check all was well before throwing it back.

Hope refused to shed the disguise of reason. It must be the Pakistani; Mamur was simply the guide. He would have been held back at a safe distance. Yes, it is the Pakistani they have found. Why then did Mamur not hurry home? Because he has hidden the mine components and does not want to associate his home with an act of war. *Brave Mamur. Well done.* There was the time when his neighbour came to collect a debt and Mamur had herded the largest of their sheep in with the women. He was quick with his wits.

But not only was hope a suspect actor, anguish heckled the performance. If Mamur was injured, Janan would have said so.

His eldest son... and all for twenty dollars. What choice did he have? The Haji had soft hands but they throttled all the same.

He felt a powerful urge to urinate. Calling out to Janan, he moved to one side of the track and fumbled to release himself. Hitching the long kameez and untying the drawstring on his shalwar,* he squatted down. Janan was pacing around impatiently. Gul Khan turned his back on him, bashful even in the dark. At first it would not come. Perhaps this impulse had been just a way to delay the inevitable, an excuse to move slower and savour the fantasy – however remote or futile – that Mamur was spared. The urine flowed heavily. It sounded like one of his animals, spattering on the dust. He stood, empty.

Taking that as his signal to continue, Janan strode on. Gul Khan was forced to tie his kameez on the move. He had not shaken himself properly and urine trickled warm down his thigh. They hurried along the canal, past the mosque. It was deserted even though first prayer was due very soon. Piety and superstition were unleashed. 'I have not been prayerful but my boy has,' he entreated under his breath. 'What has he done to be punished? I am the one being punished.' All the little slights and tricks against his kin eddied to the surface. Even the pleasures he had taken from younger boys during the years before his marriage, when unfulfilled desires burned in him. 'Spare my son and I will do anything you ask.'

They pushed into the alley between two large compounds just as Mamur had done earlier that night. Somewhere in the neighbouring village a muezzin chanted his recitations. Gul Khan knew he had neglected his obligations: *Woe to the worshippers who are unmindful of their prayer; those who delay their prayer.*** It was one of the few Quranic verses he knew how to form on paper, yet he had never managed to inscribe it on his heart.

---

*   **Shalwar Kameez**, long knee-length cotton shirt (kameez) and baggy pyjama bottoms (shalwar) ubiquitous to South Asia.

**   Quran 107:4–5.

Entering Janan's field, torch beams played in the trees beyond, figures bustling among them. As they drew near, Gul Khan could discern two men trying to drag something heavy from the irrigation ditch. They were tugging at it and exhorting each other to greater effort. One sounded like Janan's brother-in-law. Neither of them seemed willing to get into the ditch. Gul Khan stopped and tried to compose himself. Sensing this, Janan spoke for the first time since the gates, extending a beckoning arm.

'Peace be upon him, cousin. That is the Pakistani. Mamur we have already gathered. Come.'

Half a dozen men were standing around a bundle on the ground, about fifteen paces from the footbridge leading into the hamlet of Kasim Kalay. Gul Khan could see the Mullah in his white turban. Everything was filtered blue-grey, torches increasingly redundant in the steadily improving light. His breathing refused to conform, at once tight and shallow, then like the bellows of a blacksmith. These were the last few steps with Mamur in his life.

Foolishly, he had imagined a shroud like his father's. All the years of war should have prepared him for the truth of these things.

Those with their backs to him turned in unison, expressionless behind their dark beards. They deferred to the Mullah, who embraced Gul Khan and muttered his condolences.

'May the peace of Allah be upon you dear friend. And may He grant you the forbearance to accept the pain of this separation from your son, and extend to his departed soul the hand of paradise.'

The soft words glanced off his shocked stiffness, like

autumn leaves hitting a branch on their way down to the ground. 'May *you* take the goodness, Mullah Sahib.'*

A numbed serenity befell him. Stepping between them, he knelt down and drew back a corner of the blanket they had used to cover Mamur. It was not his son. Not anymore. Once it had been: his little round cap was the only recognisable piece of clothing. They must have found it in the field. There was no sign of his head. A leg, scarred with innumerable abrasions, still had its foot; too small to be the Pakistani's. Gul Khan put out his hand. The foot felt tough and dusty, like the bald parts of an ox. How could that be the foot he tickled when Mamur was a child, kicking and writhing?

Someone rested a hand on his shoulder. Gul Khan looked up. It was Janan, standing over him. The aspect was symbolic: though younger he had always been the taller of the two when they were growing up; the more measured.

'I'll fetch my tractor. We will get him home.'

Gul Khan rose and wandered towards the bridge. The crater was visible, a couple of paces wide. One of the men called out to him.

'Be careful near the bridge! We're not sure where the Pakistani put the mines.'

A few curious souls were gathered on the outskirts of Kasim Kalay** but they did not approach. They probably feared the mines too. Everybody knew that nocturnal explosions around there generally related to mines, directly or indirectly. He stared at these ghouls, remembering all of the times he had played

---

* **Sahib**, a mark of respect bestowed upon elders, teachers, Mullahs or the owner of a home/business when one is being hosted.

** **Kalay**, Pashtun for 'village' or 'hamlet'.

the spectator while the valley's brutal way of life unfolded around them. Every so often, the misery visited upon your own home. Allah's will was something you had to both trust and endure.

To his left, they had finally succeeded in freeing the Pakistani's corpse. It had been tossed into the ditch by the blast and become entangled in the thick vegetation. They were dragging it towards where Mamur lay. Strangely the Pakistani was not as badly mutilated. Mamur had probably borne the brunt of the missile's fury. Still, one side was so mangled they had to haul the Pakistani not from the head or feet as one would normally, but longways, by one arm and one leg. The shattered thigh trailed at an absurd angle to his body as they toiled across the field.

Gul Khan was touched by empathy for the man's family. Did he even have one? He was one of only a handful of foreigners in the ranks of the Movement here. They did not even know his real name. No father or brother here to take possession of him. No burial on a knoll overlooking the village where he had scampered, grubby and curious, towards manhood. Whoever did know him or love him would probably never find out what became of him. They will see out their years in patient but diminishing hope that he may one day plod wearily up the long, switching path to his mountain settlement. Many men journeyed from the tribal areas to fight the 'infidel'. Gul Khan respected their distinctive bearing and their devotion. But not their brutality. The Pakistani and his ilk were agents of dark, unforgiving forces. Their romance beguiled youths closeted in compounds and bonded to the land. This is what made them so dangerous. Yes, it was the Pakistani's family he felt for now, not the man. Without these hate-filled journeymen,

Mamur might be weeding their fields this morning beside his father.

He almost winced as the loss cut through his reverie. His conscience spoke in condemnation:

'You sent him Gul Khan,' stabbed the voice. 'You sent him for twenty dollars. And your wife knows nothing of it.'

Janan's tractor could be heard revving into life and soon it came into view framed by the rising sun, now casting slender, generous shadows across the landscape. Janan stopped short of cutting into the field. The young ankle-high wheat was his livelihood.

The two men dragging the Pakistani paused to catch their breath and changed direction to intercept the tractor. One of the youths standing near Mamur trotted over to assist them. Returning to his son, Gul Khan suggested they put Mamur's remains on the blanket they had used to cover him. In the improved light there was more grisly detail, and as it grew warmer an invasive odour twitched their nostrils and caught in their throats, making them work faster. Mentally Gul Khan detached himself as best he could, grateful that the others were too respectful for exclamation. Gathering the corners of the blanket, they formed a large sack that could be dragged towards Janan.

Yet all the dignity of the pre-dawn response was fast giving way to shrill excitability. More and more people were spilling from Gul Khan's village to witness the event. They crowded the tractor's sides, jabbering useless instructions as the men tried to lift the Pakistani's cadaver onto its flat trailer. The throng included dozens of children who ranged around the periphery, gawping. Gul Khan dreaded he might see his youngest son, Imran, among them. The Mullah waved and muttered ineffectually at these young onlookers to leave. Wide-eyed, they ignored him. A round barefoot toddler in a filthy anorak was being marshalled by her older sister but strayed too close to the men at the back of the trailer and received a soft kick that toppled her over. Shocked, it took her a few seconds to start crying, by which time her sister had gathered her up and moved to a safe distance.

With a man on each corner of the blanket, it was easier to convey Mamur. Janan and another man stood on the trailer, bent double to assist from above. When they'd slid both bodies into the centre of the trailer, some in the mob set off back towards the village, getting a head start. Others loitered around the trailer on tiptoe, transfixed. A violent death was nothing novel to them. But it punctuated their life in the valley. They paid heed to those black exclamations and bidden pauses.

Gul Khan had to get home. Signalling to Janan with a nod and a point, he set off at a jog. He knew the fact of Mamur's death would already have reached his wife. You did not need radio to broadcast up and down this valley. But women never wanted one fact, they wanted them all – every last one. He could hear his father's simple wisdom; the wisdom that always tanned his backside as a boy. 'Tell the truth Gul Khan. Tell the truth under Allah.'

People called out to him and he paid no attention. Stumbling, one of his loafers flew off and he struck a rock with his bare foot. He hooked his foot back into the shoe with a curse and hobbled on. The sharp physical pain was enough, at that moment, to break something inside him, small but pivotal. Gul Khan wanted to howl; to give vent to the maelstrom of guilt and anguish. This tragedy bore no relation to the loss of his infant daughter to illness all those years ago. He and his wife had met that with stolid acceptance.

In the distance beyond the canal he could see cars along the desert road en route to the city. 'It is days like this that the mundane things wreath themselves with meaning,' he thought.

'Why are we so cowed by all these people? Why should we pay tax, to travel for oil and rice? Why should we give up our sons to be sacrificed to other men's beliefs? Is our poverty so great that they can play us like fish for a week's wages?' A flood of indignation consumed him.

At the point where he turned off the canal path into the village, Imran emerged at a run and shouted 'father' in instant recognition. He latched onto Gul Khan, his face a contortion of distress and disbelief. Looking up, he braved the question:

'Baba, is it true what they say about Mamur?'

'It is. Hurry with me.'

Imran was a strong and intelligent child, unusually composed for his twelve years. Gul Khan felt less alone. Responsibility was a form of armour. It did not diminish his emotions, it re-ordered them.

Before father and son reached their compound, they heard the women's ululations. The wailing was more angry than plaintive. Breathless and limping slightly, Gul Khan paused before pushing open the gates. His neighbour's inadequate son was hanging around outside like some Kuchi nomad soliciting labour at harvest. It was tempting to snap at him. Instead he used the opportunity to test his balance, like the pleasantries extended before expressing difficult opinions in village council meetings.

'Thank you Mir Hamza but there is nothing you can do here. Get busy with your field.'

Steeling himself, Gul Khan stepped into his courtyard. His wife was kneeling on the straw mat by her mud tandoor. The only place she could truly call her own. Janan's wife stood at her side. The goats had formed a huddle as far removed as possible from the inhuman sounds they were unaccustomed to. The dog maintained its tireless tirade at the sky. Breaking free, Gul Khan's wife struggled to her feet. Torment manipulated her like a puppeteer. Advancing open palmed, he told her what she already knew.

'My love, Mamur has been killed in an explosion. It happened this morning near Kasim Kalay.'

'Was it a mine?' She was hoarse.

'No. We think it was the foreigners.'

She doubled up again and Janan's wife stepped forward to take her by the shoulders. Gul Khan felt useless, out of place. It was strangely reminiscent of a birth. They would leave the women to women's business and sit with the men. There was no role for a man at a time like this, except to dig a grave and present the dignified face of the family – just as he had done for both of his parents. He so wanted to hold her – as much for his own need as hers. But the time for that would be later, when the real questions came. Instead he drew Imran to his side, squeezing the boy's narrow shoulders to signal that it was alright to cry now.

Gul Khan tugged at his beard. The distance to the grieving women opened wider. She'd carried him, suffered the agonies of his birth, and nurtured him to his feet. Mamur was her life's work. More than a house, more than fields – the open spaces where men laboured. Hers was something so tiny and close, like the inward world of a craftsman. She had trusted Gul Khan with the walls of this world, and he had failed her. Her emptiness now was something so open and cold. But it was also pure. She was blameless. He was not.

Janan's tractor came into earshot. Guiding Imran towards his mother, Gul Khan turned and made for the gates. Janan had stopped short on a flat open space at the junction of the alleyway so that he would be able to back his trailer with the bodies up to Gul Khan's compound. He was struggling with the gears when two motorcycles sped down the track, bouncing on their suspension. They skidded to a halt needlessly close to the gathering of villagers. A few of the more timorous characters leapt aside.

Each motorcycle carried two men. The pillion passengers dismounted. Neither driver cut the engine: they turned the machines around in preparation to leave, resting on one foot and surveying the scene over their shoulders. Their shawls conformed to the shape of short assault rifles.

The taller of the two passengers swung a weapon off his back. Between a black turban and dark beard, his eyes menaced with the power and invulnerability of youth. The other was in charge. He wore an embroidered round cap and his beard was thin. He carried no weapon.

Despite being under thirty years old, Haji Mansur already had a slight paunch under his olive shalwar kameez. Extending short arms, he greeted Gul Khan formally.

'May the peace of Allah be upon you Gul Khan.'

'And also with you Haji Sahib.'

'Console yourself that your boy is in the bountiful arms of Allah now. He is a martyr who has brought great honour to your family and our noble Movement.'

'A martyr?' Gul Khan thought. 'I don't agree. I gave my eldest son, who had seen just fifteen winters, to your Pakistani as a guide. You gave me twenty American dollars. And your noble Movement? If I had refused, your thugs would have beaten me in front of my wife or shot me like a lame dog.'

Janan looked down from the tractor, his eyes eloquent: *be careful cousin*. The Mullah, as always, had somehow slunk away.

Haji Mansur took Gul Khan's silence to be respectful assent. He was used to that with these ill-educated farmers. So he took his next step.

'You must exact your revenge on the foreigners Gul Khan. Our ways demand it. Don't insult the centuries.' The Haji gestured to his audience, as if they represented all of mankind, inviting their confederacy. 'We will assist you.'

Gul Khan was surrounded by these neighbours yet he had never felt more alone. They were attentive for sure, but they might as well have been listening to a bard. The motorcycles idled. He was tugging at his beard again. The pause weighed on them all. In Gul Khan's mind, his father smiled, 'Honour is made of stone but you have the power to carve it.'

He knew what he had to do now.

'With respect Haji Sahib, the foreigners did not kill my son. I did.'

Waiting was always the worst part. The soldiers knew Taliban fighters were most likely in the trees and buildings beyond Kasim Kalay, plotting an ambush. For the past few minutes, the patrol had watched farmers evacuate their compounds, gathering up toddlers and moving briskly across the fields. Women, covered head to toe in long turquoise burkas, tripped occasionally on the hem as they negotiated the rough ground.

'That's them complete, I reckon sir.'

The soldier's voice was even and business-like. He lay on his belly under the mottled shadow of a lush treeline, eyes remaining fixed down the sight of his machine gun, even while he spoke. Others in the line fidgeted, shifting equipment on their shoulders and craning their necks. Birdsong lent an incongruous spring gaiety to the scene. It could have been rural England on a glorious day, verdant and mild. The fields to their front were small – no wider than a football pitch and just as flat. Flooded ditches divided the properties into medieval portions, tilled mostly by hand and nourished by the water their deep boundaries distributed.

Nick acknowledged the sentry's report. Inside he was vexed. The only purpose of coming down to Kasim Kalay was to follow up on last night's incident. Now there was going to be a fight.

Unbidden, his hand touched a cigarette packet in his thigh pocket. He was not even a regular smoker. Habit came as a feature of his surroundings. After a couple more similarly pointless movements, his mother swam into his mind, nagging him at breakfast about his constant distracted fidgeting. 'For God's sake Nicholas, stop swinging your legs.' It irked him being addressed like one of her pupils. Nobody ever called him Nicholas, except teachers and generals. And she knew well enough why – and when – the restlessness had started.

He chided himself. *Focus Nick*.

That morning the major had issued him clear direction. 'Get down there and find out what the locals know about the IEDs* near the footbridge.' At the briefing the major had pointed to a photograph of a smiling middle-aged Afghan in a woollen Pakol cap. It was one of dozens that lined the wall of the briefing room.

'The head honcho is our man. Kasim. Easy one to remember. He'll square you away.'

It sounded straightforward. In prospect, it always was.

Kasim had met them on the edge of his Kalay, effusive as the proprietor of a struggling tourist restaurant. Nick could never fathom how genuine Kasim was. One day he had braved Taliban fire to bring them a hunk of grilled goat wrapped in flatbread. It was the size of a rugby ball and fed a dozen

---

* **IED**, Improvised Explosive Device, military terminology for homemade landmines emplaced by insurgents. They take many forms but broadly are either victim operated (pressure plate) or command initiated (lanyard, radio control etc).

men. Next he appeared in an intelligence report as a Taliban informant. 'Welcome to Helmand' was the major's response to all that.

Once Nick had exhausted his basic Pashtu phrases on Kasim, their interpreter stepped in to translate the conversation. Kasim explained that he knew of only one mine by the footbridge and had marked the area with sticks laid out on the ground. He had heard that one of the dead insurgents was local to Shingazi – the larger village south of Kasim Kalay. Besides that simple information, all Nick could elicit was a shrug. These farmers were too wily to be seen imparting insights in public.

All the while Kasim's children played around his legs like pilot fish, thrusting grubby hands at the passing soldiers and repeating 'chokallat'.

Kasim was as good as his word. The sticks had been there alright, pointing towards the dip in the bank where Nick and his men sometimes waded across the stream. It was clear that the insurgents had been observing their patrols, and spotting the patterns. Error. Even twice was too much.

At first, the atmosphere was relaxed. A few farmers toiled away at the weeds in their fields, tugging and slashing at them from the squatting position with small sickles. One or two possible Taliban scouts were identified in the far distance but that was normal. So, with nothing untoward going on, Nick decided to have a go at finding the mine and making it safe. It would be a blow to the Taliban if they lost two men emplacing one, only to watch it being removed.

First Nick reached for the transmit button on his radio, to raise his deputy. It was dangerous for anyone to approach something that could be some kind of bait. The Taliban might have a means of detonating the mine from a distance. Sergeant

Langdon was in charge of a second team, moving in a wide circle around Nick's band of a half dozen soldiers. This practice was supposed to keep the Taliban on their toes.

'Advance up to the next treeline while we investigate this device. We've got you covered from here if you need to extract in a hurry.'

Sergeant Langdon's column was strung out in single file, the half dozen British troops in the lead, with a gaggle of Afghan soldiers trailing behind. The unhurried Afghans cut a motley dash, weapons hefted onto their shoulders and many wearing plastic flowers in their shoulder straps. They did not carry as much baggage as the British soldiers, and moved with the insouciance of teenagers.

As soon as the gaggle entered the next field, the farmers stood up to greet them, a cultural confusion of welcome and alarm. Nick heard Sergeant Langdon shouting distant reassurances, which the Afghans echoed in their own tongue. Sergeant Langdon's column strode on and spread out into cover. The Afghan soldiers reclined behind their weapons with casual disinterest. The farmers returned, distractedly, to their labours.

A London accent sprang into Nick's ear.

'We're all set here. Nice view towards the canal.'

Sergeant Langdon's reports were always upbeat. He might just as well have been calling Nick to say which table he had found in a pub garden.

With this safety blanket in place, Nick called forward their sniffer dog, Merlin, a black and white spaniel. The dog was adored by the soldiers. There was not a man among them who would refuse to adopt him. Merlin's handler was Corporal Grant – a jovial, heavy-set man who chuckled constantly.

'Right as rain sir,' he'd said to Nick before releasing Merlin onto the stream bank. Merlin nosed and wagged around before looking back for permission to swim across the stream.

'*Git on Merlin!*' Grant was almost reproachful.

Merlin plunged in with a satisfying splash and scrambled dripping up the other side, pausing to give himself a good shake under his bulky nylon harness. Poking his nose over a fallen tree, the dog pawed at the bark and yelped, seeking Corporal Grant's approval with a cant of his head. Merlin had found something. With evident relief, the handler voiced appreciation, and called the dog back.

Private Brogan knew what was required now. As the operator of their metal detector, he would still have to go and confirm the presence of a mine beyond doubt. Nick turned to him, and gestured towards the fallen tree.

'Take your time Pat,' he said.

Brogan's metal detector squeaked like a child's toy. Nick heard him swallow hard as he lowered himself into the stream. Up to his groin in bracing water, the soldier tried to sweep beyond the fallen tree. The slim, tubular detector was long enough to reach but its oval head sat at the wrong angle for this approach. He reached forward to fiddle with it and tried again. Now the tree trunk got in the way. An Irish blasphemy sprung him a couple of paces further forward, up to the blank spot Merlin had indicated. In his heavy body armour, sodden legs drawn up out of the water, Brogan scrutinised the suspicious patch of soil, lying across the fallen tree. Tiny tributaries flowed from his boots, mapping a delta in the dust.

Peering over Brogan's shoulder, Nick felt convinced that someone had been digging there. They all knew the signs. Man's mark: disturbed earth, unnaturally straight lines. Now the Taliban had learned not to put any hard metal in the mines anymore – just copper wire or carbon fibre rods – excavation by hand was going to be the only way to be certain.

Brogan bit on the fastening of his right glove. Tugging it free, he reached down and dug a shallow channel with his fingertips. There was a pause while he sniffed at snot that was not really there. Then, sifting every millimetre of soil, he burrowed towards the dormant danger. Behind him, Nick caught a whiff of human excrement. It flared his nostrils. These water courses doubled up as sewers.

Overhead there was a buzzing sound like a neighbour's electric hedge trimmer. It was a tiny plane launched from the helicopter pad in their fort, a sophisticated cousin of the sort that model enthusiasts crash in the park at weekends. Nick was glad of it and waited for the distant operations room to relay live video feed from a small camera in its belly. The Taliban knew that the little plane had keen eyesight and would try to avoid a battle for as long as it was airborne. Brogan seemed to ignore it and tunnel on. His world no bigger than a doormat.

Brogan must have nudged something firm, because Nick saw him withdraw his fingers, scratch his upper lip, and pull out a small decorator's paint brush. Painstakingly, Brogan swept the soil from around the obstruction to reveal half an inch of white plastic. That was enough for them all to be certain. Brogan regarded the mine for a moment, six inches from his nose, before clambering back across the stream, water sloshing from his boots as he settled into cover.

Nick exchanged a nod and a thumbs-up with Brogan. One of the other helmets twisted around in Brogan's direction. 'Nice one mate,' it said.

But then the exodus had started. It spread across the vista with a seemingly unspoken telepathy. The farmers in the fields were the first to go. Then the nearest compounds started to empty, with the women, struggling under their bright burkas, children in tow.

Nick was faced with a dilemma. He now wondered whether he could keep the Taliban at bay long enough to dispose of the mine. He could withdraw, but coming back for the mine a second time would involve greater risk for the bomb disposal team. The Taliban would treat the mine as a tethered goat.

Stay or go?

The plane's camera revealed nothing of relevance to his decision. The silent patience of all the men around him only served to increase the sense of responsibility. Whichever choice he made, the men would be exposed to danger.

Fruit trees shifted in the breeze and Nick could hear a cockerel. Unfailingly a cockerel somewhere.

Then the gunner's laconic report. 'That's them complete, I reckon sir.'

Five years in the army did not seem to count for anything in these situations. His previous experience in Iraq as a brand new lieutenant felt like a poor reference. There it had been very urban and procedural. Being new, he had spent much of his time as a sort of taxi despatcher in the operations room. Here you did not judge things so much as try to sense them. Nick sought the major's counsel over the radio.

'Only you can call it,' said the distant and disembodied major. 'We've got your back.'

Nick pulled out his map, more for show than for answers. It gave the impression of doing something officer-like, buying him time. Each kilometre was the size of his palm, and they had roamed across this tiny area incessantly. Pretty much their whole world was reduced to a page – an area no larger than a city district, end-to-end, maybe half an hour at a brisk walk.

He looked back for the young Afghan officer, who was chatting with the interpreter and eating peanuts. Nick and his team were advisors to this man. Technically speaking, he was in charge. Nick raised a hand to wave him over when the radio filled his ear again. The first part of the message garbled. All he caught was, '...the camera is malfunctioning. We've brought it in for...'

A hefty thud slugged Nick in the torso.

He was enveloped by a sudden brown-grey cloud. His mouth filled with gritty dust. His ears seemed deadened. Somehow he was on his belly, trying to free his weapon from underneath him. A boot came into view, kicking out on the ground in frog-like strokes, and then was gone. He felt as if he were submerged at the bottom of a muddy torrent.

It must have been a rifle grenade, he thought. They were fired from a sort of outsized shotgun set under the barrel of a Kalashnikov. The Taliban often started their attacks with a salvo of them.

But the first thing to reach his ears was a furious staccato snapping: streams of machine gun rounds passing above him. A cacophony of zips and whines followed each burst as the rounds ricocheted off walls and branches. Nick fought to regain his self-control. Instinctively he reached for the transmit button on his radio to report 'contact'. When he tried to speak, his mouth just made shapes. Nick was immured by sound.

He slithered through the dust cloud, visibility improving. Brogan was shouting unintelligibly and pointing towards

Sergeant Langdon. Nick gripped himself. *Kneel up, kneel up. You're useless face down in the dirt.* The incoming fire persisted. He knew he had to get a grip of what was happening.

Every fibre resisted his will but he managed to peer up over the ditch's edge. It formed a low bank to hide behind. One by one, without prompting, his men returned fire. The long black machine gun hammered quick bursts. Nick could see the outline of the gunner's helmet, shaking with the recoil and shimmering with a fine dust thrown up by the furious energy of his weapon. Small clouds were being kicked up in front of their muzzles by the pressure of escaping bullets. Empty bullet cases flicked and winked through the air like tossed coins.

The attack appeared to be coming from somewhere to their left but ahead Nick could also see Sergeant Langdon's gaggle firing to their front. The Taliban were coming at them from at least two directions.

Nick's next thought was for casualties. It was pointless shouting to check. He looked around, counting heads. At the far end of the line was an unmistakeable huddle over a prostrate soldier. Shrill cries of 'man down!' started to slip through the din. When he rose to investigate, an angry sound filled his right ear and he ducked back down.

Prioritise Russell. It was as if some patient, expressionless instructor loomed over him again on the hillside of a Welsh training ground, hands rooted in the front pockets of a camouflage smock.

There was nothing more he could do about the wounded soldier right now. First he needed to get Sergeant Langdon back across the field. Nick sent clipped and rapid instructions. The reply shed any conversational tone. Sergeant Langdon was breathless.

'I've got a casualty here. ANA.* He's serious.'

The operations room wanted detail. Neither man could give it yet. They asked Nick for coordinates of the Taliban firing positions. When he reached for his map, he could not find it. Then he recalled that it had been in his hand before the salvo of rifle grenades impacted. Dread whispered in his ear. *You're getting out of your depth.* A shade of panic crept into Nick's explanation on the radio. The major intervened, measured and avuncular.

'No pressure Jack. Just get back to me when you have what we need.'

Using nicknames was the major's way of calming people.

Bent double, Nick scurried back to his initial position and spotted the map half covered in dust on the ground. Corporal Lennon was controlling the fire now and it was just the Afghan soldiers who continued a spirited fusillade. Taliban fire slackened to a few 'cracks' overhead. But it was still very furious up front, where Sergeant Langdon was. Nick knew he had to extricate them and their wounded Afghan.

He yelled for the mortar fire controller, a broad ginger sergeant. Word carried down the line and the controller lumbered up at a crouch, the whip antenna of his radio dancing to and fro. Thrusting a marked map under Nick's nose, the controller launched straight into a brief delivered at the range of a kiss. It carried on stale cigarette breath.

'I've taken the liberty of preparing our response sir.' A smile was trying to get out.

The deference and aplomb of this opening lifted Nick.

---

* **ANA**, acronym for Afghan National Army. The most common reference used by Western troops.

Not for nothing was the controller's nickname 'The Anchor'. Experienced men like this were... well, where else would he be? The controller rattled off coded target numbers. He would drop smoke bombs to blind the Taliban. High explosive bombs would follow if there was any attempt to manoeuvre around their flanks. Nothing would fall in villages, he said.

'I'm confident on that score sir. My barrels are waiting on your order.'

'Fire.'

The controller turned away and delivered another torrent of coded language into his radio. Nick moved to the wounded soldier. It was Private Dixon. A round had passed through his right forearm, leaving a large exit wound at the elbow. The patrol medic, Private Mailer, was putting the finishing touches to the field dressings. Bloody flaps of shirt sleeve spread from Dixon's arm like the petals of a flower. He stared straight ahead, fixated by the pain. Nick needed to know if morphine was administered.

'No sir,' grinned the medic, 'Dix refused it. He said the needle might hurt. Can you believe that?'

There was a deep 'pop' as the first smoke rounds impacted in the fields around them. Almost immediately the Taliban fire desisted. Nick could see Sergeant Langdon's party gathering itself to move. They had extended the folding stretcher and a limp Afghan soldier was being rolled onto it. Two of their machine guns chattered away extravagantly as the remainder started moving.

Nick managed a lucid-enough report to the operations room. He had ascended to a vaguely detached state of exhilaration. But he knew it was a fragile grip. The Taliban were simply re-posturing, and Sergeant Langdon's wounded Afghan was in grave condition.

The interpreter appeared at Nick's side with the young Afghan officer in tow. After a brief exchange in Dari, the interpreter spoke, pallid with nerves and his helmet askew. Mohammad was a trainee accountant from the capital. He had not told his mother about this job on the front lines.

'Sultan says we should be attacking now Mr Nick. You are a coward to run all the time.'

Nick was used to the officer's questionable acumen. He even sympathised with it. Sultan needed to assert himself. When things got serious, the British tended to make the decisions and this hurt the young Afghan's pride. But for all that, Sultan was always reluctant to lead. His own commander hardly ever left the fort. Sultan himself barely had any training. This was hardly a place or time to build confidence slowly and steadily. Nick spoke directly to him with measured tone.

'Let's get our wounded back to safety and then we can think about what to do next.'

Mohammad translated and Sultan assented with a sage nod. Nick checked on Sergeant Langdon's progress. Four Afghan soldiers manhandled the stretcher, set against a cinematic backdrop of billowing white smoke. The mortar barrage was in full flow. Sergeant Langdon trotted up and down the column, lending encouragement.

Nick's half was already on the move too. He ordered Corporal Lennon to secure somewhere to land a helicopter on the 'friendly' side of Kasim Kalay. The patrol found its stride. They were practised at loading their casualties onto these clamorous and cavernous saviours.

Sergeant Langdon's bedraggled chain approached the treeline, their progress painfully slow given the urgency of their situation. His British followers were carrying at least forty kilos of equipment each, and the field was soft underfoot. They had left a ladder in place across the stream as a bridge and were able to send most men straight over. The stretcher was too wide for their makeshift crossing and its bearers would have to go through the stream. But the Afghans refused to get into the water. They hated getting wet on patrol. Nick wondered if it was the sewage that bothered them. A row flared up with Sergeant Langdon that Mohammad struggled to keep pace with. From where Nick was kneeling, it looked like removals men arguing over the best way to shift a wardrobe. Sergeant Langdon surrendered in exasperation, calling back his uncomplaining acolytes to take over the stretcher from the Afghan soldiers.

When they reached Nick and his team outside Kasim Kalay, fresh hands relieved the stretcher bearers. Sergeant Langdon and his team clambered over a low wall in a muck sweat, breathing with great rasps and profanities. Weapons clattered on the sun-baked mud. Nick put a hand on Sergeant Langdon's pack.

'All well?'

A glimmer of delay, and the smile returned. 'Never better.'

Nick examined the wounded Afghan, a scrawny youth in voluminous camouflage fatigues. Sultan was making a fuss over him and quizzing his companions, as if a clear explanation might aid the soldier's recovery. One bullet had clipped the soldier's face, opening up his cheek into another bright blossom. Another had gone into his side just below the ribcage, exiting through his stomach close to the edge of his small breastplate of body armour. Inexpertly bandaged and barely conscious, the soldier had a waxy complexion that alarmed Mailer.

'This man can't move just now sir. I need to stabilise him.'

Without waiting for any response, the medic unzipped his rucksack and started ripping open the sterile packets that sustained his labours. Nick conferred with Sergeant Langdon.

'If you secure this corner of the field and catch your breath, we'll get Dixon to the HLS.* Once Mailer's satisfied, join us. I'll leave the Anchor with you.'

At the mention of his nickname, the controller leapt up exuberantly. Nick had lifted the smoke barrage for the time being. An armed helicopter was inbound, arranged by the distant operations room. If it maintained some kind of visible holding pattern, things tended to quieten down.

Hurrying up the main track through Kasim Kalay, Nick heard the helicopter before he saw it. Its American designers had called it the 'Apache' in honour of the infamous Native American tribe. But most people likened them to hornets or birds of prey. Certainly that was what they resembled, hovering menacingly in clear skies, with their whirring blades. Even so, Nick always thought instead of sharks. It was their malevolent curiosity: any blood or commotion and they appeared, nosing around for a kill.

Corporal Lennon made short work of organising a place for the helicopter to land. Dixon was insisting on boarding the casualty evacuation helicopter under his own steam.

'It's alright sir, I've still got legs,' he said.

Nick saw no reason to refuse him that dignity. Sergeant

---

* **Helicopter Landing Site**, the military term for any place – temporary or permanent – where helicopters come and go.

Langdon's casualty was the priority for the stretcher bearers anyway. The major informed them the evacuation helicopter – a heavy twin-bladed Chinook – was circling at a safe distance and would make its run on Nick's command.

Before long, Sergeant Langdon's force fell back through the village, leapfrogging around the stretcher. Mailer jostled alongside the wounded man, holding up an intravenous fluid bag clear of the turbulence, as if it was a pitcher of beer in a crowded bar. Now that the Apache was acting as guardian angel, the tension dissipated. There was a palpable lull. Nick gave clearance for the companion Chinook to approach.

Having gathered both casualties in a protective cluster, Nick waited for his cue to toss a coloured-smoke signal grenade. The distant beat of rotor blades gave him plenty of warning. On command from the radio, he strolled into the open, trying to appear casual to his men, and lobbed the grenade ahead of him with an underarm throw. Identifying the roiling pall of emerald smoke, the Chinook's pilot banked hard, speeding low over the flat landscape.

Landings were necessarily ponderous on such uncertain terrain. The Chinook flared over Kasim Kalay, the downdraught whipping up straw and items of laundry into a giant invisible saucer. Nick spared a thought for the village this fat noisy contraption settled over, while it made up its mind, beating the air into submission. On landing the winds were hurricane force, buffeting and deafening the stretcher party. Two or three men draped their bodies over the casualties to shield them from the stinging hail of grit.

A crewman hopped off the ramp, trailing a long flex, like an umbilical cord. He beckoned urgently for his human cargo. The man's face was hidden by a broad black visor but his mouth issued soundless commentary from behind the boom microphone. The next minute was long and frenetic while they rushed forwards with the stretcher. Dixon went on under the arm of a fit comrade. As quickly as possible, the stretcher party scuttled clear, stooping and stumbling. Their visiting alien bounded back aboard with a practised hop and the pilot re-applied power. The Chinook spun away with remarkable agility for such a large helicopter, speeding away again over the treetops, barely at the height of a double-decker bus.

Unfortunately, the Apache had to go with it. They were alone again under the clear blue sky.

Four minutes later, the battle resumed.

The sunlight stretched itself across the desert, picking out folds and rocks. These licks of shadow were as precise as the tip of a calligrapher's brush. An isolated mud compound sat in the lee of a gentle rise. It was boxy and coarse. The desert dust was claiming this dwelling for its own, less two small, irrigated fields marked by a knee-high bank of sand. These fields defied the desert's encroachment with bright green growth. One was a dense herbal bed of lush alfalfa, destined for the animals. The other revealed young reaching shoots of poppy, destined for the dealers.

Cars plumed dust along the desert road below. But here the only sign of life was the farmer's son, and a clique of scrappy goats. The boy flicked his stick, and the goats contrived to ignore him. Their passage home for the night assumed the manner of a negotiation.

Baitullah remembered this chore only too well. But his younger brother would be calling and clicking at their goats now. Baitullah's destiny lay with Haji Mansur, who was sitting, alone on a short, sun-bleached section of tree trunk, strangely out of place in this desert. The trees all stood far in the distance, an emerald sheaf, hemmed between the canal and the river. Perhaps the tree trunk was part of the farmer's furnishings, and passed for recreation in his simple life. A place to sit and take snuff, as Haji Mansur was doing now, in patient contemplation.

Baitullah and the other fighters knew when to give the Haji his space. They squatted and reclined in the warm sand, close to their motorcycles. Sadiq had a bag of fried chickpeas he was kind to share. These were contented moments: weary limbs and sometimes a slight headache. Another day to be proud of. They had packed the Tajiks and the foreigners back to their fort, with a price to pay. The big helicopter always signalled that success. A just vengeance for Sher Mohammad, the Pakistani. He was the only one of them destined to be Shahid* that day, thanks be to Allah.

But their commander always had more than the business of one day to contend with. He grappled with their future, and carried the duty of reconciling it with their past and their present and their sacrifices. They knew the world weighed heavy on him. They tried to share the burden but it was not a matter of carrying sacks and weapons. As they saw it, the Haji's duties bore down, not on his shoulders, but on his heart, and his soul. And what could the young Baitullah do to lessen such exalted concerns?

Haji Mansur was waiting for a car that could take him to a meeting, where he was due to spend the night. The rest of them would sleep in this desert compound, by prior agreement, and the Haji would join them again in the morning, after prayer, for breakfast. It was their duty and their honour to protect

---

* **Shahid**, the Arabic for 'witness' is an honorific in Islam for martyrs who are deemed witnesses because they have died out of passion for truth.

him up to the point of his departure. Only then would they rest and eat.

None of them knew where the Haji was going.

'You all grasp the wisdom,' he would say. 'A secret is your prisoner. Once revealed, it imprisons you in turn. I will make neither jailers, nor convicts of my brave sons.'

Haji Mansur's intuitive feelings for his men were something Baitullah and his friends talked of with reverence. Everyone had seen how moved he was by Sher Mohammad's departure. The two men had fought together for three summers and two winters. Of course they were accustomed to death among their friends. They were resigned to it. Martyrdom was the journey they professed to accept. They sought its blessing. But the weaknesses of human nature still squirrelled through gaps in their fortitude. Zealots too can grieve.

On the news of Sher Mohammad's swift end early that morning, Haji Mansur had retreated to one side and squatted peacefully under a tree for a few minutes, motionless but for the click of crimson beads through his podgy fingers. They knew he was affected because normally he would say something rousing about their martyrs. Not on this occasion.

Now the Haji was sitting apart from them again, waiting for the car. And still he had said nothing.

It was rumoured that only Sher Mohammad had enjoyed the privilege of questioning the Haji's decisions. Not that a man of his daring and experience made many bad decisions. Baitullah's favourite story was of Haji Mansur scouting an attack on an American checkpoint by visiting it, claiming to have valuable intelligence.

'He walked right into the lion's den I tell you,' Sher Mohammad assured them.

True, nobody had actually witnessed the event. But they liked to believe it. The tale was convincing. Although the portly Haji Mansur was an unlikely-looking soldier, his continued survival spoke much for his cunning and prowess.

It was a fool who crossed him. They even had a name for the cold rage that foreshadowed his decisive acts: 'the veil'. All the warmth and charisma seemed to detach itself from his face in stages. First the eyes went grey, then the nostrils narrowed and finally his mouth and jaw hardened beneath that narrow beard. When the veil fell, his usual visage appeared to retreat somewhere distant inside his being. And then the malice arrived.

Baitullah had only left home to join the Movement three weeks before he witnessed his first execution.

Haji Mansur deduced the man's guilt on the basis of a mobile telephone. He was a simple tenant farmer who lived close to the canal footbridge they used when replenishing arms caches from the desert road. Poor even by the standards of the valley, his miserable subsistence yields left him short every year. Like the tenant in the compound where Baitullah would be spending the night, this man only met his rent through seasonal work harvesting poppy. His wife was a cousin. You could never raise a bride price on that kind of income. As if to underline his ill fortune, the farmer endured a wearing stammer. Under the stress of the Haji's interrogation, it rendered him a blithering, defenceless simpleton.

'How can a man like you afford this telephone Wakil?' the Haji had asked. 'What would you even do with it? The foreigners gave it to you didn't they? They gave it to you to spy on us – to report our movements.'

Wakil's eyes had an answer, but his jaw and lips merely

quivered a stream of gibberish. Something about getting work as a driver. Baitullah never found out.

Once the veil came down, it was irrelevant. Haji Mansur flicked the turban off Wakil's head, revealing a rough crew cut. He slapped him and said 'it is finished'. Wakil was then marched over to a tree and pushed into a seated position, his head darting around in search of salvation while his jaw blathered on. The Haji was passed a Kalashnikov. He put it into his shoulder. Wakil saw what was coming and raised his forearms as a pathetic, instinctive shield. Haji Mansur pulled the trigger, pummelling the farmer with a deafening stream of bullets, a few of which went wide into the canal, spouting little geysers of green water. Wakil's body surrendered to death with a few jerking spasms. Handing his implement back, the Haji gave a curt nod to one of the older fighters who then stepped forward with a large knife and hacked Wakil's head from his neck. An inexpert butcher, the man struggled because the crew cut gave him no purchase for his fingers. He was left tugging at Wakil's ears, as a man might tease a boy.

It was not the very first time Baitullah had seen something like that. He came from the north of the province, which had been lawless when he was a child. The Russians left before Baitullah was born. His parents told him the invaders had never ventured much to his village anyway. Either way, their departure unleashed a kind of torture of the land, and its people. Bandits roamed, taking what they wanted. Baitullah had just scraps of memory, hardly to be trusted. But some things took form.

The neighbour with no nose and hands. The day the bandits came for him, terrible sounds carried over the walls. There was pleading and screaming. At the time, Baitullah had no knowledge of the world whatsoever. He knew nothing of what it is to take a woman's virtue. Looking back though, with the sense he now had of his own body, some of those sounds reached him again, with renewed force and meaning. The utterances of men reaching a summit of raw, unholy pride.

Then, *thanks be to Allah*, the Movement arrived. This, Baitullah remembered much more clearly. Some of those same bandits – were they the same bandits? – tethered by their feet to the tail of a 4×4, heavy, naked and grey after being dragged from village to village. Such evil inside those men, the wide-eyed Baitullah remembered, that even their blood was black, where it had flowed from their headless necks and mixed with the dust. Then, from the back of the 4×4, the smiling students manoeuvred a heavy basket onto the tailgate, like a load of watermelons. It was full of the heads, they said, but Baitullah was not tall enough to see. The crowd celebrated with prayers.

For all this, Wakil's death still refused to leave Baitullah's eyes, irrespective of where else he cast his gaze. Where one minute there had been a man – living, breathing, with a future – now there were the brutal sounds of his animal dismemberment. Sucks and cracks. He saw the face of his father and brothers in Wakil's sightless eyes, the head perched on the ground as if there was a body buried upright beneath it. They dragged the corpse to the canal bridge and left it there with the telephone sitting where his head should be. There was no chit pinned to his kameez. No need of a cardboard sign. The act had its own voice. Later, from a distance, they had seen the farmer's young wife lying with the corpse in an embrace, too weak and miserable to move it before help arrived.

The Haji had noticed his young recruit's distraction at supper that same night. He beckoned Baitullah over for a private conversation.

'Do not be troubled by what you saw today young Baitullah,' the Haji had said. 'These first steps into the world of men are the hardest. Wakil was guilty of our greatest crime: infidelity, disloyalty. Call it what you will. He betrayed us...'

Here Haji Mansur grasped Baitullah's upper arm and repeated himself for emphasis.

'...He betrayed us, men of his own kin and godly creed, for material wealth. He was tempted by the greed and cheap pleasures of foreign ways. Simple people like him need strong leadership, our enlightened guidance, to show them the right way. It gave me no pleasure. But his death, and especially the manner of it, will spread a stronger message than sermons, where weak men daydream. His family will receive alms. And if we treated him unfairly in any way, and I don't believe we did, Allah in his infinite grace and knowledge will have compensated him in judgement, where paradise awaits, for eternity.'

The Haji had waited for his words to sink in.

'Nobody has lost anything today. Just, perhaps, your innocence my boy. Unfortunately innocence is like being curled up with a blanket over your head. It is snug in there for sure. But no man can undertake a journey – follow the path set for him by Allah – lying down, blinded by this covering.'

Baitullah could never imagine being that wise and resolute. Certainty flowed into him like hot, sweet tea. He felt himself age and grow. Yet the talk was just like taking such tea in the fields on a winter's afternoon. The sustenance proved temporary. Wakil's decapitation refused to leave Baitullah's dreams.

He just had to be brave and resolute.

Baitullah's childhood had been peaceful for a time. But then the Americans came. The students went to fight them. None of them returned. At least none of the ones from Baitullah's village. And soon the bandits were back, some of them wearing policeman's uniforms this time. Baitullah had yearned to fulfil his duty to Allah, and honour the memory of the students who delivered his village from that time of torture.

By the time he came of age, the Movement had recovered itself. This had to be the hand of Allah. Baitullah's destiny was upon him. His time was now. Fear was simply part of the test. The Haji assured them of this. He invoked holy scriptures to steel his sons.

'And go down from it, all of you. And when my guidance comes to you, and whoever follows my guidance, they will have no fear, nor will they grieve.'*

Before long, two cars arrived. Haji Mansur was beckoned into the rear one. He put a hand to his sequined cap as he climbed into the back seat. But not before acknowledging his men with a kind, knowing wave. Now they felt ready to eat, because the Haji had nourished them.

Janan's neck was stiff. He yearned to curl up with his wife. Zarmina would arrange their bedding and bring him hot

* Quran Sura: 2–38.

sugared goat's milk, then caress the hairs on his forearm and hum softly by lamplight. There was no chance of that now. It was already past nine at night and he hadn't arrived at his meeting yet. In fact, the friend did not even know he was coming.

'Duty always takes more than a man has in his pockets,' he sighed.

The day just would not end for Janan. Since dragging those miserable misshapen corpses across his field, it had been a series of collisions.

First there was Gul Khan's charged exchange with Haji Mansur, which had troubled the elders. It didn't help that the old men swallowed the story regurgitated from the throats of their fawning gossips. One would be forgiven for thinking that Gul Khan had slapped the Haji. Janan understood why the white beards feared the Movement: they valued their necks. But the relationship was as carefully balanced as the scales of a saffron merchant. If they got too close, someone would denounce them to the long-fingered thieves sitting in the provincial government. Next thing they would send the narcotics cops to destroy or 'confiscate' their poppy crop. Or worse, seed some lies into the ever twitching ears of the foreign jackals. Then there would be a raid, and arrests, or an explosion, and fresh turned earth. Either way, the elders lived on their knees. Honour was losing its meaning in these modern times.

Respecting Gul Khan's bereavement, the elders had riled on Janan instead, as if he was master of his cousin. Then the elders had 'requested' that Janan deal with the dead Pakistani. Any man in the village could have done that. Janan should have been with Gul Khan and his family. This confused the careful hierarchy attached to paying respects, as if the Pakistani had been Janan's kin. Worst of all, it troubled Janan that Gul Khan might feel abandoned by his friend when there was so much to do.

Mamur and the Pakistani were buried before the next sunset, as things should be. They agreed to inter the Pakistani first. It seemed appropriate to place him alongside the itinerant Kugyani tribesman that had joined them during the war with the Russians, when Janan was a boy. They used a corner of the graveyard reserved since those days for outsiders, among the whispering long-needled pine trees.

Janan had expected Haji Mansur to be present but the Pakistani's comrades did not return. Their only formal representative was one of the Haji's scouts, posted up at the graveyard because it was on a low ridge dissecting the river valley. The fort was visible from there and, with an old pair of Russian army binoculars, the scout was able to see the foreigners to-ing and fro-ing from its gates. Doubtless the Haji had his spies in that village too, but the soldiers were alert to people operating radios and telephones. It had become a perilous thing to do in their company.

The scout – a youth in sky-blue shalwar kameez – evidently had spotted what he was looking for, jabbering excitedly into a walkie-talkie and hopping on a motorbike while Janan was still digging. The Pakistani went into the ground without incident. While they were gathering for Mamur's funeral, the neighbouring hamlet emptied in their direction. People around Janan dithered over whether to go and seek shelter in their compounds: vantage points like the graveyard were not a safe place when the shooting started. Presently, the thud and crackle of battle cast the deciding vote.

Stray rounds parted the little crowd like a dog among grazing goats.

'The final insult,' spat Gul Khan dejectedly.

The two friends sat out the battle in the lee of the knoll, waiting for the world to leave them alone just long enough to bury what was left of Mamur. They knew what it meant when the helicopter with two blades sped past at eye level. Someone else was dead or wounded.

'That vulture is never sated,' said Janan.

Gul Khan had nodded wryly. 'Yes cousin, we are never alone in our suffering.' With his head bowed, Gul Khan selected small stones from the ground and flicked them absentmindedly with thumb and forefinger. And then he confided in Janan.

Now, six hours later, Janan was breaching that confidence.

Janan always approached his clandestine meetings under the cover of darkness and had a standing agreement that he could turn up without appointment. Timely information was what the foreigners needed, and it was what they rewarded him for. He looped around the fort in order to arrive from a misleading direction, lest he be seen by anyone observing the gates. Mines were not a concern on these nocturnal forays. Janan gave enough information to the Haji and his men that they trusted his sympathies, believing him to be well-meaning, if a little slow witted. Consequently they invariably warned him about the dangerous areas.

Even the greatest trees sway in a strong wind. Janan knew that to be true.

Most visits to the fort related to the presence of Haji Mansur's fighters and tax collectors. This was how the relationship had started. Janan kept a mental note of the time and place he had seen the men and then related it to a model of the village kept in the British fort.

The British commander was at least the fourth – or maybe it was the fifth – that Janan had cultivated. They changed over with the harvests: one for the maize and one for the poppies. Now Janan was having difficulty separating these men in his memory, unpicking the strands from that rope that had bound them these recent years of the long American war. At first the soldiers came and went, rare but noticeable, like strong dust storms. Outsiders with beards in angry-looking 4×4s, covered with weapons. Some strange joke, that. It was exactly how the Taliban had come, the first time, during the war that followed the Russians. Outsiders with beards in angry-looking 4×4s, covered with weapons. Both parties arrived bearing peace and hope. In turn, both proved to be a perishable gift, like fish or very ripe fruit.

One day the British arrived from the desert in a long snaking caravan. Huge trucks that followed one another ponderously, just like Kuchi camels. They established their fort. First there was the large man. 'Ed.' Not 'Eid', as some would have it, perhaps in hopes of holiness. 'Ed.' Then…well it did not really matter, which strand of the rope you choose after that. They were all gracious at least. One or two he could even say had become a sort of friend, because a friend is somebody who cares enough to be always good to their word.

Some men knew better how to be powerful than others. Janan knew that to be true too.

The important thing was they were all wise enough to not always act directly on his information. This protected Janan. The soldiers simply built a picture of the Movement's routine and tailored their own activities accordingly. And for his trouble, eventually he could finally afford a tractor.

Janan's progress through the village was signalled by dogs. He steered clear of the moon shadows in order not to appear suspicious. On a previous occasion he had blundered into a British patrol lurking in the darkness like wraiths. The fright had made a boy of him again.

Aware that he was visible to sentries in the towers, Janan walked confidently towards the gates, stopping a stone's throw away and raising his arms. It felt foolish in the darkness but he knew the routine well by now. He then moved forwards through a chicane made of tall concrete blocks, his arms outstretched, until he was under the tower. Whereupon he gestured to himself and spoke one word:

'Janan.'

The sentry replied in his own language but Janan comprehended it was some kind of message to wait. Before long there was a crunch of gravel beyond the sheet-metal gates. Chinks of torchlight played through the gaps; a jangle of keys; a sliding bolt. Finally, a small door opened, off to one side of the gate, its hinges in need of oil. Janan heard the sentry above shift his posture: he knew there was a gun trained on him. An interpreter spoke from beyond the door.

'Enter. Keep your palms open.'

Janan stepped through the space. He knew what was coming next. The door shut abruptly behind him and immediately a brilliant white light played on him from one side; from the other, in darkness, a voice again.

'Lift your kameez.' No suicide vest.

'Empty your pockets and place the items between your legs.' Out came Janan's snuff box, his old broken comb, key-ring torch and enough oily Afghani notes for the things any day might bring.

A freckled soldier stepped into the pool of light and searched him from head to toe – strong fingers but gentle, probing his armpits and grasping the shape of his calves. When this was complete, the soldier placed Janan's possessions in a clear plastic bag, said something and stepped away. The light played off Janan and onto a gap between great wire baskets of rubble. He had been in a sort of pen they used for these checks.

On the other side were his temporary British friends and a chorus of apologetic assurances. Janan did not need to speak English to know what they were saying. 'The search is a necessary formality' or some such. Hands reached out for his and gave a firm shake. Another patted him on the back. Torchlight led the party to a corrugated-iron hut erected against the side of the fort.

Inside, the single room was lit by candles in an old ammunition tin on the floor. There was a carpet but no other furniture, only bolsters and cushions arranged in the Afghan style. Blankets hung on the walls. Janan kicked off his loafers at the door and they all settled around the tin, as if it were a hearth. Aside from the commander and his interpreter, there was one other British soldier: the man the locals called 'Jaysus'. He was the commander's intelligence representative, forever writing things down. There were men like him in every walk of life. Their cunning always spoke through their smile.

The commander opened in accented Pashtu.

'Health and Happiness Janan. Tea? Cigarette?'

He tapped the end of a packet on his knee and mimed to Janan, 'have one'. The lighter was passed around. Two flasks were opened and tea poured into glasses.

It might take time to reach the point. The commander was a convivial man and Janan often wondered that he might be lonely for a normal life with his family. He liked to tease and was generous with treats: sticky cake, butter biscuits and soft sugary sweets.

'These have come all the way from London,' the commander would say with pride.

Janan had no idea where this place 'London' was really. Just that it was a city somewhere in Britain, he imagined with tall buildings like the ones Al-Qaeda had flown planes into. Janan got confused about Britain because the commander also used to say how similar it was to this valley: lush green farmland. Of course it was possible to have both cities and farms in a country, just as in Afghanistan and Pakistan and Iran. But Janan knew all British people were rich. So how could there be farms like his? Even poppy does not make a man truly rich and that was the most valuable crop of all. He dared not show his ignorance to these men. So the mysteries kept Janan company when he walked home.

Tonight the atmosphere was more restrained. 'Maybe he can see I am tired. Perhaps he is tired himself,' thought Janan. The candles' sharp shadows voiced conspiracy. As if to exaggerate it, Janan leaned forward.

'What do you know about the explosion this morning commander Sahib?'

The man put his glass down. 'You tell me Janan.'

However long it took for the interpreter to translate, the commander never surrendered his gaze. He used to nod while Janan was speaking, as if he understood. Some people in the village claimed that he spoke fluent Pashtu, and that the interpreter was an elaborate ruse. Janan didn't believe them. But the commander's manner sometimes unsettled him, especially when Janan was avoiding the truth.

That night there was no need for evasion. He explained about the Pakistani and Mamur – the fact that Mamur had only been working as a guide.

The commander interjected. 'Many insurgents start that way, I'm told.' But he let Janan continue without waiting for comment.

Janan described Gul Khan's exchange with Haji Mansur and the abortive funeral. Finally, he arrived at the pith of it.

'This man Gul Khan is my cousin and oldest friend, commander Sahib. He blames himself for the death of his son. He says that we all live like sheep, beaten by the Haji's crook and chased by his dogs. We have no honour.'

The interpreter caught up, his speech fleeting and soft. The commander remained impassive, his silence drawing more from Janan.

'Gul Khan is planning to make a stand against the Haji; to try and unite the village against him.'

Janan closed the report by dragging on his cigarette, the ash now longer than the filter. Jaysus leaned in towards the commander and muttered some English into his ear. Whatever it was, they agreed.

There was laughter coming from inside the tent. Rob Langdon heard '…next day I found my pants in the middle of the road…' before the voice was drowned out by more hilarity.

The junior officers' accommodation was often like this after supper. Some might say it was the feeling of having got through another day. More probably they were buoyed by that night's helping of sugary duff and tinned custard. One of the regiment's grey-haired colonels always referred to the lieutenants as 'puppies'. Rob loved that tag. Outmoded perhaps, but it still had a ring of truth to it.

Rob announced himself with a knock on an aluminium cross-beam and then ducked through the wide, heavy flap without waiting for a response.

'Evening sirs, I'm after Captain Russell.'

A haphazard string of bare bulbs lit the interior like a garden shed. Five domed mosquito nets crowned tired, sagging camp cots. The only other furnishings were a couple of folding canvas chairs and a makeshift bench, which had been fashioned from offcuts and was covered in dusty sections of a thin mattress, nailed down. A few footlockers and hanging fabric box shelves fought a losing battle against general disorder. Wire hooks dangled off the tent frame, supporting some combat fatigues. But most of their belongings disgorged from open kit bags on the black plastic floor matting. Rob mused. Not for nothing did the major call this dwelling 'the swamp'.

Only their body armour and weaponry toed the line – set at readiness in a neat row close to the entrance.

In keeping with the rules of most any young man's habitation in that fort, desiccated cuttings of bikini and lingerie-clad women adhered to most flat surfaces. One of the officers represented the second most reliable constituency in uniform: that of the biker. His corner formed a modest shrine to brightly coloured machines photographed in a variety of action aspects. Dance music strained through a small portable speaker.

'Here Langers.' Captain Russell emerged from his dome, closest to the door. It was noticeably tidier than the others. He had repaired the net with strips of green canvas tape. The insoles from his boots were airing on the plastic matting underfoot. A tousle of sandy hair poked through the open zip while he disentangled himself from the cord of some in-ear headphones. It was not obvious to Rob whether Captain Russell had been wearing them. He was sure he had heard that familiar laugh amid the others.

Captain Russell stood up in a pair of sports shorts and a green T-shirt. His feet made the floor mat sections crackle as they took his weight.

'What can I do for you?' he asked.

'Sorry to interrupt your festivities sir, but I bumped into the Skipper just now and he wants you to nip down to the ops room later for a chat. Any time after twenty-one thirty hours, he said.'

'No dramas. Did he say what it was about?'

'I'm afraid he didn't.'

Captain Russell's face held to the sense of inquiry. 'Have you submitted another of your spurious appeals for the long service and good conduct medal Langers? I'm not going to vouch for you again.' The other officers laughed.

'You can fuck off an' all sir.'

Captain Russell sniggered and kicked the bench. 'Go ahead and grab a seat. Mister Hutton[*] is just making some real coffee.'

---

[*] 'Mister', Lieutenants in the British Army are normally referred to as 'Mister' in lieu of using their rank, which is a mouthful (especially for the most junior 'Second Lieutenants').

Rob bought half a second by looking at his watch while he decided whether or not to linger. Hospitality was an obligation in the army, and he knew what it was like when you were in your own space and somebody interrupted the cheer. It could be a kind of grudging welcome.

The officer at the kettle intervened by flourishing a mug. 'I hope you like it strong Sergeant Langdon. My girlfriend sent us a packet of Italian roast.'

Their condescending charm convinced him a quick brew would be fun. 'That sounds just the ticket sir. I'll take it as it comes then. Black, no sugar. Cheers.'

He sat down on the bench rather too heavily and it gave out an alarming crack. Springing back up a couple of inches, he squatted over the suspicious structure in the attitude of a sumo wrestler.

'Is this fucking thing trying to have me?' Rob peered between his legs to inspect its integrity.

'It's stronger than it sounds.' Captain Russell gestured to one of the canvas chairs. 'Take one of these if you prefer.'

Rob chuckled. 'No, no. I'm loyal to my own kind. Old and complaining.'

Captain Russell weaved his way over to the upturned box that passed for a kitchen. The two officers fussed about like a married couple, somehow managing to get in each other's way. The electric kettle gargled and then clicked. Soon a pleasing waft of fresh coffee reached Rob's nostrils, in his view second only to the smell of fresh baking.

The third officer in the room was a little self-conscious and reabsorbed himself in the task of cleaning his rifle. He ran a shaving brush over the innards of its trigger mechanism and then blew into the cavity sharply. A pop song filled the space between them. A man kept repeating 'she knows she wants me; I'll come right on time' in a high-pitched whine.

Rob tried to break the ice. 'That geezer sounds even more sex-starved than we are.'

The officer's face creased upwards. 'It's Nuttal's favourite. He's obsessed with it. I hear him singing it twenty-four seven. Even on patrol. He was doing the dance moves in the scoff* queue earlier.'

'He auditioned for a TV talent show that kid,' Rob mused, almost to himself.

'Yeah but it was a wind-up. He can't sing for shit. The lads just *told* him he could. A fascinating experiment in psychology really... He fell at the very first hurdle. They'd created genuine self-belief. Nuttal still thinks he was robbed!'

Rob remembered it well. He had even been witness to the conspiracy. But the officer had joined only recently and was forgetting that life in their company pre-dated him.

'Those shows are a form of blood sport in my book,' said Rob. 'They should be banned. It's cruel to build dreams, simply for the smashing.' Realising that he was embarking on one of his rants, he changed tack. 'My missus on the other hand... She can't get enough of it. Pays that quid to vote. Even buys the fucking albums.'

Captain Russell came back with two mugs. 'Sorry it's a bit dirty Langers,' he offered.

The streaked sides of the mug bore the logo of a household tea company. The captain clocked Rob staring at it.

'We got sent these with a massive box of teabags. Mister

---

* **Scoff**, British military slang for food.

Hutton wrote a bluey* to the chief executive saying we were – how'd you put it Tom? – "deprived of quality leaves"?'

Mister Hutton piped up from the back, eagerly. 'The tactic works better for teabags than swimwear models, sadly.'

Captain Russell flopped into the nearest chair and said 'cheers' as if the coffee was beer. It tasted good. Thick and rich, not at all bitter.

'There are biscuits if you want one,' he said.

'No worries sir, I'm still stuffed from scoff.'

'Hey, thanks for boxing up Dix's kit earlier. Any word?'

On hearing this enquiry, the other two officers turned away and went back to doing their own thing. Everybody shared these concerns about their wounded. But there existed a tacit barrier around the people that had actually witnessed specific deaths and injuries.

'Not yet,' Rob said. 'But he should be fine. We've all seen worse. The Skipper may have more for you later.'

Captain Russell wrinkled his brow. 'It's amazing what you can get used to isn't it Langers? Somebody loses the use of their hand maybe, and it's "good" news. Back in the war people must have got to a point where they felt the same sunny thing about "only" ten blokes being killed.'

The thought often occurred to Rob too. Over the years he had met quite a few veterans from the Second World War and their modesty made his own story seem even less impressive. The twinkle in their eye always reached beyond the carefully edited highlights they were prepared to share. The scale of such battles needed no explanation.

---

* **Bluey**, a British military issue aerogramme nicknamed after its powder-blue hue. Postage is gratis for servicemen deployed on operations.

'Those were hard yards.'

Addressing Rob in a low voice, Captain Russell proffered something. 'You've been in a while Langers. How do you explain all of this when you get home? What do you tell Rosie?'

Rob laughed. 'Fuckin' hell sir. I don't tell her nothing. She thinks I'm at the back with the spare ammo.'

Captain Russell smiled back. 'No Langers. You *tell* her you're at the back. She's not stupid. What about your father? He was in the army wasn't he?'

It was easy for Rob to picture his old man – the typical bar-stool philosopher – spinning such bitter topics into candy floss. These days he even attracted a few misfits from the morning shift he supervised in a multi-storey car park. They hung on his every word. The funny thing was his father's constant moralising commentary had long since driven Mrs Jeanette Langdon to find her happiness elsewhere. You can be too upbeat in life, Rob always thought. Too watertight. Not that his father subscribed to that. The divorce was soon shunted into the trophy cabinet of challenges 'overcome'.

'Yeah, the old man's pretty good about it,' Rob said. 'Doesn't press too hard. You know the drill sir. Drown it all in lager and put your best foot forward.'

Captain Russell had his brew to his lips so he didn't say anything. Rob kept moving.

'Truth be told, there's no use trying to bring other people into it. I think it's selfish personally. They wouldn't know what to say if you laid it on thick. Told 'em what it's really like. Rosie would worry more and probably try even harder to get me to leave.'

Captain Russell creased his eyes into a knowing smile. 'How's that one going?!'

'You ever basked in someone else's shadow sir?'

Captain Russell threw his head back, shaking it in silent mirth at the contradiction.

'Well, she earns way more than me. If we ever get around to a wedding she'll probably pay for the whole fucking jamboree. She's got that tosser she works for wrapped around her little finger. So her bonus keeps taking another chunk out of the mortgage on our place in Leyton. I love watching her push to the front.'

'I'm sensing a "but" coming Langers.'

'Yeah, I s'pose.' Rob put his coffee down and clasped his hands together. 'Once a woman writes the cheques as well as making the decisions, what are you left with?' He paused for a rueful chuckle.

'I'm still not registering the problem here Langers,' Captain Russell said, laughing along.

Rob could see the captain was trying to make light of it – respecting the invisible line. But a man who asks an honest question deserves an honest answer, right enough.

The tinny music blared on. All the other officers were absorbed in their own business.

'D'ya know sir, she refuses to have kids until I get out. And I just can't blame her for that.'

It came out more bitter and grave than he intended. Rob left it hanging but Captain Russell failed again to kill the pause. In fairness, it was an unusual confidence he had just unleashed.

Rob felt himself filling in the last box on an Army Form entitled 'Confessions of a Fuckwit'.

'The thing is I've got my pension to think about,' he said. 'I've earned that bastard, and it's getting closer. I love this life.' He threw his arms wide. 'It's what I know.'

Rob might have added *I count for something here*, as his final flourish. He certainly would have, if drunk. But his expansive gesticulation caught Mister Hutton's mosquito dome a blow, knocking the dust free with a thwack. Inside it, the officer leapt with surprise and nearly spilled the remnants of his coffee.

'Fuck, sorry sir,' Rob said.

Mister Hutton pulled a headphone off one ear. 'We under attack?'

Smiling at the sarcastic enquiry, Rob spied the opportunity to leave, and stood up.

'Only from me gentlemen. Thanks for the brew. Always good to see why they call it an officers' mess.' His tired, weak pun was met with theatrical groans. 'I'm going to catch the CQ* and see about those clothing exchanges.'

Captain Russell ducked back towards his bed. 'Hold on a second Langers. Seeing as you're down there, would you mind bunging this bluey in the mailbag for me?'

He pressed it into Rob's hand with a kindly kind of look. The 'to be continued' kind.

---

* **CQ, short for CQMS – Company Quartermaster Sergeant**, army term for the soldier responsible for a unit's administration, supply and welfare.

B Company, CF2
FOB Bussaco
Op HERRICK
BFPO 639

Dear Dad,

I've just made myself an enormous brew and tucked into the remnants of your last parcel. It's been a long day and I feel like your company for a bit if you don't mind. Dixon collected a Blighty earlier so he will be on his way home soon. Sergeant Langdon and I have just been boxing up his kit. Whenever we do that, it's always strange to see everything just as they left it, expecting to return. Anyway, enough of that. What can I tell you?

It's strange to think that we are already more than halfway through the tour now. By the end we'll have done very nearly seven months. You have to take your hat off to the American special forces that passed through here the other day. They endure anything from a year to fifteen months. You'd think it would make them more cautious but I certainly didn't get that impression from these characters. They all wore beards and mixed uniform. They could have been the armed faction of a biker fraternity. Whatever they are getting up to in the Bad Lands north of us, they make a great deal of noise. We get a free fireworks display most nights.

Langers and the boys are in good shape. Morale had a boost because our two chefs have rotated. The old ones came to the end of their tour. Not before time! They were starting to run out of ideas. The new guys are keen to make a good impression. Langers is happy because they make an effort with the porridge. He can't complain about being 'fucking Oliver Twist' anymore. It was starting to sound like a broken record.

We never did manage to get another kerosene heater for our tent after Tom Hutton's disastrous attempt to dry his wet kit on it. But it's not really necessary now. I never expected it to rain so much here. Of course everything is made of dried mud and it turns back into sludge after a while. Some of the checkpoints looked like trenches from World War One. But the sun has been out for a while now and lifted everybody's mood. The feral cats in our FOB are stretching themselves on the roof.

I think our Afghans are the most relieved to see the sun. They don't do duty in the checkpoints and outstations, so they've been spared the sludge living. Even so, with their admin and hygiene that would have been a disaster, and they hate rain! All this has been a blessing for us as their advisors, because it means we don't have to work in those places either. But now I'm not sure all my lads would agree anymore. We can see how those stints give people a break of sorts, from the raids and patrols. Sultan is still hiding in Kamran's pocket, which is quite frustrating. There is no progress on my scheme to get them to do a simple patrol on their own. Sultan would be up for it I reckon but Kamran won't put his blessing on it. It feels like the time I couldn't get Mum to sign the consent forms for that rugby tour to France. She was absolutely right of course – everyone that did go ended up face down in the gutter, which is exactly what she predicted. But, as we both know, that was never the real reason to refuse. Well, I've reached the end of the 'bluey'. I'll go and pop it in the bag now so it's sure to make the helicopter later. Thanks for being on the end of my pen.

Love, Nick

'Evening Jack, I didn't disturb you I hope?'

'Not at all Skipper. I was coming this way to post a bluey to my old man.'

Major Lockley beckoned towards a green canvas chair and handed Nick a cup of sweet instant coffee. Powdered milk made it cloying and slightly liverish: leagues apart from Tom's earlier masterpiece. They were alone in the 'intelligence cell' – a curtained-off compartment of the company's headquarters bunker. Its low walls were papered with maps and enormous aerial photographs. A whiteboard at one end was a confusion of scrawls, arrows and symbols as if a physics professor had just finished a tutorial in there. An alcove served as what the wry intelligence corporal liked to call his 'beverage station'. The major prepared himself a coffee, distracted by the découpage of semi-naked magazine cuttings that adorned it.

He chortled. 'I'm never sure this pantheon to our nation's goddesses is entirely helpful. No use lighting the stove all the time if you're not going to cook anything.'

Finally the major settled into a chair opposite Nick, resting one leg over the other. He smiled benignly.

'So have you heard from your brother recently? Leeds isn't it?'

Nick came back with good grace. 'Of course I haven't. You know students. Pete's in the throes of a love affair with lager.'

'Weren't we all,' mused the major. 'With no cash left for a taxi. Maybe that's why we all ended up in the army, trained to march eight miles home on an empty stomach.'

'I had a teacher at school who always said that most boys join up because they're too idle to think of anything else to do.' As Nick related the comment, he could almost see the twinkle in his old master's eyes: a favourite, provocative quip.

'I like that,' said the major. 'Isn't it what they say about teachers?' The retort had never occurred to Nick before.

One of those gaps imposed themselves, when everyone knows it is time to change the subject, and address the purpose. The major rubbed his eyes.

'Before we get on to my scheme, you'll be glad to hear that

Dixon is in good shape. He'll keep his arm. He flies home to the UK tomorrow. Still uncertain about our Afghan friend I'm afraid. You did well today though.'

'If you say so Skipper.'

The major smiled again. 'I know you hate praise Jack. Sometimes I wonder whether it's a clever scheme of yours. You pretend to squirm so that we'll take delight in it, and throw more kindness at you.'

There might be something subliminal in that, Nick conceded to himself, wryly. But the conscious truth felt different. For all the Skipper's sound judgement, he knew little of Nick's life. In fact nobody in his regiment knew about the accident that boyhood summer – how it ruptured Nick's family and how it still dragged him down. Yes, that was a suitable frame for the reality Nick had lived with for so long. 'Dragged down' was exactly what did for the young Andrew Alderson, in that pond, while Nick swam for his own little life.

The army had presented a branch for Nick to grasp. Strange how the institution even used that word: to describe the trades you could choose when you were joining. University proved to be more of a waiting room than a springboard. A place for Nick to change the landmarks he took his bearings from, and find a voice he was happier to hear in public. Then, in the army, the real process began. Almost like a snake, it made him grow a new skin and shed his old one. With the surname 'Russell', immediately he was issued the nickname 'Jack', like the canine breed. His personal qualities were reverse engineered to fit the template. Nick was not even particularly small.

The sense of rebirth began on the very first day. A few of his friends from university were destined for the same vocation and they all arrived together at the military academy on a Sunday in September, towed by parents almost as self-conscious as they were.

It would have given Nick's father great pleasure to join this flotilla to a New World. An excuse to don that threadbare Civil Engineers Club tie. Those sorts of occasions were a challenge to the advancing diffidence of a man living alone. But, churlishly, deliberately, Nick drove himself to the academy.

Once commissioned Nick plunged into the rapids of military service and, like many young officers, was happy to be swept along. Being based in Germany, he saw his father only when leave came about. Even then, there were often other draws: road trips and skiing holidays with brother officers. Iraq was the biggest distraction of all. Six months spent driving tentatively around the city of Basra, with rocket attacks to break the routine of keeping watch in an airless operations room.

When they returned Nick was posted to instruct at a training depot in the north of England. Becky found him one night when dancing with the other nurses from Darlington Hospital orthopaedics department.

She was a little older than Nick and more self-possessed. Shades of Rosie and Langers there, Nick sometimes thought. He surrendered to the drift winds of unaccustomed comforts, like Sunday nights sitting on a sofa rather than behind the wheel of a car. At Christmas he built a little sleigh for her Labrador and filled it with presents for her patients on her ward, clean forgetting there was no way the ward Sister would let a dog deliver them. Still, the gesture moved her to tears.

'You are such a sweet man Nick,' she had said. 'But that's not why I'm crying.'

His impending return to the battalion in Germany gave them both an excuse to dangle in front of friends.

Then Afghanistan muscled into the battalion's collective existence. They all got sucked in by the prospect of it, married and single soldiers alike. They yearned for it. They feared being on the wrong side of this institutional divide – those who had served there, and those who had not – almost to the point of anxiety. Some people were impervious to these forces. The wise ones? The secure ones? Maybe the lucky ones. Regardless, it washed one or two of the insusceptible soldiers out, and they left the army. For the remainder, the word 'Afghanistan' invaded almost every conversation for nearly a year while they trained. Week-in, week-out, they mounted buses, perpetually on the road, like an enormous touring band.

After one such course in England, he travelled up to see Becky for the weekend. Pent-up desire made a charade of their guarded civility. She suggested they make tea. The cramped kitchen created a little intimate ballet of steps and reaches. Becky was wearing her favourite earrings: tiny enamel daisies. Nick touched one as he commented on it.

Two full mugs cooled side by side as they drew on their familiarity. In the end she confessed to spending longer choosing her outfit than wearing it.

But loneliness had deceived them both. The aftermath was awkward. One especially combative girlfriend of hers cut across a restaurant to harangue him theatrically, sticking a thumb in his pudding as the bizarre finale. The Labrador upset Becky even more by making a huge fuss of him. On the second night, Nick made a bed on her sofa. It felt almost righteous, simplifying his commitment to the company, to his men, to face the whole thing unencumbered.

On, on, the funnel narrowed. Fewer were the touchpoints with anything alien to their purpose. Sometimes, on the busiest of days, ingesting the almost ridiculous surfeit of instruction, Nick clean forgot about Andrew Alderson.

But there and then, under the major's friendly jibe, the boy was firmly in view: his dimpled countenance and thick brown hair; tanned colt-like legs crowned by red swimming trunks.

When finally Nick replied, his eyes were directed at a random spot on the floor beyond the commander's foot.

'You know Skipper, we had to relearn a few old lessons in Kasim Kalay today. That's unforgiveable. We were static too long; too focused on the IED. And that was a punishment for setting patterns around that footbridge. When they hit us it always seems to be at a time and place of their choosing. Then I was slow to react. I just scrabbled around in the dust on my belly. The Anchor was more decisive than me I think. I just wish we could anticipate these situations more – get on the front foot.'

Buying time with a sip of the suspect coffee, the major picked his responses with care.

'Don't be hard on yourself Jack. As a commander you have more to think about than anyone else. The boys play their roles and you play yours. Ops are always about compromise, the balance of risks. Something has to give or you'd never achieve anything.' The major looked up, reaching for an analogy. 'How much money do you think… investors would make without going near the edge? Play it safe out here and that's exactly how you pass the initiative to the enemy. That's when we bleed for nothing.'

The major put his mug down and picked up a notebook. He might have said *'here endeth the lesson.'*

'Something has come up that could put us on that front foot of yours. I'm interested in your opinion on it. A friend came to see me earlier. Things are getting interesting south of Kasim Kalay. A local down there lost his son in that strike this morning. According to our information, the boy was acting as a Taliban guide and now his father is on the warpath. A man called Gul Khan. I'm told he was a pretty determined Mujahideen fighter in his day. Potentially there's going to be a punch-up between Gul Khan and our old friend Objective Stocktake, the artist formerly known as Haji Mansur.'

Both men turned their eyes instinctively to the Taliban network diagram on the wall, with a grainy clandestine shot of Haji Mansur alongside the tag bearing his intelligence codename. He had only recently been promoted to the official target list.

'Here's where I'd value your input Jack.' The major continued, without actually inviting comment. 'It's a tricky one. An indigenous resistance to the Taliban has much greater credibility without direct association with us as foreigners. On the other hand this man, and whatever followers he persuades to join him, will almost certainly be crushed without our help.'

Nick had to admit to being dragged from his introspection. 'I'd say it's all about timing our run.'

'That's what I've been thinking. As soon as this man Gul Khan nails his colours to the mast we will spring down and establish a base in the village, preferably before any shots are fired. I'd want the ANA to garrison it, which means you and Sergeant Langdon living down there to support them through the early days when it's most vulnerable. What do you reckon?'

'No dramas. It'll be a busman's holiday for us.' Nick's

bravado sounded unconvincing to his own ears, and the major pushed on regardless, still almost rhetorical.

'In the meantime we can't afford any dealings with him or we'll frighten the horses. It's not certain that he wants anything to do with us either. But he's more likely to listen once his life depends on it, I guess.'

'I see the logic,' said Nick, 'provided your contact can cue our operation at the right moment.'

'He believes so. This is the land grab we've been looking for.' The major picked his mug up again, and peered into it. The result seemed a disappointment. 'Well, everyone is tired now so we'll sleep on it,' he said. 'It's late. Tomorrow morning I'll need to sell the basing plan to Kamran. We can go across for *chai*. Don't mention the Gul Khan bit or it may leak. In fact, let's choose an entirely different village for our discussions: Torzai fits the bill. Then we'll plan the operation mid-morning in case things move fast.' The major's energy contradicted his stated intention to sleep.

Nick stood up. 'I'll say goodnight then.'

'Go and get your head down. I've got a turgid report to finish.' Then, inevitably, the parting shot. 'Jack.'

Nick turned back. 'Yes Skipper?'

'People don't deal much in facts when contemplating themselves. Learn to trust us.'

The Kalashnikov rifle was an object of beauty to Gul Khan: its wooden stock aged and smooth like a chestnut; the sweep of the greased magazine; edgings of the metalwork polished to silver. He uncloaked it from a threadbare red blanket and travelled back to his youth. Indulging the reverie awhile, he sat against a cushion and rested the weapon across his thighs, as he had done so many times during the war. *Patience*. That was his abiding memory. Hours spent among the rocks on a hillside waiting for the snake of Russian trucks to wind its way into their trap. Long, cramped winters in Pakistan watching the flanks of mountains in anticipation of thaw.

His long-dead comrades waved at him from across the vale of time. Saki Dad the jester who took two days to die on the back of a mule. Qudrat – extraordinarily talented with a rocket launcher but a man who ruined anything he was ever given to cook, even tea. He had disappeared one day at the white heart of a shell blast and they never found so much as a scrap of him.

And now Mamur had joined that family of treasured phantoms.

Gul Khan tried to imagine his friends welcoming Mamur into some sort of paradise. They'd make a fuss, he was sure of that. 'How you look like your father! Join us! We were just reminiscing about the day he managed to start an abandoned Russian tank and drove it into a wadi, smashing his nose? I bet he told you that scar was from fighting...'

Banishing such wishful thinking, Gul Khan returned reluctantly to his predicament. It had been a mistake to confide in his wife. As always her wisdom had shone through, Gul Khan playing the stubborn child clinging petulantly to a hopeless position. She had deconstructed his argument with the care of a street mechanic repairing an unfamiliar engine.

To her parents she had been Balbala – nightingale – but Gul Khan's wife had not set eyes on them since she married, that same year the Soviets turned tail.

Gul Khan finished the war in mountainous Kunar, far from the low-lying banks of the Helmand River. His group of Mujahideen held sanctuary in a remote forested valley, where the community had gifted him a small compound. He had no stomach for the civil war that spun in the wake of Soviet departure. As he saw it, his duty was fulfilled. It was time to return home and help an ageing father till the soil. Moreover, he would return as a man: not merely a seasoned and respected warrior but as a husband who had raised his own bride price without credit from money lenders. Truly a man who could look others in the eye unflinchingly for the rest of his days. With inestimable pride, Gul Khan had negotiated a fair settlement for the fresh, spirited Balbala – then little more than a girl. A hillside upbringing gifted her strong legs and the perseverance of a goat for finding water.

Gul Khan's relatives did not make the journey for their wedding. Instead the Mullah recited the necessary Quaranic verses under the affectionate gaze of his wartime family, or its remnants at least. The two Arabs had sung a lilting nuptial ballad in their classical, guttural tongue. Later he asked them what the words meant.

'Husband and wife will rest in groves of cool shade, reclining on thrones of dignity.'

Forgiving himself for the blasphemy on account of youthful ardour, Gul Khan had felt the very presence of the Prophet Mohammad (peace be upon him) blessing the union. And he was sure to give silent thanks for his survival.

Time was not theirs just yet. For seven days and seven nights they remained in his tiny home. And then, as tradition dictated, she returned to her family for the same period. Normally this was a symbolic farewell. But for Balbala, leaving with him for distant Helmand, the days were her last amid the surroundings of her upbringing.

It was a time of mutual discovery. The great mystery revealed. On their first night she had not winced as his older friends said she would; just bitten her lower lip, smiling with her eyes all the while. Later while they journeyed south, she abandoned any passivity, gripping him with her muscular thighs and clawing at his flanks. The memory of her wet heat fired him even now, nearly two decades on. Afterwards, still coupled, they recovered their breath with him weighing upon her: sweaty chests sticking then peeling with the rise and fall of their ribs. Gul Khan always savoured the musk of their secretions – a redolence muddled with earthy travel clothes and the dusty interiors of cheap accommodation.

Yet for all the passion, there was a distance in his new wife. It wasn't indifference to her husband – or resistance to the fate she had been prepared for since early childhood. It was independence taking hold: growing with every stride further from her sisters in Kunar. Gul Khan respected it, understanding that he would come to draw on her strength. In his daydreams on long marches with the Mujahideen, he used to imagine he would nickname his wife 'Ghotai'. Gul Khan – flower prince – wedded to Gul Ghotai – flower bud – from which the seed of his loins would flourish. But during that journey Balbala instead became his 'Sanga' – the stem. His support.

In the early years of their marriage he would kick and whimper at night, reliving the Soviet attack helicopters tearing his friends asunder with cannon fire. Sanga wrapped her limbs around him like a wrestler, humming in his ear as he woke – a peculiarly powerful form of tenderness so fitting of her personality. Now, though streaked with the first few silver threads of age, and sapped by grief for her firstborn son, she had struck the same balance with the tone of her arguments.

'It's not that I don't understand honour my love... but first yourself, then the universe. This stand will be futile. Those dearest to you – most vulnerable – will be hurt the most. There is more to life than tomorrow, and talk of you. There is today to think about too.'

'This is not my legacy Sanga. It is *our* legacy: the legacy of a village to its young and unborn.' Gul Khan then attempted to lever her maternal instincts by using the affectionate honorific for a wife.

'Dearest Mother of my Sons, we make choices on behalf of those that cannot choose,' he said, all grave and earnest.

'You mean *son*...' She left it hanging, brutally, punishing his pomposity. But immediately reached across and ran her fingers softly behind his ear, tickling the ear lobe with her little finger. Gul Khan intercepted her hand and kissed it. It smelt of flour, of family, of all the things he stood to lose. They had succumbed to a natural silence and shifted closer on the cushions to compensate.

Now Gul Khan was scared. Sanga's persistence had unpicked the logic of his position. But that alone could not weaken his resolve. He recalled the old proverb, 'you cannot do anything by doing nothing.' Yet, whether by accident or design, she had introduced fear. What had been clear to him was now clouded by dark imaginings: of Sanga on her knees mumbling prayers as one of the Haji's thugs casually lined up the muzzle of his Kalashnikov against the back of her soft brown neck. The neck he kissed in lamplight. Gul Khan had seen these things. Worse, he had *done* these things.

Not to women and children, but unarmed men for sure. One day they had captured a foraging detachment from the Communist Afghan Army. There was no torture or anything barbaric, that time at least. They just opted to shoot the soldiers by a brook. Some were disdainful and proud. That made it easier. But others were pitiful creatures blubbing openly, mucus streaming from their noses and clinging to the moustaches they had cultivated as men, reduced to condemned infants, mewling for a mother's embrace. Their disfigured faces haunted Gul Khan now that he was older... softer. The brook – something ordinarily of such grace and gentleness – seemed so totally indifferent to the act. It just flowed and bubbled on regardless, like it had looked the other way.

Yes, thought Gul Khan, it is shameful to avert your eyes or turn your back on those things that should concern you. Either agree or disagree. That is the courage in everyday living. And it is most courageous of all to lead: to start the debate and encourage weaker men to use their voice. Fear is Allah's way of telling you that you are on the right path.

He must walk it alone for the time being. Janan could borrow a car and drive Sanga with Imran to stay at Gul Khan's sister and brother-in-law's house in the city. They would be safer there.

It had been a good idea to heft his old rifle again. Gul Khan was reminded of simpler times. Violent and regrettable as they so often were, one dealt in straightforward currencies: decisiveness, selflessness, trust. The world around you was dangerous but it was comprehensible. Everybody knew their place in it. Only a fool harboured illusions that death could be outfoxed.

Addressing his rifle not as an object but a servant, Gul Khan spoke quietly. 'I was lucky to live through those days and you've waited patiently during my long pleasing rest in the bosom of a family. It is time we went back to work, old friend.'

It was not a formal Jirga.* The large village council meetings were held outside the mosque on a patch of beaten earth. Age conveyed you to the centre of proceedings: beyond the core of white bearded elders was a throng of ever decreasing years until you reached dozens of children ragging on the margin and paying scant attention to the grave adult matters being discussed within.

---

* **Jirga**, an open consultative council used by Pashtuns to decide social, legal and political issues. Jirgas can be convened at the village, clan, tribe, regional and even national level.

Although Gul Khan's agenda warranted the broadest possible consensus, a full Jirga was impossible. Haji Mansur would arrive to start the killing long before a decision was even reached. Instead they met in private, gathered under the broad mulberry tree in Haji Abdul Baki's compound. There were eleven men present: four principal elders, with the balance made up of wealthy and trustworthy characters of their sons' generation. Janan was Gul Khan's only companion. They arrived last.

As Gul Khan had come striding around the corner to their rendezvous Janan was both proud and perturbed by his cousin. Gul Khan had dyed the grey from his beard and swopped his turban for a woollen Pakol cap. The Kalashnikov was slung muzzle down from Gul Khan's shoulder with some decorative green ribbons tied to the swivel for its sling. He conveyed the mildly unhinged cheer of someone who has just lost everything in a bet.

Walking straight past Janan, Gul Khan chirped, 'Peace and health cousin. And so it begins.'

They were ushered into Haji Abdul Baki's compound. The tall yellow gates voiced their disapproval. It was late afternoon so shadows stretched themselves out across the open space within. A flurry of pleasantries accompanied the usual reserved embraces and handshakes. Repeatedly Gul Khan placed his right palm across his heart to emphasise the earnestness of his impending submission.

Haji Abdul Baki's nephew was attending to the guests. He scooped sugar generously into sturdy fluted glasses before hosing them confidently with tea. Green leaves tumbled in suspension as the steaming measures were handed around. There were dishes with candies that resembled chips of quartz.

A few others contained sweets in wrappers. Feeling awkward, Janan busied himself with one of these, in an act of diffidence.

The men savoured their tea in silence for a while. Apart from a vociferous little bird in the tree above them, the only sounds were a few slurps and sighs of approval at the quality of Haji Abdul Baki's leaves. The boy was quick to refill their glasses from his dulled tin pot. Janan noticed how he had outgrown his sandals: adolescent toes were clawing over the ends like a hawk resting on a rail.

Their host opened the debate. 'So Gul Khan, you wish to beat the drums.'

Janan watched Gul Khan reach instinctively for his beard. But not wishing to betray any sense of doubt, instead he scratched under his Pakol. The Kalashnikov was lying under the right knee of his crossed legs. Gul Khan answered with a question.

'Where is the Mullah, Haji Sahib?'

Haji Abdul Baki cackled and his tongue quivered behind his few remaining teeth. It reminded Janan of a parrot. 'I spared you his cowardly counsel, Gul Khan. We all know what he would say. Besides, he borrows Haji Mansur's ears on occasions such as these.'

Others joined in the mirth. Of all man's emotions, Janan found laughter the hardest to falsify. As soon as one forced it out, the genuine feelings scuttled free as well – sycophancy, boredom, guilt… The slightest mention of duplicity seared Janan, as if branded. Sitting there, he feared that his face might transfigure into the British commander's. But for all they knew, Haji Abdul Baki himself would relay their conversation to the Movement. Beyond one's family, trust was folly. At least the notionally confidential nature of the meeting bought them time. Haji Mansur would want to protect his sources, just as the foreigners did.

Whilst reluctant to disrespect the Mullah in public, Gul Khan evidently felt it was worth adding his derision of the man, to warm up the elders.

'Well, we all know that empty vessels make the most noise,' he quipped.

There was more laughter. Some of the men were taking green tobacco from mirrored snuff boxes and using the lid to flick delicate quantities behind their lower lip.

They did not have time for the usual leisurely overture so this brief exchange at the Mullah's expense was the extent of their levity. Gul Khan seized his opportunity while the men were still digesting his humour. For dramatic emphasis, he lifted his rifle so that the butt was resting on the ground and he could lean into it like a staff. That captured everyone's attention. He asked Janan to pass him a snuff box and then held it up in his left hand so the sun caught the tiny mirror.

'When a man regards himself in the lid of his snuff box, what does he see? A tiger or a lark?' Gul Khan didn't wait for an answer.

'I remember when the Movement first came to this valley. We welcomed their moral stance, their swift justice for the bandits. Not just the ones that roamed the desert roads. The fattest ones in the cities too. But those of us who had travelled with their ilk on longer roads – roads from Pakistan – knew what was coming and chose to deny it. Now look at us. We live like the lark again.' Pausing, Gul Khan passed the snuff box back to Janan.

'Our arms, once strong behind the trigger…' he slapped the metalwork of his rifle sharply '…have turned into wings so we can take flight when even a pebble is cast. This is shame enough but now we have to swallow the humiliation of foreigners defending our valley. The British no less! Who can teach us anything about them? Just imagine what our forefathers would say.' He placed the rifle down again and leaned forward.

'I do not sit here in judgement of you. I sit here in judgement of myself. When the Movement turned sour we didn't resist because we were weary and we were weak. I was weak. It was too easy to pretend that our taxes, and a few of our sons, would protect us from them, especially when it was other people being hung and beheaded. I am the most experienced warrior in this village. It was I who travelled far and learned the ways of modern war with its rockets and mines. But I was seduced by the dream that I could turn my back on death and raise a family in peace, fattening up on the yields of maize and poppy. I even impressed myself with a few Mujahideen tales around the kettle, as if a man might rent the deeds of his past to pay for the obligations of today.'

At this point, Gul Khan was interrupted. Haji Khan Mohammad, a wizened miser always clever with money, let out a shrill derisory cry and clambered awkwardly to his feet. The others asked him to sit down, but he dismissed them with a pawing motion of his long narrow hand.

'Good luck with those obligations Gul Khan. What a fine funeral you will have!' Flecks of green tobacco flew off his lips, some catching in the white of his beard. 'We'll be sure to tell our grandchildren all about your exploits. The kettles will boil much faster for the entertainment. I intend to die in my bed. Presently, if Allah wills it.'

He fired the last quip as a parting shot but one of the younger men stood in his path, glowering. Haji Khan Mohammad was a picture of white. Even his buff waistcoat was part obscured by the tail of a blemishless white turban. The challenger was wearing a charcoal shalwar kameez piped at the collar and hem with red thread, his turban and beard black. It was a contrast for the eye that underlined the tension. The challenger spoke first.

'You are wise as a fox Haji Sahib but foxes will always suffer a hundred hungers before facing up to a dog.'

Haji Khan Mohammad responded with a weary caustic wit. 'Haven't we had enough of the animal kingdom for one day Saifullah? I can't have wings *and* whiskers.'

Janan could see the younger man burning with indignation. Evidently he had taken Gul Khan's lead in conjuring a proverb from the lips of his elders and looked pleased with himself as he said it. Thankfully nobody laughed or there might have been violence. Janan nudged Gul Khan to mediate but Haji Abdul Baki got there first.

'Let him be Saifullah. Khan Mohammad has earned the right to speak his mind and you will honour it in my house.'

'With respect Haji Sahib, I also have the right to speak my mind at this meeting.'

'And so you shall, so you shall.' Haji Abdul Baki gestured for Saifullah to sit.

Haji Khan Mohammad mumbled unintelligibly as he shuffled towards the gates, leaning into the base of a small fruit tree and hawking a string of green spittle in among the roots. The discussion continued without him.

Turning towards Gul Khan, Haji Abdul Baki maintained his conciliatory tone. 'You have spoken with the conviction of a man who knows the true weight of his words. I see so much of your father in you. We understand you. There is no need for further explanation. But what would you have us do? We did not invest in the Movement, like our tribes to the north. We don't have those ties. And it is plain even to a child that we don't have the means to stand up to them. I see only a destructive path.'

Gul Khan drew breath. 'First of all, if I see Haji Mansur again I will cut him down. The consequences of that act are for Allah to decide and me to suffer. As a community, you can stand with me or betray me to his avengers. I will not judge. I ask only that you protect my family.'

Some men shook their heads at the futility of this proposal but one of the more taciturn elders – near deaf and a beard dyed orange with henna – voiced his approval. With uncharacteristic ferocity, he raised a weak quivering fist, speaking a little too loudly: 'I am frail but my heart is as mighty as the night I took my first wife like a bull, and the day I killed the Wazir that disrespected her. Let them come for the Barakzai. Khan Mohammad was wrong. Better to die quickly on your feet than slowly in your bed!'

Janan could see he wanted to say more but his wits failed him and he fell silent again.

Gul Khan's reply was old fashioned, obligatory ingratiation. 'Thank you for the support Kaka.* Such tales of your virility precede you everywhere.' The old man smiled graciously and toothlessly. Yet, heartening as this bellicosity was, it failed to address the practical question, to which Gul Khan returned.

'As for our village, Haji Abdul Baki is correct. We don't have the means for a sustained resistance. There are, however,

---

* **Kaka**, affectionate honorific to an elder man that means, literally, 'uncle'.

the foreigners to consider. It troubles me that we might have need of them now...'

'Nobody invited them.' The orange beard had found his voice again.

Gul Khan's riposte was patient and respectful. 'Not so Kaka. We invited them when our old Arab friends flew planes into their buildings. If your guest steals cattle, you can expect the aggrieved man to knock on *your* door. The Movement brought this on us all by abetting those acts.'

The old man concealed his defeat with a digression. 'I hear those buildings were ten storeys tall!' His naivety amused Janan who knew well enough that the towers had reached into the clouds. The old man had never been further than Quetta. Gul Khan continued.

'Nobody wants the government up here. Those dogs never stop feeding. Yes, foreign soldiers are an insult. But I fear we have dithered too long. Indecision isn't practical in these times. It is dishonourable. We must decide who to support. At least the British are just. At our bidding they will build a checkpoint here and we can enjoy the security and prosperity of our cousins neighbouring their fort.' There was one elder who had not spoken yet and he chose this moment to air an opinion.

'The foreigners will leave Gul Khan. They always do. Then we will be at the mercy of the Movement or the fat thieves in Kabul. It is not a pretty choice. And if the Movement prevails, they will be less than forgiving of our association with the foreigners.'

Janan could see that Gul Khan was weary of being the lone proponent. If he was not so self-conscious, he might have weighed in. His cousin waded on to conclude his argument.

'If we help the foreigners then the Movement may *not*

prevail Haji Sahib. Perhaps I did not make myself clear enough. Haji Mansur and his ilk are not a choice. They are a blight. I have made my case. My actions are clear to you. I will not be living on my knees, kissing Haji Mansur's plump fingers. The village must decide about the British.' With that he fished around in the nearest dish for a sweet to fit some random, unvoiced precondition.

Haji Abdul Baki broke the impasse again. 'There is one more thing to consider here. I am amazed that our neighbours living with the British have not made more trouble. After all that has passed between us – the rape twenty years ago, the disputed sluice gate – I would have expected more lies and agitation. If we join them in the British fold, they will not be able to speak with forked tongues about our loyalties.' There were nods and grunts of approval. He changed tack.

'Who here has met the British Khan?'

Janan flushed with dread, terrified that his body language would give something away. Salvation came in the form of Saifullah, who piped up confidently.

'I have spoken with him in my fields Haji Sahib. He is small – not an impressive-looking man. The men around him seem obedient though. That is probably a good sign.' Emboldened suddenly by the reference to farming, Janan proffered one innocuous but convincing comment. 'I've met him in my fields too Haji Sahib. He seems honest. They never take any tax.'

'That may be so but these men change more often than the leaves on the trees. What about the National Army commander?' Everybody shrugged their shoulders. Only Saifullah offered anything. 'He's a typical Tajik warrior Haji Sahib. I would imagine cheaper than Haji Mansur... for the time being at least...' He started chuckling wryly at himself. 'Until the police get here too.'

A few of the elders nodded sagely. Others shook their heads.

Haji Abdul Baki spoke for them all: 'My years tell me we should mull this over but I suspect there is no time. If someone here doesn't warn the Movement, that little bird will.' There were some knowing sniggers as he pointed into the mulberry tree above them. 'Each of you must now state his view. It is safe to assume what Haji Khan Mohammad thinks.'

There was no simple vote. The meeting stretched for a further hour while each man present exercised the full gamut of his opinions on the matter. Gul Khan and Janan did not speak again. This was the Pashtun way. The subsequent debate was almost an indulgence. It changed nothing fundamental. Consensus had been reached deceptively early in their deliberations. It was only the impending evening prayer that compelled them to close the meeting.

With an air of gravity, Haji Abdul Baki set the village on its perilous path. 'If there are no objections, I will arrange for a message to reach the British tomorrow.'

Janan knew there was no need.

'Right, is everybody here?'

This was a polite way of bringing the room to order. The major had already made a mental note of the faces arranged around the map table.

'Good. Don't look so glum! This is going to be a cracker.' He grinned. 'Even the intelligence officer is coming along.' Mock indignation animated the tired lieutenant's face. There were smiles and a few light giggles but the major knew everyone was tense about an operation that would be paid for in some way.

It was cold. Dawn was hours away and the sterile strip-lighting only augmented the sense that they were sitting in a meat locker. A generator hummed in the background.

The major had slept badly. When the watch-keeper roused him softly – breath visible in the torch beam – it was like waking to remember a crippling debt or some other pervasive affliction. He never conquered the wrench of shedding the snug cocoon of his sleeping bag, where things existed only in the past or in prospect. It was a refuge from which to commune with the woman he loved, curling into the folds of memory where her lips nuzzled his ear, and her fingers traced his bones.

The major could even summon notes of the bergamot hand cream that scented them.

Now he scanned the earnest, weathered faces of his people. He knew many of them had no appetite before these offensives. Breakfast had been a distinctly monastic affair: benches, silence, porridge, joyless chewing. For some, it would simply have been a cigarette under starlight, washed down with contemplative sighs. His inner monologue spoke. Which of these faces is going to be carried into the back of a helicopter today? No use dwelling on it. Purpose is what they need.

'Nobody can sugar-coat it. We all know it's going to be a fight today but the Taliban battle hardest where we hurt them – and this *will* hurt them. Today's operation is the language of progress. As you all know well enough by now, we're going down to Shingazi to put a patrol base in. And this is the part I want you all to take away: the locals have invited us. *Invited us.*'

The major indulged in a pause, to let that sink in.

'We've been patient with that village; bloody patient. All the nerve-wracking forays into those fields are now paying off. They want what the locals around here have: stability, generosity. Don't underestimate what a tough decision it is to side with us. Stocktake and his crew will try and punish them for it. It is up to us to make sure we live up to the offer on the table and make it worthwhile. And when the Taliban show up, we'll hit them hard, clinically and as cunningly as possible – like always. It's going to be public. Insurgents respond most aggressively in the early days and the local residents will be watching. Christ, some will probably be in the firing line.'

This drew a few dry titters. A voice could be heard at the

back. 'Get to fuck.' The major raised his voice, to silence any more commentary.

'So we're going to have to be especially careful. You all know how tough that is when you're really getting smashed. But we just cannot afford any civilian casualties on this one.'

He ranged his eyes around the room, holding people's gaze for a glimmer apiece.

'So... before we crack into the detail, here's the outline. Our contact was at the meeting yesterday, where they decided to ask us for a patrol base. There's an ex-Mujahideen in Shingazi called Gul Khan. We don't have a photo yet. He's the impetus behind this one. The intelligence brief will cover it shortly. Suffice to say, his son was part of the IED team we killed last week.'

A voice – different this time. 'Seriously?'

'I know... bloody lucky we didn't make another insurgent. It's more complicated with this guy. He's got it in for Stocktake. All very Afghan; all very personal. We're turning it to wider advantage. The white beards are planning to send a messenger up here later today. That's all too late in my view. When the insurgents get the word we're inbound, they'll IED every viable compound in the area – and probably more besides. So we're going to beat them to the draw. I've had this op hatching for a couple of days now in anticipation. The second-in-command has been sitting on it like a hen.'

The major patted the captain on the shoulder.

'I won't steal his thunder. Usual method of approach. The patrol base will be on the southern edge of the village in the vacant compound numbered P-4C 37 on your maps. Codename is "Sally".'

The company named compounds and hamlets after past

loves. It was quicker than the long-winded codes printed on their maps and provided an opportunity to travel elsewhere for a few seconds during briefings.

'Care to enlighten us Doctor?!'

'Sally' had been the medical officer's first lover in medical school. He had offered the name at a planning meeting. Now, wreathed in laughter, he was more bashful. 'She was a bit of a tomboy Skipper; all cider and pork pies.'

'Well she's earning her spurs today.' The major let them relish the humour for a minute. Ribald comments were batted back and forth like squash balls. A young female medic was the most lewd of all. Inevitably though, the sun had to go back behind a cloud. The major restored decorum by rapping the table with his pointer.

'You know the score on how we skin these tasks. The rifle platoons will isolate "Sally" for the engineers to search, clear and fortify. Obviously we'll all lend a hand with the latter. The quartermaster sergeant will be following up with the vehicles containing all the stores we need. Jack Russell and his advisors will be the first residents into the new patrol base, with their dirty dozen of ANA. No reminders necessary on the importance of putting them front and centre on these things.'

Sergeant Langdon raised a hand, cheek written all over his face. 'Who's paying the deposit on our rental sir?'

The major laughed. 'I am – so no sub-lets and no parties after midnight. In case there was a serious question hiding in there Sergeant Langdon, the owner lives in the city so I'll be squaring the dues.'

His introduction was coming to an end. 'One last thing before I hand over to the team. When the main body withdraws before nightfall, a stay-behind force will remain concealed on the Taliban's favoured approach to Shingazi. We might catch them napping. Nasty surprises from the outset will deter anything too brash later on.'

Heads nodded everywhere.

'Happy days. I'll summarise again at the end.'

Sitting down again, the major retreated back into his doubts.

―――

The men clustered in their detachments – a coalescence that was almost magnetic. Looming indistinct in the darkness, the quiet groups reminded Nick of cattle in the corner of a field at night – betrayed by their shuffling mass and exhalations. Gravel laid down on the helicopter landing pad to suppress dust crunched under everyone's feet. This open area in the centre of their fort was where they always gathered before departing on an operation. Torch beams swept over the scene, resting briefly on items of equipment and squinting faces. Nick never understood why people always seemed to forget that a head lamp will blind the person you are looking at. Some of the men squatted over radios, checking the inaccessible displays and battery housings for a third or fourth time. There were occasional muted curses as people stabbed their faces on the unseen antennas. Innumerable cigarette tips glowed like the lights of a fishing village on a distant shoreline.

'Have you had one of your small cigars yet sir?' Brogan upbraided the major with a friendly, concerned tone. There was a superstition in the company that things would go badly if their commander failed to light one of his habitual cigarillos during the preparatory muster.

Sergeant Langdon answered on his behalf. 'Don't worry

Pat. He's already put away two of those terrier turds this morning.'

Nick piped up with scepticism. 'Read any chicken entrails lately Pat?'

'The cigars don't hurt sir,' he retorted.

Nick chuckled. 'Don't they? I've heard some medical evidence might suggest otherwise.'

With that he lit a cigarette of his own, the flare captured under the rim of his helmet. In that moment his thin reflective countenance could have been an Orthodox icon, hanging behind a candle.

The major moved to the next group, inviting himself into the circle by putting an arm around the shoulders of a young corporal. A ripple of forced laughter followed. This tactile tour of his soldiers preceded all of their trips beyond the gate. Sometimes he seemed to try too hard. Perhaps he was as nervous as the rest of them.

Nick was always carried back to his sporting schooldays at these moments: pre-match nerves, bonhomie. The parallel was a total cliché. Henry Newbolt's poem sprung to mind, the one about the Victorian public schoolboy stepping from sports field to beleaguered infantry square: 'Play up! play up! And play the game!' Even the campaign was an echo of Victorian misadventures. But he could not shake the strong reference to his past. Nick almost smelled the close leathery boot room again, buzzing with nervous energy.

Nick's packet of smokes did the rounds, his lighter passing in its wake at the rate of some ancient coastal beacon chain. The Anchor vocalised his gratitude with a loud 'don't mind if I do sir.' Only Private Alewa refused.

Handing the packet back to Nick, Alewa repeated his

habitual graciousness. 'Kind of you sir but I don't burn cancer sticks.'

'I'm not sure it's cancer that's going to kill you out here Jojo.'

Teeth beamed a rejoinder in the darkness. Alewa made the lamest comedian feel funny. His laugh rested on a hair trigger. He was Brogan's best friend and one of the most popular men in the company. The two men were always shoulder-to-shoulder: queuing for food, clambering onto transport – even on patrol together if they could fix it.

Everyone, regardless of rank, called Alewa by his first name. He told them it is tradition in Ghana to recognise the day that a child is born. 'Jojo' is a Monday name. In barracks it became their byword for the start of the week. 'I'll see you on Jojo mate' was a common refrain. Like many soldiers recruited from the British Commonwealth, he was older and better educated than most men of his rank. He had a family and studied part time for a law degree while contemporaries were pickling themselves in bars and clubs. Yet somehow Jojo managed to be the life and soul. Dance lived in his bones. The exhibitionism was totally at odds with his natural deference.

Nick's mind remembered an occasion Jojo had entertained the entire battalion. They were formed up on the parade square one winter's morning to board a fleet of coaches before an exercise. But the coaches had not arrived. This was exercising the Transport Officer, who paced up and down in front of the ranks absorbed in a mobile telephone that he had already used half a dozen times. His agitation was betrayed all the more by plumes of condensing breath. The veteran puffed up and down their ranks like an obsolete locomotive.

A mischievous corporal nudged Jojo, who at that stage

had only been in the battalion for a fortnight. 'Go and see if he needs any help Jojo.' The Ghanaian hesitated. 'Seriously. He might need a runner to wait at the gates. Go and ask him.' Breaking ranks, Jojo made his lonely passage across the tarmac, pursued by a few anticipatory sniggers. The Transport Officer turned to meet him, incredulous. Nobody could hear what was said but Jojo remained rooted to the spot when the officer barked and strode away. Realising finally that this was a practical joke, Jojo took his cue and broke into a hip-flexing, quick-stepping series of dance moves. The boys cheered and the moves became more expansive – Jojo's face turning to bronze in the rising winter sun. Eventually the Regimental Sergeant Major marched over and dispatched him back to the throng, carried on the wings of their laughter.

'Are you going to dance for us this morning Jojo?' Nick asked.

'Not wearing this shit sir. I would not do it justice.' His West African accent broke the words into distinct syllables. But even as he spoke, Nick could hear Jojo's feet starting to shuffle in the gravel.

Brogan cut in. 'Jojo's gonna come with me to Kildare one of these days and show us all how to dance sober. It takes me a skin-full to make me shapes but old Jojo here, he does it when he's brushing his teeth.'

Jojo stifled a giggle. 'I can't help him sir. He needs professional assistance.' The last word came out as 'ass-is-tance'.

Brogan guffawed. 'Will you see that sir? Loyalty. I'll get my Celina to teach me then. She was a dancer back in Poland…' He interrupted himself, pointing at the others. 'I know what you's are thinking, and it ain't what you think.'

'Judge us by your own standards why don't you Pat.'

Sergeant Langdon was uncharacteristically quiet. Nick was just about to bring him into their mirth when he discovered why.

'I think we'd better be forming up sir.' The sergeant extinguished his cigarette by pinching and twisting behind the tip. Without waiting for comment he shut the door on their conversation and moved over to where the rest of the section was lingering, cuffing Corporal Lennon playfully.

'Oi! Beatle! Where the fuck are our Afghans? Let's get a jeldy* on then.'

A soft kick. 'On your feet Mac.'

The hustle proved infectious and soon the company was lining up in their pre-agreed order. Their operations room initiated a radio check and all the commanders piped up in order. Being so close, Nick could hear them both on the air and conversationally, just as one did with cheap toy walkie-talkies. The major paced about consulting the luminous dials on his watch. As if waiting for their cue, the two dozen ANA appeared in a snake with Sultan at their head. Sergeant Langdon nudged Nick on the arm. 'Look sir, another vagrants' fashion parade.'

Torch beams converged on the party. To a man they were wrapped up against the chill in a jumble sale of balaclavas, scarves and thick gloves. Their helmets – ill-fitting at the best of times – perched incongruously atop these woollen defences as an afterthought. Nick rose to meet them, beckoning over Mohammad the interpreter, who was similarly overdressed.

---

* **Jeldy**, army slang for 'hurry', derived from Hindi and dating back to colonial times.

Opening with some good-natured pleasantries in Dari, Nick alighted upon the thorny question. 'Where's Commander Kamran this morning?' The major was nearby but evidently choosing not to interfere. Sultan looked shame-faced even before Mohammad had translated it. There was a brief exchange. Mohammad turned to Nick.

'He says that Kamran sends his apologies Mr Nick but he is not feeling well today. Something about a headache. The usual bullshit.' In his accented English the last word came out as an elongated 'bool-sheet'. One of the soldiers within earshot snorted with humour. Nick cut him off.

'Shut it Stephens.'

Turning, he spoke directly to Sultan even though Mohammad would be delivering the message in Dari after.

'I understand, Sultan. We're very fortunate to have someone of your courage and energy in command of Kamran's warriors.'

The major had been monitoring the conversation and he spoke into his radio. Towards the front of the column, the men rose to their feet and snapped helmet-mounted night-vision scopes down over their right eye. Short ladders were hefted onto shoulders, machine gun bipods folded away and heavy packs given one last shrug into a comfortable seat on their backs. A few final cigarettes arced away with a flick. There was a ripple of cocking weapons, spreading up and down the line like a chorus of crickets. The second-in-command was destined to control things from the operations room. He had come to the back gate to see them off. It clanged open and, in the manner of an elderly relative waving off weekend house guests on a Sunday evening, the captain lingered there as the company filed noiselessly past him into the alleyway beyond.

They hadn't moved twenty yards before the dogs in the

village alerted one another. It was of no concern to them in safe territory. Each man viewed his surroundings through the myopic lens of his night-vision scopes. Everything was a brilliant green monochrome, grainy and lacking depth. It rendered their movements deliberate and sometimes awkward.

It took less than five minutes to clear the village and they were into the fields, following a mud track, baked hard as concrete by the sun. When the rains came it turned to soup but for now it was a pale band of comforting solidity. Any attempt to dig mines into this surface could be spotted yards away. There were other risks attached to using obvious routes – ambush, different types of mine initiated by an observer – but speed and the cloak of night made the relative highway worthwhile.

The major's plan took them along this road for half a mile to the canal whereupon they planned to split: the main body hooking into the desert over a bridge, to approach from the east so the enemy would be firing into the rising sun. Meanwhile, Nick and the ANA aimed to follow the canal along its western bank and take a direct line onto 'Sally'. This would threaten any insurgents trying to ambush the larger force from the fringe of vegetation.

With close to eighty men strung out on the road, the column was ungainly. Caution at the front end forced constant short halts and the tail closed up behind like a concertina. For most of them, the whole journey was either a trot to catch up or a spell waiting on one knee wondering what the hold-up was. During the waits, sweat cooled rapidly under their heavy body armour, leaving them uncomfortably cold and clammy.

Planting the butt of his rifle into the ground, Nick leaned forward onto it, straining to relieve the pressure on his shoulder and collar bones. Only twenty minutes into an operation that would last twelve hours or more, and they were already aching. The man in front of him was scanning the countryside slowly and diligently through his monocular. His exaggerated movements gave Nick the impression of a leering pantomime villain seeking some hidden heroine.

Nick reached up and pushed his sight into the rest position. With one eye adjusted to the dark and the other temporarily blinded, it disorientated him. Yet it was also a release: the devices always struck him as a form of alternate reality, like an ability to see ghosts. Back in black and white, all but the closest of his companions disappeared. Last night's thin moon had set below the horizon. He could hear a couple of the ANA chatting in Dari and he decided to leave them to it. Objection would only create more noise. The dogs had calmed down back in the village. In addition to the two gossips there was a high-flying warplane passing somewhere overhead, invisible. A flick of his wrist. 0457hrs on Saturday morning. Half midnight back in England. Nick smiled at the likelihood his younger brother would be roaring drunk somewhere, trying to disarm the girls with his guileless sarcasm.

He heard people rising awkwardly to their feet and pushed the sight back into place, reuniting himself with the company. As each man moved forward he turned to ensure the next was moving too, communicating with a whisper or low whistle. Only the ANA officers wore night-vision scopes, so their soldiers always halted closer together, rousing neighbours with a tap. Nick settled into the rhythmic cadence of their advance: muted footfall, creak of rucksack straps, the clink of an aluminium ladder against the bearer's rifle, his own gently elevated breathing.

A squat fortified checkpoint presided over the canal bridge and its daily traffic. There was no sign of life but Nick knew the sentinels within would be alert to their approach. Sure enough, as the line passed under the apertures of its bunker, the soldiers exchanged hoarse, whispered greetings.

'Eh! Who's that on stag?'*

'Clark. Who's that?'

'Oz. You alright mucker?'

'No. Shite. Watch yer'self today Oz.'

Nick didn't need an order to split the column. His lead pair knew to pick up a narrow footpath between the checkpoint and the bridge, following the canal bank while they were still covered by the bunker. The inky, placid waters of the canal were only disturbed by an occasional pebble dislodged as the soldiers tracked along its embankment. A few minutes passed before Sergeant Langdon appeared in Nick's earpiece from the rear of the diminished column.

'That's far enough sir. We're losing the checkpoint now.'

There was no hint of reproach but Nick knew he should have been paying more attention to the detail of their progress. Hissing to the men up front, he crept forward and found Corporal Lennon who was third in line. The lead team second-guessed the reason for the halt and were already on one knee, breaking out and extending the metal detectors. Once beyond the surveillance footprint of the checkpoint they were, for the first time that night, vulnerable to mines. Footpaths became a serious liability. Now they must cut into the fields and pick a random route to 'Sally'.

Tiny infrared lights were attached to the heads of the metal

---

* **Stag**, army slang for sentry duty.

detectors, invisible to the naked eye but bright spots in their emerald world, so that the operators could discern their sweep accurately. Brogan and his fellow operator started clearing a path. Every few yards, Corporal Lennon dropped other little chemical lights to mark the safe lane. They moved at the speed of a casket bound for the altar.

Tedious as this was, there was no trace of impatience. They all appreciated the anxiety of mine detection in darkness. Even with night-vision equipment it was near impossible to read the subtle disturbances to the ground that often alerted them to mines. Placing one foot in front of the other was a leap of faith. Nick found himself subconsciously light on his feet as if that would somehow reduce the likelihood of initiating one.

Every man in the patrol – ANA included – cast repeated glances over their left shoulder, willing on the dawn. The glow behind distant mountains augured well, yet there was something cruel in its painstaking advancement. Nick sensed the irony in this. Whenever they spent the night emplacing covert observation posts, the dawn seemed to hurry towards them with total abandon. Just as it always did when he was lingering on the sofa trying to pluck up the courage to kiss a girl at a summer party, talking drivel with music on loop.

Nevertheless, open fields were relatively safe. The impending treeline was what preoccupied Nick most of all. At their tortuous pace it took a quarter of an hour to reach it. These were classic places for mines – and especially dangerous being the first treeline after a checkpoint. Overgrown with wild grasses, it was pitch black inside the wooded cage and they could hear a brook busying along within. Nick weighed up his options with trepidation. They had discussed it at the briefing and the major was content for them to wait until daybreak if

Nick wanted to. But darkness aided surprise further on. Every minute spent here would be a gift to the Taliban preparing their reception.

Nick consulted with Corporal Lennon and his pair of metal detector men. After all, they were the ones who would be first into the foreboding vegetation. It was harder than usual, not being able to see their faces.

Clearly on edge, Brogan was punchy. 'I'll go sir.'

Corporal Lennon countermanded him. 'Nonsense Pat. If anyone goes now it'll be me.' Turning to Nick, he said, 'Sir, it's dodgy as fuck. Let's do it properly at sun-up and take our chances with the small arms* later.' The second operator – Private Stephens – stayed silent. Sergeant Langdon arrived to stand above the kneeling huddle, bathing them in his levity.

'What's with the traffic jam sir? I'll fuckin' vault it!'

Nick chortled. Sergeant Langdon's hand rested on the top of his pack. 'I say we wait. Beatle's right. If we hit an IED now we're going to blow the entire op. Twenty minutes – max – and we'll have enough light.'

It swayed Nick. 'That's settled then,' he said. 'Let's get some sentries off to the flanks.'

Brogan's sigh signalled audible relief. A quick message to the major was acknowledged with a measured 'make up the time as best you can.' When Nick explained his decision to Sultan, the young Tajik wore the expression of someone listening to a conversation about people they don't know.

The men lay down among young green wheat shoots and shivered while the sky paled to grey. After a time, bored, Nick

---

* **Small arms,** military terminology for weapons that fire bullets rather than bombs or shells: e.g. pistols, rifles and machine guns.

sought out Private Brogan. An officer is never supposed to have favourites but Brogan's easy nature and Irish philosophy made him an excellent companion in these open-air waiting rooms. He was at the head of the line, reclining against his kit and whistling a soft lilting ditty whilst drumming a beat on the shaft of his metal detector. His fellow operator, Stephens, was on sentry duty so Brogan unsurprisingly had gravitated towards Jojo, who was humming along with him.

Brogan looked up. 'Hallo sir.'

'What are you singing Pat?' Nick sat down next to him on the cold ground.

'*Come by the hills.* Remember a band called The Fureys? "Come by the hills to the land where fancy is free, and stand where the peaks meet the sky and the lochs meet the sea"... No?'

'Do people your age really still listen to that stuff?'

'Sure. We don't just listen. Me Da and me play it. I'm on the bodhran and he's on the banjo. The best set is always right now, the hour before the dawn, when the whisky's running out. That's why I thought to play it here – on me *Helmand fiddle*!' He patted the metal detector. 'There's meaning in those songs sir – not like the crap most of these lads listen to.'

'Why aren't you in an Irish regiment Pat? Or your own army? I've always wondered that.'

'I left Ireland to get away from Ireland sir, not find a smaller version. I'm happy with all of yous, and Jojo, me African connection!' He kicked the affable Ghanaian and they exchanged smiles.

Nick mused at the incongruity of this friendship: Ireland and Ghana sitting in an Afghan field. He drew a mental triangle on a school map.

Brogan clapped his gloved hands together, to try and warm his fingers. 'Strange to think we're going to fuckin' roast after sun-up isn't it sir?'

Nick twisted to the east and craned his neck ineffectually. With the weight of his equipment he was a tortoise on its back. He laboured to his feet and appraised the conditions once more.

'What do you reckon lads? Light enough?' he asked.

It was as bright now as it was through their devices. Early cooking fires would soon be lit inside compounds. They would hear the first prayer. Wise as they had been to wait, it might not feel that way in half an hour. Nick unclipped his monocular and zipped it into a pouch on his waist.

Corporal Lennon piped up. 'We can probably work Merlin by now. We'll be good to go by the time he's done.'

'Just what I was thinking,' assented Nick. 'Pass the word back to Corporal Grant.'

The jolly handler pushed his way to the front with Merlin straining on a lead clipped to the front of his equipment. Dog and owner shared a spaniel's scruffiness: the ripped and scraggly strips of green cloth and scrim, designed to break up the shape of Grant's helmet, dangled below its rim. His paunch was attempting to break out from beneath his body armour.

'We're ready sir. Where do you want to work him?' Merlin's tail swished the wheat shoots.

'Go for the horrible-looking patch over there. Merlin will enjoy getting dirty.'

'That he will, sir,' smiled the handler.

Brogan tested the detector against the eyelets of his boot laces and waved its crown towards the thicket. 'Come on corporal, I'll take you over there.' Part sigh, part battle cry.

Both men kneeled down ten yards from the proposed breach and released Merlin, who bounded forward into the vegetation as if in pursuit of a rabbit. Emerging again with a cant of the head, Corporal Grant waved him back. 'Git on boy!' The spectators were, as always, rapt with curiosity and concern. Nick gripped them.

'Observe your arcs lads,' he said, reproaching.

Guiltily, they faced outwards to scan for insurgents.

Merlin trotted back with a few twigs and leaves in his fur. *All clear.*

Brogan called out to Corporal Lennon. 'I'll do the home bank and get a ladder in over the ditch.'

Corporal Lennon gave a thumbs up.

With the lonely tension of a track athlete staring down his lane, Brogan started to sweep carefully forward: angle of the head set at a perfect horizontal, consistent height above the soil, walking toe-to-toe so he didn't get his feet ahead of the cleared band. 'Fuck I'm tired of this,' he thought.

Concentrate.

But there was no way to banish his inner monologue's running commentary. His gut told him the field was safe. Nothing pointed to danger. But that ditch... He pushed the detector head into the long grass. Plenty of light now. A quick glance left. Sun will break the horizon any minute. He examined the base of the grasses – where the peril would lie – scrutinising the roots like someone deciding whether they need to re-dye their hair. Old IEDs got overgrown: thicket was no guarantee of safety. Penetrating deeper, he encountered the lip of the ditch. It was just over a stride wide and deep, with vertical sides, over half a metre to the water. Not a brook at all. Fast flowing and manmade for irrigation. He retreated to call for a ladder, but Steveo was already standing there, holding one out to him. Beatle paused on his shoulder clutching the talcum-powder bottle they used to mark cleared lanes in daylight.

'That ditch is fuckin' deep lads,' Brogan said. 'It's not going to work getting Merlin over. We'd struggle to fish him out if he fell in.' He offered his free hand. 'Give over the ladder Steveo. I'll get it set.'

It was tight working both the detector and the ladder. Brogan swept the far bank and felt better by the minute. Nobody would think to mine this spot: the grass was equally abundant leading into the next field. Laying the detector lengthways between his legs, he set the stubby ladder on the home bank and lowered it carefully into position on the far side. He stood up and placed a boot firmly on the first rung.

Nick had his head down in his map when he heard the crash of Brogan dropping into the ditch. Corporal Lennon and Stephens sprang forwards. His detector was resting on the beaten-down grass but there was no sign of him, or the ladder. Stephens was first to the ditch, already on his knees. The top of Brogan's helmet was out of the water but the rest of him was submerged, wedged by his equipment between the narrow sides of the ditch.

Something acidic and revulsive invaded from the shallows of Nick's memory. Brogan was drowning.

His left arm flapped around, desperately clawing at the steep, slimy sides. The other was caught under the taut sling of his trapped rifle, useless. Stephens could not tell whether

Brogan's feet were on solid ground or not. Because he was effectively damming the stream, water banked up against his head like a rock in rapids.

Corporal Lennon peered down and swore before twisting back towards Nick and the others.

'Man down!' His voice cracked into a feeble screech on the second word.

Quickly he unslung his weapon and thrashed violently to free his heavy pack.

'Right! Steveo! Hold my belt OK?'

Stephens set himself against a tree stump, praying that Brogan had cleared that patch of IEDs. He hooked both hands into Corporal Lennon's belt and steadied the descent of the larger, stronger man as he slithered his upper body over the lip.

First Corporal Lennon tried to free the weapon but it was still attached to Brogan. Instead he let it drop into the water on its sling, which at least gave the victim use of his other arm. Instantly Brogan's free arm joined the futile flap and, finding its rescuer's bicep, grabbed the sleeve, hindering them both.

'For Christ's sake stop struggling Pat!'

Lennon managed to get hold of Brogan's shoulder straps and heaved with every ounce of strength. Brogan shifted a few inches, bringing his mouth half out of the water. Spluttering and gargling sounds joined Corporal Lennon's grunts. Stephens added encouragement creating a curious cacophony of exertion.

It became a tangle of commotion in the thicket. More people arrived from the tail of their column. They were able to take Brogan's outstretched hands and assist with the dead lift. Brogan was coughing like a consumptive, peppered with unrestrained profanity.

'Jaysus…' Cough. 'Wanker…'

As soon as his shoulders were clear of the ditch, he was able to kick out onto the far bank and propel himself clear. The men on his arms dragged him unceremoniously into the field, his weapon trailing, where he lay sodden and steaming in the first shafts of morning sunshine, while they leaned on their knees panting. Once it was apparent he had escaped harm, the ribbing started.

'What the fuck Pat?! There are easier ways to get a wash you know.'

'How much of that piss did you swallow?'

Brogan ignored them, rolled onto his side and retched: partly to expel ingested ditch water, partly a release of nervous energy. For the first time he noticed his lip was bleeding from where the ladder had kicked up into his face on the way down. The ANA stared at him impassively. Cold mornings dampened their usual mischievous effervescence and that irritated Brogan more than laughter.

'What are you's cunts looking at?'

Nick wandered over with Sergeant Langdon. 'You OK Pat?'

'Yeah… I'll be fine sir. Sorry about the ladder. Think it's still down there somewhere.'

Sergeant Langdon cut in. 'Don't be daft son. You're alright. We've got two more. Sit this one out for a bit. Jojo will take your Vallon.[*] You carry his kit.' He whistled and waved at the Ghanaian.

'Right,' Sergeant Langdon said. 'We're going to need to get

---

[*] **Vallon**, metal detector on issue to British forces in Afghanistan from 2009–12.

a shift on now the sun's up. Are you good to go Pat?' Brogan simply nodded and spat.

They were on the move again within minutes. Jojo and Corporal Lennon replaced the ladder and cleared a bridgehead into the next field. The major came up on the radio requesting an update on their progress. His main force was already approaching the outskirts of Shingazi. Nick explained the short delay.

'Roger. Sounds like you were lucky,' the major said. 'Keep moving, best speed.'

As is my habit. Nick knew he, personally, had done next to nothing about Brogan.

Haji Mansur tore a strip of flatbread and dunked it into some thin, tepid yoghurt. He loved the burnt edges best, and the tiny, charred craters where the dough had bubbled in the tandoor. Thankfulness for such simple pleasures was the mark of a devout man. Chewing noisily, he reached for some raisins and settled back against the compound wall, flicking them into his mouth one at a time. It was his favourite spot for breakfast. A morning suntrap with views east towards the mountains. A view no man could take for granted. Strong tea, fresh bread, reclining in the company of his loyal lieutenants, and all in the service of Allah. He felt an urge to say something good-natured.

'Eat Baitullah! Where is your appetite?' The youth was sipping his tea absentmindedly.

He looked up. 'I'm sorry Haji Sahib, what did you say?'

'I said eat boy. The bread is warm, the yoghurt is fresh and you are among friends.'

'I was waiting for you to finish Haji Sahib.'

'Nonsense. We are all equals in the warm embrace of morning.' Haji Mansur gestured towards the sun. Everybody saw the slight fallacy in his magnanimity.

But Baitullah reached forward to the pile of flatbread

in the centre of a blue cotton shawl they had spread on the ground. The picnic was framed by weapons strewn casually at their feet. A long rocket-propelled grenade launcher leaned on the same wall as Haji Mansur, like a totem among them, its olive-green nose cone sharp against the drab khaki mud. Their motorcycles, ticking as they cooled after the journey to this daily rendezvous, rested at angles in a row nearby.

The host emerged with a tea pot, obsequious and edgy despite his long familiarity with the fighters.

'Fresh tea Haji Sahib?' he said. 'You will be thirsty taking the fight to the foreigners.'

A snotty child peered warily around the doorway from which the host had emerged, in awe of the dozen warriors grazing against the wall of his father's house.

Haji Mansur put his right palm to his heart. 'Your generosity fuels our courage Hikmat. Please charge the cups of my men before attending to me.'

Haji Mansur enjoyed those pastoral exchanges with his men. It brought them closer to him, to a place where he could judge their fears and talents effectively. The Movement's inferiority in technology, compared to the foreigners, increased the value of things like the guile and courage of its fighters. Looking at them now in the golden morning sunshine filled him with pride. There was an aura to their youthful appetite and playfulness, some sense of enchantment maybe he had created. The kettle reached him and he offered his glass.

Yes, these were his sons.

Allah had not blessed Haji Mansur with a boy of his own yet, just two daughters. But this atmosphere was no different from contented hours passed basking in the uncomplicated love of his little girls. They were still at the age where anything he said or did could provoke peals of laughter. Their worship, obedience and total reliance didn't seem so different to that of his youngest fighters. Just his wife was missing from the picture. The nourishment of her admiration. He had not felt her embrace for over five months. He could not call her even if she had a telephone – they avoided all personal communication – and writing was no answer either. He moved constantly to stay ahead of informants and she was almost illiterate. Instead he reached out to her in his most private moments: settling down to sleep, gripped by fear under bombardment, reflecting on the loss of friends. Eventually he might get time to visit Pakistan where she sheltered with the girls. More likely he would be martyred before that. The thought of never holding them again saddened him deeply, picking at the seams of his resolve. One must trust to Allah's will, he reasoned, and the gravity of His heavenly purpose.

A handheld radio on an unnecessarily strident volume setting interrupted his reverie.

'Powenda! Greetings! Are you there? It is Sarbaz.'

The scout's voice was shrill and excitable. After a stream of white noise, Sarbaz relayed the message again, impatient for a reply. Obviously the foreigners were up to something.

Powenda – a Pashtu term for nomad – was Haji Mansur's codename on the Movement's communications network. As he picked up the radio with calm deliberation, the commander addressed the men around him.

'It is time brothers. Picnic's over. Mount up and take what bread you can carry.' Haji Mansur then keyed the handset. They all had a habit of speaking loudly as if that might help carry their message over the airwaves. 'Greetings

Sarbaz the vigilant! Well done my boy. What can you tell me?'

'The foreigners are coming for Shingazi, dozens of them. Their Khan has been seen. This must be big. Most are emerging from the desert on foot but we think there might be more north of the town. No sign of any Tajik dogs in the desert so it could be them in the fields.'

'Any Porcupines?* I hear no helicopters.'

'Nothing yet Powenda, just the pink donkeys with all that stuff on their backs. Will we attack?'

'Of course. We are coming. I will get more men from over the river.' That last bit was a deliberate lie. Haji Mansur knew the foreigners were probably listening. Drones might now be wasted monitoring the bridges and boat crossings. He would send a courier to fetch fighters from further south, resting near the city, to come up the desert road.

'Stocktake is on the team-sheet today lads,' Nick said. 'The Skipper just relayed it to me.'

Nick was sitting against a low mud wall and had leaned back to call it over his shoulder to the men behind.

Corporal Lennon answered for all of them. 'The more the merrier, I say.'

They were now parallel with Kasim Kalay, in the fields east of where they had been ambushed a few days ago. This close to the outskirts of Shingazi, Nick's force had split, leapfrogging

---

* **Porcupine**, Taliban nickname for British 4×4 vehicles armed with multiple machine guns.

so that one portion could always cover the other across open ground. Nick was waiting for Sergeant Langdon and the ANA to move up to them.

Private Stephens scanned over the wall through his rifle sight. He broke the short silence. 'I hear Stocktake is fat.'

Nick did not answer at first. 'Sorry Steveo. What was that?'

'I said I hear Stocktake is fat.'

'From what I've heard, chunky more like,' replied Nick. 'Think of a retired rugby player, who hasn't readjusted his appetite. Unusual around here, I grant you.'

'Right... Only I knew a really aggressive fat bloke back in Nottingham once. He was built... kind of like a beach ball. He'd kick off on a whim. Everyone always underestimated him because, well, he looked so harmless and friendly. It's funny – whenever they mention Stocktake, I picture his face.'

'What can you see out front?' asked Corporal Lennon.

Stephens looked down from his rifle sight. 'Sorry, I *was* concentrating, I promise. Pretty quiet. Most of them are still milling around their compounds having breakfast.'

Not having joined the army until his mid-twenties, Stephens was older than most men of his rank, and the steadier for it. There was another pause, filled by persistent flies.

'You'll like this sir.' Stephens took it upon himself to continue. 'The guy was called Brian. It just didn't fit. I think his dad worshipped Brian Clough. You know, the football manager. Anyway, one day we were absolutely smashed – really sweet cocktails like chicks drink, they were on offer – and he started on me and I just couldn't take him seriously. He had such a nice face, even in a rage. So he put me on my arse. I probably could have had him but it would have felt like mugging a children's TV presenter. I'm sure that's why he never lost.'

But Nick was elsewhere. A similar temperature. Just a different time of day; a different continent; a distant decade. He was wet, and skinny, and breathless – his ribcage rising, stretching sun-tanned skin. There was the overturned canoe, a slick glossy yellow, streaked with green lichens. There was one of the paddles, bobbing briskly on the ridges of brown pond ripples. There were his feet and calves, slimy and grainy from his panicked amphibian flapping. There was his track through the reeds and silt to a cold flattened bank of bushes. There was the burn of the brackish water dragged through his sinuses.

'Great story Steveo,' Corporal Lennon said, curling with satisfaction at his own sarcasm.

Sergeant Langdon approached, with the ANA column. The Afghans' weapons balanced on their shoulders like big-game hunters. They grinned and chatted with each other. It broke Nick's reverie. He noticed Sultan was still some way back, remonstrating with one of his men. Sergeant Langdon whistled at him, swinging his rifle with a beckoning action. Realising the gaggle was leaving him behind, the officer surrendered whatever petty issue he had pursued and trotted to catch up.

Sergeant Langdon smiled at Nick as they drew near. 'It's like the fucking *Sound of Music* this lot.'

He knelt down close to Nick; a big man with a low centre of gravity. His belt and pouches hung low as well – grenades, magazines, all manner of impedimenta. A Christmas tree decorated by small children, with all the largest baubles at the base.

'You OK sir?'

'Sorry Langers. Yes, I'm fine. That business with Brogan just now…' He gathered himself. 'It's all good.'

The two men plotted their next move, gesticulating between map and landscape. Nick welcomed the familiar flood of practical considerations. The major's half of the force had settled on a low desert ridge commanding the canal. They were waiting for Nick to catch up so they could achieve a simultaneous entry into Shingazi. There was one more bound to go.

'I'm going to leave Merlin with you for this one Langers,' Nick commanded. 'Corporal Grant tells me he's knackered. It makes sense to give him a breather before all this gets going properly. The Anchor may as well hang on with you too. Better for him if he's got a good vantage point.'

Nick called over to him. 'You stay here Anchor. Line up the target information for smoke to the south-west. I think that's the most likely avenue for drama.'

'Great minds think alike sir. The mortar line has the target numbers. We've got your back.'

Nick's party of nine clambered stiffly to their knees, making room for Sergeant Langdon and the ANA to cover them from behind a low wall. They chose to trend towards the canal slightly. That way the major would be able to pick them out, moving in the fields. It would reduce the risk of fratricide if fighting broke out. Jojo and Stephens were leading with the metal detectors, swinging confidently now in the broad daylight.

Nick started to loosen up. The sunshine lent their surroundings a benign air, the way early morning commutes are so much easier in the summertime. There was none of the usual dramatics from the farmers, which meant the insurgents were probably not yet in their vicinity. Then at once it made him paranoid, like he was missing something.

'Don't switch off lads, just because it's sunny and quiet.'

Corporal Lennon glanced back with the look of an adult son being reminded to wear a vest.

The obvious waypoint was the corner of a compound, where someone had parked their battered white Toyota among the potholes. After that sarcastic response, Nick dared not remind Corporal Lennon that it would be a bad idea to stray too close to it. IED layers preyed on man's tendency to move between recognisable landmarks. Nick willed himself to let the team exercise their initiative and experience.

Get on with something useful, he thought. *Nobody likes backseat drivers.*

He strained for a glimpse of the major's force on the desert horizon just beyond the canal. Good to get a good bead on them. *Safer if something kicks off.* There were trees in the way so he stood still, leaning left and right to improve his perspective.

When he looked back again, Corporal Lennon's team were abreast of the Toyota two or three paces from the corner of the compound. Private Stephens, in the lead, had turned back towards Corporal Lennon, gesturing with his shoulders, as if to say 'where to from here?' Jojo swept on towards him.

Nick flushed with annoyance, more at his own reticence than their oversight.

'For fuck's sake Beatle,' he said. 'You've taken us way too close to that compound. Think about your drills.'

'Don't fret sir,' came the reply. 'I'm all over it. We'll cut east along this treeline for a bit.'

The tower of dust was visible to Haji Mansur before the thud reached him, clearly audible even over the pitch of his motorbike engine. He beamed, tapping the driver on the shoulder and pointing. His lieutenant grinned back, so close on the seat that the Haji could see mashed bread between his teeth, from breakfast. The motorbike revved on faster up the canal road.

―――――

It could have been the force of the blast that knocked Nick onto his backside, or simply shock. Only later would his senses start to catalogue everything that had seemed to arrive at once. Vanquishing sunshine, the core of the explosion was a brilliant, instantaneous light like a giant camera flash. The sound and shockwave that came with it were indistinguishable, flooding his mouth, nose, ears and stomach with malevolent energy. It revived incongruous memories of surfing, and being blindsided by a huge wave.

Every single window in the Toyota scattered in tiny cubes as if the glass was not solid matter but a shoal of panicked silver whitebait. With a flick, the blast conjured a wall of dust higher than a cottage. Within it, Nick saw Jojo's body twisting and spinning up to the first storey.

Recovering his wits, the first thing Nick heard through a dull ring in his head was Corporal Lennon screaming, 'Jesus, fuck, MEDIC!' Then Sergeant Langdon came up on the radio, to the major, laconic.

'Contact IED.' He must have seen Nick incapacitated.

Spitting some grit from his mouth, Nick was actually up with remarkable agility, his equipment weightless. Corporal

Lennon was already kneeling over Jojo, hands waving above the injuries as if his palms were sensing on behalf of his eyes. The Ghanaian lay partially within the crater, no larger or deeper than a small paddling pool, churned to moon dust and still smoking faintly, as if it were volcanic. Ammonia from the homemade explosive tingled in their nostrils.

Thankfully, Jojo was completely stunned and therefore still largely oblivious to his injuries, gaunt under his shroud of grey dust. Something, probably his weapon or metal detector, had knocked his front teeth out. He mumbled through swollen lips. His sleeveless right arm was partially severed below the elbow, hanging on flaps of flesh, its open gloved grey hand already lifeless. Shielded by his body, Jojo's left arm was intact, although missing the little finger. His legs followed a similar pattern. The right was completely missing, replaced at the pelvis by a dense shapeless mash, still pulsing with the blind commands of his circulation. His left leg had been amputated below the knee. Shattered leg bones protruded like the leftovers of a carved joint. The soil drank his blood thirstily.

As was, Jojo had about two minutes to live.

Throughout this survey, both Nick and Corporal Lennon were already removing black Velcro tourniquets from Jojo's medical pouch. These were his lifeline. Nick called out to Private Stephens, still prostrate beyond the Toyota, unharmed save for some small cuts in his face, and visibly in shock.

'Sorry sir, I swear I cleared it, I fucking swear I did.'

'I know Steveo. These things happen. Stay where you are. Don't move.'

Corporal Lennon's mantra of profanity rolled on under his breath as he busied with the tourniquets, punctuated with occasional assurances. 'It'll be OK Jojo, we've got you.' They seemed as much for his personal encouragement. The clean arm and leg were straightforward to tie off; he was practised. But the pulpy mass had no shape, nothing to get the thin band around.

Bellows of 'coming through' announced the arrival of Private Mailer, the medic, pounding up the line of soldiers lying static, waiting for the order to assist. Tense faces creased with concern. Somewhere within also a dark, secretive, shame-inducing relief. *Not me*.

'Field dressings* Beatle,' Mailer said. 'Pack it out with field dressings and we'll fashion the tourniquet around that. I'll get fluids in.' The medic swung his bag off and burrowed inside it. Jojo was struggling. Losing. His eyes rolled back. His skin went waxy. The medic swore. He was not a man to swear normally.

'Fuck,' he said again. 'I'm going to have to put the fluids direct into his sternum.'

'Do whatever you've got to do Doc,' Nick offered helplessly, as he tore open bandages. Corporal Lennon spoke again to Jojo, his voice choked by emotion.

'Oi Jojo! Come back mate. Look at me! Don't give up.'

For the first time they heard Brogan. He had moved forward unbidden and was kneeling up nearby.

'Think of your wife and boy Jojo, for fuck's sake. You don't want to die in this shithole.'

As Nick looked back, he spotted Jojo's boot lying on the roof of the Toyota.

---

* **Field Dressing**, absorbent pad the size of a paperback, attached to a long bandage that wraps around the limb or body to apply pressure.

'Jack, I'm going to have to press you for some detail. We can do the running to get you a helicopter but we're powerless without the basic information…'

The major let the radio message – his second – hang as if there was something else, but then simply added '…over.'

'Powerless' summed up his whole demeanour. The tact and patience of the soldiers around him almost made it worse. Whilst not appearing to share his frustration at being unable to help, they did. On big operations the major always moved with the army engineer search team – seven men who specialised in finding IEDs where they were certain to be encountered. The deputy of that team had lost three limbs clearing a compound only a month before. Other teams in their close-knit unit had suffered fatalities. Memories were raw and they faced the prospect of another search at 'Sally'. This incident was a decidedly unwelcome appetiser.

Nick came up, more preoccupied than flustered. 'Roger. I'm on it. There's just nothing left we can find with his zap* on it. The blast… Wait.'

The commotion was audible in the background. A voice could be heard saying 'no, no, the other way.'

'Sorry… we can't roll him over… his pelvis… hold on… his pulse is somewhere between weak and none… I'll get back to you… Out.'

Sergeant Langdon intervened from his vantage point, swift and coherent on the radio. 'I've got the bare bones of it. Zap from my notebook: Alpha-Lima-Five-Four-Nine-Six. IED.

---

* **Zap**, code used to identify individuals over radio nets, derived from a combination of their name and army personnel number. Full names of casualties are not used.

Blast amputee, multiple. We'll be using the emergency HLS I sent up to the ops room ten minutes ago. Acknowledge grid please. Approach, obstructions and method of marking to follow. Over.'

From the distant operations room, the captain closed it off – 'got all that Skipper' – and read back the grid.

The major knew instantly who they were referring to and formed Private Alewa's name, trying not to picture the athletic Ghanaian's effortless victories on the running track.

There had been some consideration of whether to send him home the previous month. From time to time the distant bureaucratic system reached into the major's narrow field of view, servicing the interests of 'normality'. It was never obvious to him who had the upper hand: the exigencies of their daily struggle against the enemy, or the army that existed between – behind – such ungainly distractions as a war. They had decided to hold onto Jojo Alewa. A reliable man, his posting could wait, they agreed. No use being short-handed, they concluded.

It was pointless to confront all this now. The major had more than enough exposure from the Balkans and Iraq to know how such thoughts were best left alone. They stretched and reclined in the preserve of one's private quarters, never in a hurry to find the door, and always ready to impose a sheaf of glossy portrait photos. The soldiers smiled at him in those mental snapshots. He wondered: was that solace or revenge?

The major beckoned to Mister Hutton. 'You good Tom?'

'Yes Skipper. What do you need me to do?' There was incongruity in the young lieutenant's weathered single-mindedness. His was a face that belonged on a terrace, drinking beer in a T-shirt, carefree and animated.

'No change to the plan, I'm just advancing things. We've

caught the Taliban napping this morning but that IED will be sure to draw them up the canal. Bounce the road bridge with your platoon and get in their way. We've got your back covered here. As soon as you're set, we'll push through you, onto "Sally".'

'Happy days Skipper. It's been crawling with civvies this morning. Looks clear.'

'I'll put Seeker up along the canal road and try to spot their motorbikes for you.'

Restless with the tension of impending battle, Haji Mansur ambled over to a tree and rubbed his free hand up and down the bark, savouring its dry roughness against a clammy palm. Bringing a handset to his lips, he hailed the chief scout.

'Sarbaz! Are you awake? Be my eyes.'

'Praise be to Allah, Powenda. The foreigners triggered a mine and now they are waiting for the helicopter to carry their dead into the sky.'

'Praise indeed Sarbaz but I saw that for myself. What of the donkeys coming from the desert?'

'They are approaching the Shingazi Bridge. We must do something. Where are you?'

'We are already at Uncle's place, gathering eggs.'

This was code for an arms cache they maintained within a walled orchard south of the village. A shoulder-high stack of dried poppy stems in one corner served only to distract unimaginative searchers. At the base of the north-facing wall, almost always in shadow, lay a rough trapdoor camouflaged with dirt and chaff. The others unearthed their stash: a used fertiliser bag for bullets – some of it in belts for their machine gun – and behind it a satchel containing more rocket-propelled grenades.

'Hurry or you won't catch them in the open. I will send Kakay to guide you. Meet him at the jammed sluice gate.'

'We are on our way Sarbaz.'

Their motorbikes were parked a few hundred paces to the rear under some trees, in dappled shade adjacent to a crossroads. They had made their way to the orchard on foot by a circuitous, covered route. Haji Mansur needed to lose any drones that might have been tracking them.

The crossroads was where they planned to rendezvous after the battle. It was the closest accessible point for the converted estate car they used as an ambulance. If they suffered any wounded, the car would make a dash to hospital in either Kandahar or Quetta, over the border in Pakistan. There were sympathetic doctors closer to the action but these men had neither the facilities nor knowledge to treat gravely wounded fighters. In truth, your chances were not good. Both journeys took hours on poor roads. Nevertheless, numerous tales of survival bolstered the illusion, and it was a comfort to know that one's comrades always persevered in trying to save a life, even if martyrdom was its own prize.

Baitullah was given the wheelbarrow to push closer to their ambush point. This was useful for getting wounded men back to the car as soon as possible. For now they loaded it with rocket-propelled grenades and bullet belts. They threw the fertiliser bag over the top, as a cover. The others shouldered weapons and then concealed them under shawls. It was important to cover it all. Too many men had been killed by snipers and helicopters just getting into position. Their paranoia precipitated a customary check over one another, tugging and tucking the flaps of material. Haji Mansur scorned it impatiently.

'Come on girls! You're like a bunch of sisters fussing over a bride. We need to go.'

He led off through the orchard at a trot, his own weapon tucked up into his armpit with the shawl over one shoulder. The short Kalashnikov with a folding stock was a status symbol that he only ever carried when going into battle. At other times it struck him as a greater mark of authority to be unarmed.

All ten fighters were acutely conscious of what might lurk above them – out of sight, out of earshot. Though futile to glance skyward, they fought a constant urge to do so. Listening so intently for the buzz of drones and beat of helicopter blades often elicited phantoms. Routine passage of harmless supply runs confused things further. The old hands swore they could tell the difference between an armed attack helicopter and the transport varieties, just by the sound. But old hands were rare now.

Worst of all were the jets. They could hear those exploring the heavens almost every hour of the day and night. Baitullah wondered if the pilots ever slept. Nobody knew for sure what all these machines were capable of – what they could see and what they could hit. Friends had disappeared into a fireball when the sky was clear and quiet, purified of pitiless contraptions. Anxiety became an outer skin: integral, protective, renewable.

Haji Mansur was pleased about the mine but in reality it complicated things. Whether his victims lived or died, the big helicopter always came, and with it an aggressive companion. He would have to wait for that to leave before he pressed his attack. Unfortunately, during that delay, the foreigners would gain a stronger foothold on his side of the canal. Maybe Kakay had some ideas.

His earlier buoyancy was a memory now. Was it naive or artful of the human mind to forget so readily that gut-wrenching anticipation of dangerous deeds? He loathed himself for these spells of timidity. He had once comforted a trembling suicide bomber by saying 'death in Allah's service is a noble destiny; doubts are simply a test.' That was true. His own indulgence – may Allah forgive – was the hope that death would be swift and painless when the time came.

Kakay squatted in tall grasses above the sluice gate, a relic of American aid projects two generations ago. Unarmed, as many scouts were, he carried only his radio.

He rose as soon as the fighters came into view. 'Peace be upon you Haji Sahib.' Skinny under his worn sky-blue shalwar kammeez, Kakay cultivated a few patches of adolescent fluff on his chin. Immediately he pointed behind Haji Mansur. 'Have you seen it?'

'Upon you be peace, Kakay. You have young eyes.'

The distant attack helicopter was no bigger than an insect. They moved deeper into the treeline and spread out, the fighters all lying down, while Haji Mansur consulted his scout.

The boy sketched in the dirt as he spoke. 'I counted twenty-four crossing the bridge Haji Sahib. The remainder are still on the east bank. We don't know how big the group is on the far side of the village but they have not moved since the mine exploded.'

Kakay's eyes gleamed. Haji Mansur had a talent for this. Without any deliberation he summoned the two senior fighters with clicks of the finger. Having apprised them of the situation as described by Kakay, he issued his orders.

'Reinforcements will take too long to gather. It is vital to hit them now, off balance. Tawooz. You're going to pin the northern grouping. Loop around Shingazi to the west and use the graveyard to get a bearing on them. Kakay here will be your guide.'

'It will be done Haji Sahib.'

'I trust you.' Haji Mansur turned to the other man. 'Sadiq. You will trouble the men beyond the ridge. Use the cover of the canal embankment. We need to keep their largest group on the desert side of the canal where they cannot manoeuvre onto us. So I am going to give you the rocket-propelled grenades. Do not be afraid to use them all, but make them count.'

Smiling, he scolded the scarred veteran. 'Not like last time, when you fired at the sun! Any more like that and you'll be paying those Baluchi thieves out of your own pocket.'

He was interrupted by the heavy beat of rotor blades. They all craned their necks. This must be the one with two blades coming in along treetops to pick up the foreign casualties. The attack helicopter was still flying very high somewhere over the river.

'We're running out of time,' Haji Mansur said. 'I'm going to take my team and hit the men at the bridge where Sarbaz has a handle on things. We'll use the machine gun and egg grenade thrower. Communicate on radio as little as possible. When I give the word, switch to channel seven: if anyone is listening to us, they'll miss the final orders. We want to try and attack at the same time if we can. Whatever you do, don't unmask your weapons while that wasp is still in the air.'

'Who will take the wheelbarrow Haji Sahib?' Sadiq asked. 'Baitullah is with you but it has the rockets in it.'

'You take it Sadiq Jan. We'll head towards you at the canal if there are problems.'

They were cascading these instructions when the Chinook helicopter raced across the landscape, banking hard towards the desert. Flares spat out of its flanks to deceive any heat-seeking missiles.

One of the fighters called out, pointing. 'Look brothers, it shits itself with fear.'

Their nerves made the joke funnier than it was. Even Haji Mansur took a second to wallow in the mirth. Its attentive armed escort was tracking away back down the valley.

The groups went their separate ways. Some of the better friends embraced, a hand gripping the back of the neck. 'Allah be with you.' Haji Mansur always tried to dismiss the dread and melancholy of these farewells. It was maudlin to dwell on it; an insult to Allah's divine will and the honour of martyrdom. Yet he could not fail to notice how few and small the stones he was throwing at such a powerful enemy. Hoisting and concealing weapons once more, they waved to him and were gone.

It felt quiet, almost lonely, with his three companions.

Stepping over the sluice gates, they followed an irrigation ditch running parallel to the canal. The vegetation was dense, a lush canopy trapping cooler air and rural fragrances. Flies flitted through narrow shafts of sunlight. A low hanging branch snagged the covering off their machine gun, Ismat the gunner snatching it back as if the tussle had been with a sibling. Emerging from this leafy sanctuary, the team picked up a wall situated perfectly to shield their approach from the ridgeline.

Haji Mansur turned to the earnest faces of his followers. 'Look out for the little plane here. They are not fools and will want to know what lies beyond this wall.' He then spoke into his radio. 'Sarbaz! Powenda approaches with friends. Meet us where we had lunch after the funeral.'

Exposed to surveillance and carrying such an obvious burden as the long-barrelled machine gun, it made sense to rush this section of fifty to a hundred paces. Second in line behind Haji Mansur, and encumbered by the heavy weapon, Ismat slowed up early, breathless. The other two crashed into him, impatient to get back in cover. Turning right into a narrow alley, they startled a young family coming towards them. Straightaway the father shielded his diminutive wife, covered in a dark green burka and clutching a swaddled infant to her breast. His eyes were unthreatening but defiant. Nobody said anything at first. Then Haji Mansur disguised his wishes as advice.

'I'd beat it if I was you. There's a storm coming.'

The man nodded and they slithered past one another, backs to the wall. He was forced to duck underneath the shrouded machine gun barrel.

The alley took them to a rickety wooden door. Haji Mansur opened it as furtively as an adulterer, casting glances left and right before beckoning the 'all clear' into a walled kitchen garden. It had gone fallow in the absence of its owner. Sarbaz arrived soon after by a gate on the far side. He was an impulsive man in his twenties, with a hooked nose. This, rather than his profession or talent, the reason for his nickname meaning 'eagle'. Time and tolerance were the currency of a watcher like Sarbaz. In spite of always appearing to be poor in both departments, he was good at it somehow.

'Peace be upon you Haji Sahib.' Sarbaz' eyes gleamed with excitement. 'I have the perfect firing position for the machine gun. We must go. I'll fetch my rifle from its hiding place over there.'

'Patience, patience, Sarbaz.' Intensely focused on the situation, Haji Mansur forgot to give the formal response to Sarbaz's greeting. 'How far from here? And what of our grenade launcher? Can we work around them?'

'Yes, I will show you now Haji Sahib. Best if we go unarmed.'

Handing his rifle to Baitullah, Haji Mansur said curtly, 'all three of you wait here.' His men sat in silence under a cloudless sky, fidgeting. The air gathered itself, thickening in preparation for a hot day. Birds gossiped. Insects pestered one another. Baitullah pondered on the sounds. All these creatures were totally oblivious to the affairs of man, to this interminable tension. 'What on earth does that fly want so badly?' he wondered. It would land among the hairs on his ankle, take flight at his swat, only to loop back around and land again, and again.

'Persistent little fellow aren't you?' he said aloud.

The latch went.

'On your feet brothers!'

In addition to whatever information he sought, Haji Mansur had found zeal on his reconnaissance. Sarbaz would take one man with the grenade launcher and flank the enemy. Haji Mansur would initiate the ambush with the machine gunner. Baitullah was their assistant, bearing extra ammunition belts.

'Sadiq is in position on the canal. No word yet from Tawooz,' the Haji said. 'Let's go.'

Beyond the garden they moved cautiously, stooped, along a treeline. The trees grew astride a dry ditch. There, they parted with Sarbaz. Haji Mansur moved right a short distance and knelt down where the ditch had shallow sides – most likely a farmer's crossing point – and waved Ismat up alongside him. The foreigners had established a ring around the road bridge, using a compound roof to gain a commanding vantage point. They were just close enough to have answered a shout. This was time to really take care. Each man could feel his own heart. They heard the little plane buzzing somewhere. Strangely it had been absent this morning.

Lifting the machine gun gently off his shoulder, Ismat drew away the cotton shawl and laid it on the lip of the ditch closest to his target. This was to dampen the amount of tell-tale dust kicked up when he fired. Baitullah placed his Kalashnikov on the ground and unravelled the shawl containing ammunition belts. Once Ismat had slithered into the ditch and extended the bipod legs on the machine gun, Baitullah handed one to him. The belt was back to front and the gunner did not notice. Baitullah's warning came out as a croak. He blushed. His tongue felt fat and furry.

Haji Mansur told them to lie flat and crawled away with his radio. He spoke into it with a strained whisper, which felt apt, even though the foreigners were too far to hear anything but a shout.

'Idris! Are you there?' Tawooz wasn't answering to his code name. Perhaps he was busy. Then the radio squawked into life.

'Greetings Powenda. They have the Tajiks with them up here. But they have split in two and I can't see where the donkeys have gone. It's those trick leaf clothes.'

'Don't worry. Switch channel now, all of you.'

Haji Mansur fiddled with the dial then waited a few seconds and signalled to his men. No answer. He checked it again. Channel eight. Should have been seven. Now they were responding.

'All of you fire when I do. Idris, wherever you are, do your best. We cannot afford to wait. Allah is Great. God is Great.' When he released the button, someone else on the radio took up the same refrain.

He crawled back to his team. 'Are you ready brothers?' Ismat nodded. Haji Mansur's fear abandoned him in that moment; a companion taking leave with a silent bow.

'God is Great,' he repeated, to the men around him. 'We seek only his salvation. Fire!'

The machine gun exploded into life, gobbling up the ammunition belt voraciously and spitting bright cases all over the ground. Haji Mansur knelt up and joined in with a long burst from his Kalashnikov. Despite the protective shawl placed on the ground, there was soon a distinctive pall of dust beyond the muzzle of the machine gun.

'Time to move! Up! Up! Go! Follow me!'

Baitullah gathered the belts and was off after Haji Mansur, while Ismat springing to his feet reached down for the machine gun's carrying handle. In his haste, he missed and grabbed the smoking hot barrel, letting out a howl of pain. Instinctively he withdrew his hand, shaking it, and fumbled instead with his left. But that put the gun on the wrong side of his body. He stepped over it.

Incoming bullets arrived. First they landed in front of him, kicking up stinging spurts of soil. Ismat froze. *To run or take cover?* A second later he was slammed to the ground.

Drawn by the crack of incoming fire behind him, Baitullah looked back just in time to see Ismat being struck down onto the path, framed by bright red flashes of tracer bullets. It had knocked the wind out of him and he could see Ismat trying to mouth something. The wounded gunner managed to raise himself onto his elbows when another burst tore into him with total ferocity, like a man hammering at a nail in some demented frenzy. The blows disfigured him: rounds cleaving through Ismat's shoulders, jaw and the top of his skull. The unseen hammer even snatched away his turban.

'Good strike Alfie. You definitely finished him with that last burst.'

'I don't know why he stood there so long sir.' The machine gunner was expressionless, his hands separated from his mind.

'Never mind that now. Switch target left.' Tom slapped his gunner on the helmet and indicated with a straight arm. 'They're bugging out along the treeline there.'

'Get the gun Baitullah! We have to get the machine gun!'

Haji Mansur ran past where Baitullah was cowering. No sooner had Ismat been killed, the serpent struck again through the trees, searching. Any movement attracted it. Haji Mansur seemed oblivious – impervious – to its reach. This shamed Baitullah. Composing himself, he tried to stand up. But his legs would not obey his will. He was a little boy again, standing on the bridge over the canal near his village: older friends goading him, crowing. It was one thing to decide you were going to jump into the water. Your inner self, the sensible part that cared not for other people's opinions, needed to agree.

Finally the humiliation of Haji Mansur's return with the machine gun vanquished this innate self-preservation. Baitullah was alongside him almost unthinkingly. They sprinted back towards the kitchen garden. Percussions of battle filled the valley beyond. Above the crackle of small arms was the prolonged whoosh of a rocket-propelled grenade and the deep crump of its impact up on the ridge. Closer, there was the thud of an egg grenade, and then another. Hurtling through the gate, both men leant against a wall, puffing. A drop of sweat fell from the tip of Baitullah's nose.

'Forgive me Haji Sahib…'

'…It is in the past young Baitullah. Can you operate the machine gun? We must cover Sarbaz back to here.' Without waiting for an answer, he shouted into his radio. 'Sarbaz! Are you there?'

At first only the clatter of a nearby Kalashnikov came over the speaker. 'We are right on top of them Powenda! I could kick one if I wanted! We have used all the eggs. Why are your men not firing?'

'Ismat is Shahid brother. Only two of us are left. We will give them another squirt so you can escape to the garden. That will be your signal.'

Baitullah loaded the machine gun with another belt, conscious of Ismat doing the very same thing just minutes ago. Haji Mansur was barking at Sadiq on the radio, demanding to know why he had only heard one or two rockets.

Neither of them noticed the little plane dipping its wing above them.

Leaving his Kalashnikov and spare belts in the garden, Baitullah followed Haji Mansur through the gate. This time they went the way Sarbaz had, towards the gunfire. Haji Mansur knew the route from his earlier reconnaissance. He ducked into a ditch.

'OK young Baitullah. No need to be afraid. We are going to use only half of a belt – just enough for the foreigners to be distracted.' Haji Mansur started arranging the belt for him.

'I can't see them Haji Sahib.'

'That doesn't matter. We know they have men in those trees. Hold down the trigger for a count of three and then run back to the garden. I will move towards Sarbaz and bring them in.'

The cocking handle was stiff. It took Baitullah two attempts. He tried to swallow. A reassuring hand tapped him on the ankle.

It was the Haji. 'You are not alone, my brave brother. Let's get this done.'

Baitullah lined up the sights on the base of a tall tree and pulled the trigger. Though firmly in his shoulder, the weapon had a mind of its own. Most of the bullets ended up in the treetops.

He heard the Haji from somewhere through the trees. 'Run Baitullah! Run brother!'

The foreigners responded with startling speed. He had pulled the tail of a bad-tempered dog. Their bullets brought autumn to the lowest branches, and carved at the ditch's rim. Fortunately it was directed where he had been, not where he was going. Ismat's machine gun weighed the same as a bucketfull of water and Baitullah fought the urge to cast it aside.

Once in the garden, he felt insulated from the chaos. Its mud walls deadened the sound of everyone else's share. A few stray rounds cracked overhead but they were harmless compared to the swarm he had just survived. Baitullah prayed Haji Mansur and the others would join him soon. Without them the refuge felt more like a prison. Navigating the battlefield alone back to the motorbikes did not bear thinking about.

Baitullah heard them before he saw them: the scuff of footsteps, Sarbaz jabbering away excitedly as ever, convincing himself that he had killed a foreigner. First through the gate, Haji Mansur smiled at him.

'Good to see you my boy. Let's find out how the others are getting on.'

There was definitely a battle going on north of Shingazi now. He squatted down and raised Tawooz on the radio.

'Hunting is good up here Powenda! The Tajiks are really angry with me!' Again, the chatter of automatic fire muscled in on the message.

Over by the canal Sadiq had stirred things up too – only managing to shout 'I'm on the move' before cutting off. Haji Mansur needed to re-establish some control. He paused and started a message.

'We've done enough for now brothers. All of you head back to the rendezvous. Idris, we will wait for you to break—'

The sky filled with a soaring shriek. Haji Mansur was still transmitting when he screamed 'GET DOWN!' Nobody in the garden had time to react. The shell detonated before he even reached the final syllable. It had been set to explode in the air, spreading splinters like a massive shotgun. Literally deafened by the slam above them, all four men squirmed into the ground – every fibre willing itself lower. It was only then that Baitullah registered the pain.

He didn't see the dirty smudge of grey smoke left by the blast. None of them did. Face down, their only sensations were punching air pressure and nakedness. The thunder clouds collected above the walled garden, each one portended by the same shrill rip through a spring sky, announcing its arrival with a clap that reverberated for miles.

And in imitation of nature's most violent storms, it passed quickly.

After prayer, Gul Khan had prepared his own breakfast that morning and made a mess of it. He could have gone to Janan's compound and fetched some bread but it was a sure way to signal Sanga's absence to his tongue-wagging neighbours. They probably all knew of course. It was more a question of form, in his life of endless obligations to principle.

On top of his cooking mishap, he had passed a fitful night's sleep, fearful that the Jirga decision, and his role within it, had already leaked to the Movement. Perhaps it would have been more sensible to stay elsewhere. It was difficult to think of a viable bolthole though. Pointedly, Janan had not suggested they lie-up together... It was enough to make Gul Khan smile. He knew him like a brother. Janan would have confided in his wife, and she would have ordered him to keep his distance.

He was feeding the goats when startled by the weighty thud of a mine. It had been loud – close – but the physical fright had everything to do with Mamur. That flat, isolated sound would make him sick to the stomach, to his dying day.

Still, his mind was too absorbed in today's fortunes not to mull over the possible causes and implications of that blast. In daylight it had to be a victim: either a soldier or yet another farmer. Another thought then occurred to him. The mine was sure to attract fighters from the Movement, even Haji Mansur himself possibly. Events were moving quickly.

Caged, blind and impotent inside his compound, curiosity had burned in him early that morning. But he knew how important it was to be patient, and stay where he was. If the foreigners were coming then the Haji and his men would be too busy dealing with that to worry about Gul Khan, and present an opportunity for his faithful Kalashnikov to sing. And only a fool would wander around with a weapon when the foreigners had their blood up.

The passing of a low-flying helicopter solved the mine mystery at least. But what were the British doing all the way down here?

Of all people to deliver salvation, it was his hopeless neighbour's boy, Mir Hamza, who banged on the gates with news.

'Gul Khan Sahib? Are you in there? The foreigners are here. Hundreds of them, crossing the desert like Mongols. They are at the bridge. You must believe me.'

In his suspicious state, Gul Khan suddenly entertained the fear that Mir Hamza had been co-opted into some kind of ruse to get him to open up his compound to assailants. He drew back the gate with his shoulder behind it, braced for a struggle, then felt silly as soon as the youth's guileless moon face came into view.

'Of course I believe you Mir Hamza,' he said. 'Hundreds' probably meant about two dozen.

'Is Imran here?' the boy asked. 'He will want to see.' Mir Hamza did that thing people do on a threshold, peering past Gul Khan to answer the question for himself.

'He won't do anything of the sort. Nor should you. Go home and stay inside.' Gul Khan started to close the gate and hesitated. 'Why are you still here Mir Hamza? Why not flee?'

'Some are, Gul Khan Sahib, like birds. But my grandmother is lame. She says she'd rather die on a carpet than a road.'

'You listen to her then Mir Hamza. Keep her company.'

He slammed the gates and took his own advice, seeking shelter indoors. Even if the action was some distance away, bullets and shrapnel had to land somewhere. A metal rain they were all accustomed to by now. Gul Khan cocked his ear to the air.

Ah! The muffled dialogue of war was like his memory talking. Distant machine guns had always reminded him of a woodpecker. His Pakistani instructor in the Mujahideen used to quip that the little birds were naturals at it. 'Listen to the discipline in their bursts,' he would say. Gul Khan sat there intently, ticking off the different sounds as if it were a test of some sort. Rocket-propelled grenade. Mortar. Artillery... but not a heavy calibre, not like those Russian beasts... He almost felt left out.

Then it went quiet. That must mean the Movement were re-posturing or withdrawing. After a while he ventured out into his courtyard. One of the foreign gunships was prowling around, master of all it surveyed. The Movement would not like that. This could be why things were damper now.

He was tracking its progress idly through the sky when he heard a foreign voice, very distinct and projected. You did not need to speak English to deduce that the man was giving an order to an underling. The British were in the village.

'I said – go a bit further Steveo! Clear up to that junction and tell me what you can see.'

'Ah, roger sir,' Private Stephens replied. Anything said to him was now competing with a high-pitched ringing, thrust into his ears by the IED blast.

Nick stood in the middle of a dirt track, between two long, high-walled compounds. His column was strung out along the full length of it. The men knelt in the dust, weary. Some bowed their heads forward, baring sun-burnished necks in a vain attempt to alleviate pressure on their shoulders. Futile shrugs joined the struggle. Swollen feet itched to be free of their boots. Sweat cleared narrow trails through the grime on their faces. A few took the opportunity to suck mouthfuls of warm water from drinking tubes. Spit balanced on the dust, too sticky to soak in.

Nick's head thudded with dehydration. Worse was the persistent, niggling stress of fresh regrets, lying atop their predecessors like a wet coat of paint, all sticky and invasive. He had so wanted to give his team a clear run this day, to prove that even the most dangerous operations could be navigated without loss. Yet everyone knew what this battle in Shingazi had to offer. Judgement and luck would dance their dance.

After Jojo was borne away, clinging to life by the fingernails of his one remaining hand, they had got embroiled in a running firefight against a small group of tenacious insurgents scuttling in and out of the graveyard. Nick thanked God for the Taliban's poor marksmanship. Sultan's ANA had used up most of their ammunition generating the usual fireworks display, so everyone was relieved to get into the village during a lull. A soldier knows enough history to realise it could always be worse. They ploughed on through the day, one foot in front of the other.

And there was Private Stephens. The cuts on his face were the only outward indication he had been knocked off his feet by an IED earlier.

'Looks clear down to the canal sir,' he called back. 'No sign of the company yet.'

'I'm not surprised,' Nick said to himself, aloud. They would still be focused on the south side of the village, where that main attack arrived from. Nick looked at Corporal Lennon.

'Let's roll Beatle. You're happy where 'Sally' is?'

'Yup.' Corporal Lennon had gone flat since the blast, as if on autopilot.

As Nick took his first steps, a set of metal gates clanged open towards the rear of the column. The nearest soldier spun around and raised his weapon. A short man emerged wearing tan shalwar kameez and a brown waistcoat. His expression was hidden by a thick beard and jaunty Pakol, unusual this late in spring. He spoke confidently and cheerfully in Pashtu. None of them could understand what he was saying. As always in these situations, eyes turned to Nick. An officer problem. Radioing Sergeant Langdon at the rear, Nick set an apologetic tone.

'I'm going to need Sultan and the interpreter. Sorry to be a pain but this is the first local we've set eyes on and he's itching for a parley.'

Nick raised a hand in universal welcome. He had a sudden recollection that NASA used the very same posture when depicting humans on the side of a deep-space probe.

'Peace be upon you. Health and happiness. My name is Nek.'

The soldier gesticulated over his shoulder with a vague sweep and said 'interpreter'. Then his halting, accented Pashtu dried up into a broad smile.

Gul Khan understood well enough. One of those performing monkeys from Kabul was going to come and work his magic. They stood in a civil and awkward silence. Gul Khan could discern voices coming from inside the man's radio. He carried a map. It must be an officer. The man was dressed for some dangerous winter: helmet, strange yellow-tinted glasses, gloves, a huge vest and pack. He stood there with the mass of a calf. Tugging his beard, Gul Khan regarded the other soldiers. They were hot and tired. He knew that look, dreaming of tea under the shade of a tree or a naked swim in a cool river.

Presently they were joined by a thin, studious-looking Pashtun dressed unconvincingly like the British. Alongside him was a young clean-shaven Tajik in sunglasses. Unlike the other Afghan soldiers, he had dispensed with a helmet in favour of his beret. Gul Khan liked that – a man unafraid of his fate on the battlefield. Nek tried to introduce his Tajik ally as the senior man but their body language betrayed him as an associate. Moreover, it soon became apparent that the Tajik spoke little Pashtu and the interpreter struggled to keep pace in both English and Dari. The conversation drifted quickly into one between Gul Khan and the British officer. It was convoluted waiting for his messages to be turned into English – a strange-sounding language. Gul Khan could not discern a single word within the streams of sound, just a few hard edges. These interpreters were like sorcerers. You had to respect their gift.

'He says he is not the British commander, just in charge of the people you can see. The commander is down by the road bridge.' He named him in English and Gul Khan struggled to make it out. Something like 'Mayghor Lokhleed'.

'He wants to know if you have seen any enemies in the village today and if you know of any mines,' the sorcerer said.

'I have seen no enemies in the village because we have all been hiding in our homes.' Gul Khan smiled. 'War is not good sport for spectators. As for mines? Not many this far south. If you ask him where he's going I can show him the paths we know to be safe.'

The offer tumbled freely from his lips, maybe too freely. To be seen assisting the foreigners in this way would be Gul Khan's first public gesture of defiance against the Haji. He listened to the interpreter. Nick laughed suddenly and nodded, grinning at Gul Khan. Maybe it was the joke about spectators.

'He says they are going to the south of the village, to an empty compound not far from Shingazi Bridge. If you don't mind risking an appearance on the sports field, he would be grateful for safe passage.'

Last chance to back out. 'It will be my pleasure,' Gul Khan said.

Placing a hand over his heart, Nek offered some more childlike Pashtu.

'Many thanks,' he said.

Gul Khan saw that Nek was a man of manners at least. Friendship with these foreign strangers was a practical matter. Water flows where the hill takes it. But there was no harm in liking them, as men.

Nick was straight onto the major on his radio. 'That's right. Gul Khan. The man himself.'

He transmitted again. 'No, no. Don't worry. We played it straight. He's bringing us down to "Sally". We'll be there in a few minutes. He's set quite a pace. Like he's late for a train.'

At first, Stephens and Brogan had tried to continue swinging their metal detectors but Nick stopped them. It would be an insult to their guide. Even so, Nick took the lead just behind Gul Khan. If he considered the risk to be acceptable, the least he could do was shoulder it himself.

It felt reckless to be moving so briskly and freely through Shingazi – unnerving in fact. None of them had tripped along with such abandon on unfamiliar ground for months. Every so often Gul Khan said something over his shoulder in Pashtu, forgetting that Nick could not understand. If it was an attempt to give them a guided tour, Gul Khan was missing something crucial: most Helmand villages were totally nondescript.

Blank, high mud walls concealed all interiors, windows and gardens. The only architectural features were solid metal gates that expressed something of a personality through simple ironwork and faded paint schemes. There were no phone lines, electricity cables, lights or manhole covers. Communal space was limited to a hand water pump and a flat concrete pad for threshing crops. The village shop was nothing more commercial than a room adjoining the proprietor's compound, with one small door and a shuttered, glassless window.

This left time and nature as Shingazi's creative influences. Successive rains had carved intricate channels through mud structures and dirt roads. Treetops peeped over compound walls and abundant vegetation encroached on the village from all sides. But for the metalwork and one or two maltreated cars, Nick could have picked any century in the last millennium.

Their tour ended when the major's cordon came into view, on a wide junction. Two snipers had put a ladder up one side of a compound and were reclining on the roof like languid cats. Immediately the troops called out to one another with their usual joshing. Private Stephens walked past a prone machine-gunner, the youngest man in the company. His eighteenth birthday had come two weeks before deployment.

'Who was it Steveo?' the boy said, softly.

'Jojo mate. A triple. He might be OK. We didn't give up on him.'

'Fuck. How many's that now?' It was a rhetorical question, posed into the blank black eye of his weapon sight. When the company arrived in the valley, they started with eight metal detector operators. Five months on, only half of those men still had their legs.

Whereas the north of the village had still been deserted, there was enough of a lull now to draw a few curious souls from the safety of their compounds. Gul Khan's manner changed around them; he was less ebullient, more formal and self-conscious. Every villager that had ever collaborated with a foreign army in history must have felt something similar. At home, these were risks only familiar to serious criminal witnesses. Here it was part of everyday life.

Fifty metres further on they saw the major, immersed in a negotiation with some elders that Gul Khan seemed to recognise. Detaching himself from Nick's column, Gul Khan jogged down the track, evidently impatient to be part of it. Nick used the radio to overtake him.

'That's Gul Khan coming down the track towards you now. I'll hold my team here and thicken the cordon out towards the canal.'

'Good work,' the major said. 'Best if you come down with Sultan though. You're the tenants.'

Relaying his instructions to Sergeant Langdon over the airwaves, Nick made unhurried progress towards the impromptu Shura,* watching Gul Khan embrace the elder men formally before turning to the major, shaking his hand. By the time Nick arrived, the major's interpreter, Nazif, was in full flow. A handsome and spruce student from Jalalabad, he had completed half of medical school in Pakistan where English is the language of academia and government. Six months in Helmand was going to fund his road to graduation. Nazif's eloquence and refinement set him apart, especially in this valley. Nick enjoyed eavesdropping on the softly spoken asides to the major, delivered with a kind of affront.

'Sir, this bandit is lying to you. There is no value in me translating his rubbish.'

The major was explaining which compound had been selected for a patrol base and the fact that rent would be agreed. None of the elders spoke. Their faces conveyed nothing but stoic ambivalence, like stock photographs selected by editors to convey third-world exploitation. Nobody yet had the confidence to show public assent, even though all the intelligence indicated that they were requesting this. Set against

---

* **Shura**, the Arabic for 'consultation' is used to refer to any meeting where decisions are sought in council. It differs from a 'Jirga' only insomuch as the term is universal to Islam, whereas a 'Jirga' is specific to Pashtu culture.

such studied passivity, Gul Khan's impatience became clearly discernible. He broke silence when the major asked village folk to stay well clear while the compound was being searched for mines.

'There are no IEDs in Haji Barader's compound. We are wasting time. I'll show you.'

Nazif exercised a form of ventriloquy, never prefixing his translation with 'he says'.

Gul Khan waved an arm and set off down the road with short, bossy strides like an ill-tempered librarian. The engineer search team were engrossed in their meticulous task, clearing the perimeter and entry points of the compound, when Gul Khan pushed past their young sentry.

'Woah, woah, woah mate. Where d'ya think you're going?' The sentry was too incredulous to impede the trespasser and merely searched around for an authority figure.

Nick met his entreaty with the apologetic look of someone who regularly chaperones an obnoxious friend. When Nick caught up with Gul Khan, he fared no better: the resolute Pashtun shrugged him off and gestured ahead.

Two men were crouching together to check the main gate for booby traps, heads down in total absorption. On hearing the commotion it took them a second or two to surface, just in time for Gul Khan to bang hard against the metal gates and slide the locking bar. The two searchers leapt with alarm. Throwing the gates open, Gul Khan took two steps across the threshold and threw his arms open in a salutary flourish. Nick's Pashtu stood no chance against the speed of Gul Khan's gabble but it must have been along the lines of 'welcome'. He then took theatrical goose steps about the courtyard, stamping his feet repeatedly to demonstrate the absence of IEDs.

Recovering his wits, one of the searchers brushed at his knee-pads, uttering, 'What the fuck! Who's that lunatic? He gave me a bastard heart attack.'

Nobody followed Gul Khan and the gateway soon became a viewing gallery. Nazif called out to him and he responded by kicking a pebble at them derisively. The absurdity of this invisible divide hit home to Nick. He realised how ludicrous they must seem to Gul Khan, all crowded together in fear. They were losing credibility. But it was like watching someone paddle in the crocodile enclosure: nobody, in some cases even the insurgents themselves, could be sure an unoccupied property had not been mined at some point. All Nick's wits – the fresh memory of Jojo's twisting body – counselled him to stay where he was. Yet somebody had to act. This man risked everything by playing estate agent to the British and they were showing no faith in him.

Nick sighed and marched into the compound, deflecting cries of reproach with exasperated resignation.

'Lads, at some point we're going to have to start trusting these people.' Then he shouted to Gul Khan. 'Luxurious! I'll take it.'

Gul Khan beamed and clapped Nick on the shoulder. The two men created an inadvertent mime act with the Afghan pointing at the throng while Nick shrugged. Having led by example, Nick was not half as comfortable for others to gamble likewise. A solution sprang to mind.

'Now let me show *you* something Gul Khan. You'll like this.'

He frogmarched the older man back out of the compound to the position where a bomb disposal team gathered around their equipment. As Nick passed the search commander he issued some hasty instructions.

'That roof on the north-east corner will be the main sangar.* We can start building it from the outside while you search the compound. It'll fool him into thinking we've taken his word for it.'

One of the bomb disposal experts was kneeling over a small remote-controlled robot with rubber tracks, a camera and a claw on an extendable arm. Nick pointed to it and smiled at Gul Khan.

'Meet our little friend. He goes places we're afraid to. From now on we're gonna call him "Gul Khan", in your honour.'

Nick had thought to use Merlin for this stunt but he was not sure the Pashtun would be so chuffed to be associated with a dog. Either way, the gesture worked. When Nazif had finished, Gul Khan giggled like a child.

---

* **Sangar**, derived from the Persian 'sang' meaning 'stone,' a sangar is a protected sentry post made from a breastwork of stone or sandbags, normally located on the perimeter of a base. The term dates back to the British Indian Army and has its roots in campaigns against Pashtun tribes.

It never ceased to amaze Haji Mansur how the human belly stowed so much offal. A shell splinter had slashed across Baitullah's midriff. His entrails – distended and glistening – bulged out of a long, widening wound. The boy's feeble attempts to push them back in came to nothing, like working the split in a bag of bedding. Nobody else wanted to touch them. The stench was nauseating. Baitullah's eyes voiced a disbelieving misery.

Haji Mansur had wrapped a shawl tightly around Baitullah's body and then they carried him. It was a struggle in more ways than one. Baitullah's injuries precluded putting him over a shoulder or onto someone's back, so they were forced to shuffle along awkwardly with one man under the armpits and another carrying his legs. Everyone's coordination was affected by the battering their senses had taken. Straw-coloured mucus dribbled from Sarbaz's ears, and the fourth fighter had copped a small shell fragment in the lower leg. Haji Mansur did most of the work at the heavier, head end. Fortunately, Sadiq had anticipated casualties when he saw the lightning barrage, and moved rapidly towards them with the wheel barrow. Progress back to the main rendezvous was much smoother after that. Once there, they took stock and waited for the estate car.

'I'm really thirsty Haji Sahib,' Baitullah said.

He was pale and clammy. They had doused the shawl in water and were fanning it to keep the flies away. That much they knew was sensible... but to drink? Haji Mansur was convinced it would do no harm. He removed his round cloth cap and reached down into a nearby ditch. Murky with silt, the water did not look too inviting. So Haji Mansur stretched for the centre of the stream where it flowed fastest. Two trips later, Baitullah was still thirsty. The cap did not prove a very efficient receptacle. But there was an ignorant consensus that two rations were sufficient.

'Don't let him have more than that,' offered Sadiq, as if he knew anything of the subject.

The 'ambulance' arrived, bucking up a rutted track. Its driver enquired after the day's wretched cargo. He was a tidy, urban-looking character in his early thirties with a silvery grey turban and clean lace-up shoes. It could have been a deliberate costume to arouse less suspicion, but his officious manner irritated Haji Mansur, who was about to say something when the driver chastened him.

'Wounded leg can ride up front with me. Brother with his gut open goes in the boot where he can lie down. Please tell me you haven't given him anything to drink.'

In fairness, the driver must have seen a lot of casualties. Haji Mansur spoke for all of them.

'He was thirsty,' he said, somewhat defensively.

'Well, you haven't done him any favours. In any case, best if you say your goodbyes. These ones don't generally make it.' The driver opened up the hatchback nonchalantly and stood idly in expectation that others would load his car.

This time Haji Mansur's veil came down. He squared up to

the driver and rested the muzzle of his short Kalashnikov on the man's ribs. Only those nearest could hear them.

'Say that again you callous sinful swine. Say that again, and you'll be the one who "doesn't generally make it". Any one of us can drive your car to Kandahar.'

The driver blanched. 'Forgive me Haji Sahib. You are right. Allah decides who lives and dies. I'll be as swift as I can. We're going via a doctor who will administer a drip for the journey.'

'Excellent. Travel safe. Remember this conversation when next we meet.' Haji Mansur's muzzle tapped the driver's chest for emphasis.

Haji Mansur went and grasped the back of Baitullah's neck. 'If Allah makes you a martyr this day, you will dine in paradise my brave brother. If he has other plans, then we fight again. You've made me proud.' The weak boy swallowed drawing the courage to speak. But after a pause, he merely nodded.

'You're right. Save your strength Baitullah.'

While the others loaded Baitullah into the rear bay, Haji Mansur went around the front to share a conspiratorial word with his lightly wounded fighter.

'Be sure to see he gets buried properly. There's a good man in Kandahar, sympathetic to the Movement. They'll show you at the hospital. I know I can rely on you... if it comes to that.'

'... If it comes to that, Haji Sahib.'

With a quick rap on the roof, the car drew away. A quarter of a mile up the track, four motorbikes came at speed from the opposite direction, dust pluming behind them like rocket exhaust. Defying certain collision, the riders braked and weaved in deft manoeuvre to squeeze past the car, one kicking the side of it to maintain balance. Once past the bottleneck, they accelerated with a buzz and were bearing down on

Haji Mansur's dwindled force in no time. All carried pillion passengers.

Their leader dismounted from the second motorbike while the others parked up in the habitual cover of trees. He removed the turban tail he had been using to shield his nose and mouth from dust, like a desert traveller during the storms, and embraced Haji Mansur warmly. They were of similar status within the Movement's loose hierarchy: fealties traded on a currency of personality, experience and patronage. Whenever a rank structure was formed, Allah upset the edifice with his gift of Shahid, like a man selecting logs from the middle of an untidy pile.

'Long morning brother? That boy in the ambulance looked bad.'

'He'll be in good company. One of my better machine gunners was martyred earlier too. Don't panic. There are more men than this. Tawooz and three others are still moving back. I've sent one scout forward again. Sarbaz. He's reliable, if a little deaf today after we got caught in the hail.'

The leader nodded. 'I think the foreigners are planning to stay in Shingazi,' he said. 'One of my boys saw Porcupines out in the desert an hour ago. No doubt. They even have a couple of those four-wheeled motorbikes with trailers. My boy says there are Kuchi clans with less stuff to carry. Don't you have spies in the village?'

Haji Mansur prickled at the implied criticism. 'Of course I do but the phone towers have been dead for days up here. Why do you think we sent a courier to get you this morning? It's alright for you lot down by the highway. Our only tower was sabotaged by Mullah Ismail's incompetent hotheads over the river. Can you believe that…?'

The bleating reached his own ears and dried up. As Haji Mansur's wife liked to say, long excuses betray a man short on wits.

'Sarbaz will tell us on the radio soon enough,' he said, drawing a line under it. 'It's time we gave the foreigners more difficulty. I'd like to recover our Shahid brother too. We didn't have a chance earlier. Did you bring the special rifle?'

'Yes brother – and the Ishaqzai who can use it. He'll impress you.'

Leaning up to check that all was clear, the engineer corporal could see everyone had crouched as ordered. They showed only the domes of their helmets, abutting hunched backs, in the aspect of clustered tortoises.

'Firing... NOW!'

The corporal dropped back down to join with the others and depressed a fat button on his exploder. There was a powerful, jolting thud – strong as a mine. Confined by the orchard, the blast dislodged blossom from the trees above them. The firing party looked up to a blizzard of white petals imitating soft, wide snowflakes. Dust drifted away from the wall to reveal a gap about a metre wide.

Nick appeared at the orchard's entrance. 'Good breach Corporal Milburn?' he said.

'Perfect sir. You've got a nice clear route to your back door now. And we've made sure it will be covered by the ANA sangar. We've got two charges left if you need anything else knocked through.' Old for his rank, Corporal Milburn's

Geordie accent smiled, even on the rare occasions his face forgot to.

'No more dems for today thanks,' Nick said. 'You can go and help your gang with home improvements.'

'Aye sir, I will. Though I say it m'self, I'm a dab hand with the sandbagging. Me and the missus do a bit of drystone walling back home in the north-east, for a hobby, like. Not having any kids gives you time for that sort of thing. The lads take the piss out of me. You know…"where's your beard and boiled eggs Millie". But it's surprisingly therapeutic you know. This'll be a happy reminder. Put my skills to good use and keep you nice and snug, for when the Taliban pay you a visit.'

Corporal Milburn sustained this ceaseless affable natter while Nick accompanied them back to the compound's main entrance. The compound and its environs played host to a bustle. Order and haste competed in a contest refereed by Company Sergeant Major Barnet, a man happiest when there was too much to do.

Vehicles were being backed up to the gates leading into 'Sally'. All the constituents of self-sufficiency came off, one by one. Cases of bottled water, ration boxes, cooking fuel, defecation bags and latrine buckets, wash bowls, mosquito nets, ammunition tins, grenades, claymore mines,[*] signal smoke, illumination flares, radio batteries and a miscellany of other martial necessities. The quartermaster sergeant garnished this heap of stores with other useful desirables like candles,

---

[*] **Claymore mine**, a surface mine full of ball-bearings that explodes in a preset direction like a giant shotgun. It is always triggered remotely by an operator, not set like a booby trap, and is best suited to covering areas not easily reached by rifle and machine gun fire.

clothes line and the real prize: a large aluminium kettle, which one of the soldiers hefted appreciatively as it was placed on the trove.

Parallel with the supply effort was something altogether more remarkable. Nick stopped to take it in.

Sandbags were the principal building blocks for their main rooftop sangar. Until a decent breastwork could be raised, the engineers constructing it were totally exposed to any enemy fire. Speed was of the essence, but their workforce was limited. Most soldiers were engaged securing the canal bridge and manning the protective cordon. All spare hands had formed a team to ferry sandbags from a nearby ditch where they were being filled, thence up a ladder on the outside of the compound, to the waiting builders. Toiling in heavy armour under a strong sun was slow going. Each sandbag weighed as much as a four-year-old child.

Gul Khan soon tired of loitering while the soldiers busied around him. Wordlessly he had stepped in and picked up a sandbag, shedding his shawl in anticipation of a sweat. It raised a spirited cheer from the engineers on the roof. He was already something of a celebrity. When other bystanders saw this, someone else joined him, then another, and another. Before long, a dozen or so Afghans from Shingazi had volunteered to swell the labour force. Strong and unencumbered, the locals were in their element.

Company Sergeant Major Barnet noticed Nick approach the compound and cut across to speak with him. The short journey was not to be wasted. On route he squeezed in a couple of 'conversations', as he liked to call them.

'Wallace! Didn't I tell you to put that ammunition in the fucking shade? Great. Nice talking to you.'

Three more paces.

'See Clark? Much easier my way in't it?'

His mood could change at the speed of a TV remote: one second adult drama, cartoons the next. He never seemed to bear a grudge.

'Hello sir. We heard your DIY next door. The local council might be getting one or two complaints I'll wager.' He grinned. 'These Afghans are gleaming. Real grafters. What I—'

Sensing something over Nick's shoulder, he flashed.

'Oi! Light that cigarette Atherton! I fucking dare you.'

Then completely placid again.

'They're worse than my foster kids these. You've gotta be some kind of fuckin' psychic. As I was about to say sir, I just wanted to check the ANA are gonna doss on the north side here, and your lads in that building, under the main sangar there. We're shifting the stores for you.'

'That's the plan sarn't major,' said Nick. 'Sultan may have other ideas. They like their space and we're shorthanded after my cock-up this morning.'

His last statement weighed too much in delivery. The company sergeant major clocked it instantly and lightened the mood.

'This beats the superstore though, don't it sir.' He gestured around.

Nick twinkled. 'How so sarn't major?'

'Well, it's Saturday morning right? Imagine what you *could* be doing. Fuckin' traffic, a row with the wife about which bloody exit to take, then that bastard maze of a car park. And you haven't got a pound coin for the trolley. Finally you get inside and it's a scrum with some mindless fuckwit blocking the aisle, 'coz he can't decide what fuckin' socks to buy. I'm telling you… think I'd rather be here.'

They shared a laugh. 'It's a good point. But I'm normally hungover on a Saturday.'

'Who says I'm not sir? It's hell on earth that place.'

Whether through necessity or pretext, the company sergeant major pinched it off there. He was off again, calling up to the engineers on the roof about how much timber they needed.

Nick sought out the major and found him at the bottom of the ladder hefting sandbags. He had Nazif the interpreter engaged in a running conversation with the Afghans around them.

'Skipper, I'm keen to bring my lads in soon, to get acquainted while we're still here in strength.'

'I understand,' the major said. 'Your lads'll be the first in once these sangars are up.' His explanation was interrupted every few seconds by the audible strain of raising the bags. 'But I can't afford to thin down the cordon till then. Everyone's mucking in.'

Nick nodded as the major changed tack.

'You're going to have an interesting time of it down here Jack. It has huge potential. But these men were just explaining how the older generation holds things up: too cautious, too weary perhaps. They won't like the pace of all this change.' He turned to the Afghans. 'It's your future we're lifting. Wouldn't you agree?'

They looked quizzically at Nazif while it was translated. Nick thought the major was getting ahead of himself with such idealistic Churchillian phrases – intoxicated on the moment maybe. He was prone to verbosity at the best of times. Yet the Afghans seemed to revel in his bombast. Smirks rippled. One of them held a sandbag as high as he could, arms quivering and turban being dusted by an hourglass seepage.

Sharp cracks split the air. Their champion dropped his sandbag and it glanced off his shoulder, soil cascading down his back. Up on the roof there was the clank of tools and a few oaths as the engineers leapt behind their half-finished sangar. As he bounded up the ladder the major addressed the Afghans in the manner of a rider calming their horse.

'It's OK it's OK. Get in against this wall.' Somehow it transcended the language barrier.

A firefight sparked off on the outer cordon just as the distant Taliban machine gunner gave it another burst over the compound. The company sergeant major bellowed at Nick from the compound gate.

'Sir! Sir! Tell the Skipper they're using the machine gun to conceal a sharpshooter. There's another weapon – distinct – and much fucking closer.'

It was too late. Shrill cries fluttered from the roof like gulls. 'Man down!'

The cries were joined by a loud, flat, 'clacking sound' as the sangar's automatic grenade launcher started working at the distant treeline. The brawny cousin of a normal machine gun, it lobbed six plum-sized grenades every second. It had been one of the first things they emplaced as the sangar took shape. Distant crumps echoed each salvo. The major leaned down over the lip.

'Jack! Looks like a two-pronged attack. Casualty is a gunshot wound, upper chest. He'll be coming down this ladder. We'll be needing more ammunition.' Then he summoned the artillery observer. 'Join me up here Sergeant Marsh. You're in business.'

Nick felt superfluous. Company Sergeant Major Barnet was in full swing, barking clipped instructions.

'Right! Everyone fucking shut up and calm down. Corporal Wallace! You're on the caz-ee-vac.[*] I want that ladder doubled up and we'll run him down between them. Medic! You'll be waiting at the bottom. Go. Clark! You and one other, get four boxes of forty-mill to Captain Russell at the ladder.'

And so on. The Afghans squatted impassively, fascinated. One even flicked stones to kill time during this intermission. Nazif found himself in an uncomfortable limbo: not really qualified to help his employers but foreign to his impassive countrymen at the same time.

Incoming fire persisted, accurate and intimidating.

Private Clark panted over lugging two large tins. Nick took one.

'Well done Clark. Let's get the lids off down here so they don't have to lean up in the sangar.'

Two more arrived, and the soldier dumped them off, chasing after the next errand he had been given. A voice reached them from above.

'Ammo!'

Clark struggled with the seal and started removing his gloves. The voice insisted.

'We need fucking ammo!'

Nick had the lid off his tin so set off up the ladder with

---

[*] **CASEVAC**, casualty evacuation; pronounced 'caz-ee-vac'. Shorthand for the process of extracting a wounded soldier from front line the way to hospital.

it under one arm, feeling decidedly more exposed at every rung. The ladder became completely exposed as he topped out towards the roof. He tried not to imagine a distant marksman adjusting posture in preparation for such an appealing shot.

'Forty-mill coming up!' Nick was a little more breathless than the climb warranted.

On the roof everyone crawled around in a supine mêlée, as if overcrowding an attic space with an invisible ceiling. The major and his observer were at the far end, peering over the low parapet to plot a barrage. Two engineers were buckling the wounded man into a flexible stretcher. His body armour had been unfastened and a bloodied field dressing lay on the ground, evidently an abortive earlier attempt to plug the injury. Nick could not make out who it was. Eager hands grabbed the tin from him and then Nick narrowly avoided a kick in the face as the soldier slithered back around towards the grenade machine gun. The gunner sat feet first behind its squat tripod, with both hands on the control bar, like a biker astride his low-ride chopper. He was higher than anyone else, at demonstrable personal risk. Fat green shell cases littered the roof, each the size of an espresso cup.

Nick started back down the ladder with relief. After a few rungs he bumped into Clark who handed up another tin. Gul Khan had invested himself at the bottom, steadying the ladder. Company Sergeant Major Barnet was supervising the placement of a second ladder alongside them. He nodded towards Gul Khan.

'I tell you sir, that fella would be on the fucking grenade launcher if he had half a chance.'

With other men beside him to share his airy peril, Nick felt strangely more secure. The pop of friendly smoke bombs carried from beyond view. There was no more enemy fire being directed their way. Only the peripheral skirmish endured and that was slackening to a few desultory shots.

The young female medic knelt impatiently around her primed gear, gazing at it like someone deciding what to pack into an overnight bag.

'Can they at least give me his basic vitals?' she asked. 'I don't even know who it is yet.'

The company sergeant major conciliated. 'They're doing their best up there. Whoever it is, let's just get him down out of harm's way first.'

The medic was young and tanned, her long dark hair held in a tight bun under the rim of her helmet. Nick put his ex-girlfriend in her place, picturing Becky kneeling there desperate to heal: the inimitable Yorkshire balance of practicality and compassion that made her such a wonderful nurse. It flooded him with affinity for the medic. He tried to contribute.

'The Skipper sent the zap number out over the radio, but I didn't recognise it,' Nick said. 'Must be one of the engineers.'

Skilfully a quad bike and trailer snarled its way down the track in reverse, ready to convey the casualty out to a helicopter landing site in the desert. They left the engine idling. It was an apt soundtrack for their collective frustration.

A flaring clamour signalled that the stretcher was ready to come off the roof. Two boots appeared first, the black plastic of the stretcher encasing his legs and body, with straps tight over the top, almost like he was rolled up in a carpet. Drag loops dangled and they grabbed at them. One of the engineers shouted down, composed but with a thick voice.

'It went in under his arm Doc. Then came out by his shoulder blade, we reckon. It must be lodged in the armour.

We dressed the holes but he's totally unresponsive.' The report sputtered into a sad sort of excuse. 'None of us could kneel up...' And then it petered out.

A long strap at the head-end controlled the stretcher's ungainly, precarious descent. The usual grunted refrains accompanied their exertions.

'That's it, more my way... Someone take the strain on the left... You got him? Wait, wait! It's trapped my hand... Back it up! OK, keep him coming...'

With every jerk, Nick hoped for cries of pain and discomfort from the wounded man, to signal he was in the fight. Then the head passed him.

Corporal Milburn. The drystone walling enthusiast.

True to their word, he was unconscious with a chillingly sallow complexion. Once the stretcher was grounded, the medic worked fast, unbuckling it and giving herself a running commentary through the first essential checks. She then felt under the loose body armour and rolled Corporal Milburn's limp form over to reach underneath.

Abruptly the medic stopped and shook her head.

'I... I... Fuck, I don't know. It's not good. Maybe it went through his heart. He's almost certainly... I can try and resuscitate here but... At some point we're going to have to get him to the helicopter. If he stays put... Well...'

She threw her hands in the air.

The company sergeant major knew what she was really saying and gripped it.

'Right lads. You heard the expert. Transfer him to the trailer and get the stretcher tied down. Ride with him Doc. Let's go!' He turned to the driver. 'Take it easy on the quad Corporal Wallace. No speedway antics.'

Much as the sergeant major tried to chivvy everyone, the reality of the engineer's condition bore down on them all. With a beckoning wave from the cordon's distant sentry, Corporal Wallace gunned the engine and moved off as fast as he dared, standing in the saddle and checking constantly over his shoulder that his passengers were secure.

Everybody watched it go and then there was a pause. A unanimous sense of anti-climax. So much adrenaline and urgency had given way, in an instant, to hollowness. The Afghans waited tactfully for their cue, Gul Khan still leaning on the ladder. On the roof they started gathering tools. The major knelt on the edge and called down – the first to speak.

'Heads up lads! You did well. Everything you could, as fast as you could. Corporal Milburn is on his way home in good hands. Chinook is inbound with an Apache that's going to stay and keep an eye on us for a bit. We've got a job to finish... so let's get back to work.'

Company Sergeant Major Barnet swallowed the inclination to add anything. People resumed their tasks, moving at first with awkward solemnity the way a cast disperses in the final scene of a play.

A young sapper[*] climbed down the ladder and sat against the wall near Nazif. He looked very young to Nick's eyes, nineteen maybe. Pulling off blood-stained gloves, he produced a roll-up cigarette from a tin in his pocket. He lit it with trembling hands and took a long drag. His head lolled back to bump on the dried mud and then hung forward. The

---

[*] **Sapper**, the traditional word for a military engineer. In the British Army it is both a rank (equivalent to private) in the Royal Engineers, and a description of the trade. Derives from old Italian for a 'spade'.

cigarette smouldered in his fingers while he appeared to cry quietly.

At first it was a question of giving him space. But as the bustle regenerated around him, the dignity of that boundary faded. He started to become the unseen drifter in an underground station. Nick and the company sergeant major had moved into the compound to organise supplies. His now leaderless little tribe were on the roof preoccupied with the build, tugged by anxiety of another shot from the unseen marksman. Then a hand reached down and rested on the young sapper's shoulder. It was Gul Khan's.

With the sudden freedom of momentary flight, Baitullah plunged into the cool, green waters of the canal.

All was weightless, and all was free. The waters muffled his ears and caressed his flesh. His bare feet and hands made strong, vigorous movements. He had found the courage again – the courage to leap. And this bracing green liberty was his reward.

After a time, Baitullah's chest started to clamour for the air that shimmered there, behind the dancing, crinkling barrier of the water's surface. He propelled himself back towards it, back to the reaching brightness of the dry, hot world beyond.

And when he reached it, he awoke.

He looked up at the roof of the car, with its ripped and stained fabric. Below it was the window, dusty and streaked. He recognised a strong smell, plastic and dense and foreign, and tinged with petrol. The jostling suspension rocked him from side to side, up and down.

But the pain wasn't there. The pain had gone. That was something to be grateful for, Baitullah thought.

And then he died.

With the sun finally slipping beyond the horizon, this day had an end after all.

Inside its peach-coloured walls, their new home bore the unkempt stillness of a marquee after the wedding. Much of the equipment remained where it had been dumped temporarily. Unused building materials lay at the base of two sangars. All the earlier commotion was relegated to a forensic scene of empty shell cases and footprints.

The men were dead on their feet by the time they had bid farewell to the major and watched the company snake its way back over the bridge into the desert, late that afternoon. Nick and Sergeant Langdon gave the men time off for weapon cleaning, supper and a cat nap. A few figures dozed on sleeping mats, twitching under the relentless scrutiny of flies.

After dark they would complete the administration by torchlight and remain at readiness to support the platoon left out in the countryside, lying in ambush as planned.

They felt reasonably secure in their new dwelling. While the cordon was still in place, Sergeant Langdon had supervised emplacement of illumination flares on tripwires across the rat-runs which insurgents might use. One or two of the men possessed the necessary guile to master this mischievous art. The skill was in second-guessing how one would be attacked. Claymore mines covered the final approaches, backed up by concertinas of razor wire to prevent insurgents from scaling the walls.

The ANA were responsible for the northern sangar, which dominated the rear aspect and back gate. Sultan had agreed to billet his men in the small rooms underneath it after all, one draw being the owner's mud oven, to do their own cooking. Packet rations and tinned food were not popular with the Afghan soldiers. They preferred flour, oil and rice to prepare their own meals, supplemented by meat purchased 'on the hoof' from locals. At Nick's request, the quartermaster sergeant had sourced a volleyball net for them too. Everyone looked forward to the spectacle of their unique take on the game: limitless teams, fratricidal tackles and all competitors seemingly in league against the ball. Not their usually talkative and playful selves this time of the day, the ANA slumbered too.

Passing his men curled up on their thin foam mats, Nick observed how soldiers' faces rediscover their innocence in sleep. Corporal Lennon was awake, arms behind his head, staring into space. Nick nodded to him, sensing that the man did not want a conversation. Sergeant Langdon sat on the far side of the compound with his mountain of ammunition, as if worried it might walk away under its own steam. He had one boot off and was dusting a wiggling white foot with talcum powder.

Nick climbed the ladder up to the sangar where Brogan was on duty. The sandbagged emplacement had been covered with a camouflage net draped over a wooden frame. In time they would build a stout roof but for now the net prevented any snipers from identifying movement within, as a veil conceals a face. It was shaded and musty under the netting. Brogan had to assist Nick as he crawled through the entranceway. The net had a habit of snagging on anything that brushed against it.

'How are you doing Pat?'

'Quiet enough sir. I like this time of day. Not hot, not cold. You've just had your scoff.* Everyone takes a breather.'

Brogan sat on a forty-millimetre ammunition tin and Nick squatted next to him. It was a well-organised little office: night sight resting on the parapet, illumination flares and the claymore firing switches within arm's reach. Brogan had snapped a chemical light inside its packet and ripped a tiny hole with his teeth so that he would be able to find the stash easily once enveloped by darkness. The grenade machine gun brooded on its mount, bleeding oil after a brisk clean.

The sweet, woody smell of evening cooking fires filtered up to them. Shingazi assumed a Mediterranean character in this light and temperature. Nick thought about that idle hour before dinner when on holiday.

'Imagine a bath eh Pat? Clean shirt, cocktail, an early night between crisp white sheets.'

'You telling me a palmful of warm water across the back of your neck didn't cut it?'

'Yes I am.'

Brogan let out a characteristic wheezy chuckle. 'If I might say, you're confused sir. It's me that's supposed to be complaining to you.'

Nick looked around. They had cleaned up the roof after their skirmish. Yet memories were fresh, and shell cases must have been Afghanistan's answer to cigarette butts: they reappeared everywhere, even after a thorough sweep. Nick

---

* **Scoff**, army slang for a meal.

could see plainly where Corporal Milburn had been dragged across the dried mud. A dark patch revealed where some of his blood had been sluiced away with water.

The major confirmed his death over the radio about an hour after the evacuation. It was a formality. Anyone witness to the incident could see his fate had been sealed within seconds. The event formed an almost physical presence between the two men as they perched where it had all played out. It soon elbowed sufficient space to compel some kind of acknowledgement.

As the senior man, Nick took it upon himself to succumb first. 'Too bad about Corporal Milburn isn't it?'

The banality of his understatement mortified Nick as soon as he had uttered the words. But there was no easy way to express it. He did not want to appear melodramatic in front of one of his soldiers; nor did any of them know Corporal Milburn well. In a strange way, that increased the obligation to discuss it. The closer the bond, the less there was to say. All those years ago Nick had learnt the well-worn adage that small woe is talkative, while great sorrow is dumb.

Sergeant Joyce's death in the first month of their deployment had renewed that wisdom for him. Joyce had been the finest soldier any of them knew – a byword for competence and grip, decorated in Iraq for breaking cover to take control of a stricken vehicle and rescuing its gravely wounded driver. During one of their earliest major engagements in Helmand, a single bullet in the face had transformed Sergeant Joyce from master of chaos to two hundred pound deadweight; all in the time it took his body to reach the ground. If it could happen to him, what hope did the rest of them have? Loved as he was, nobody wanted to dwell on it.

Brogan understood what Nick was trying to say.

'Not the best day of my life sir, I can tell you that. I feel terrible for *not feeling* more crushed about Corporal Milburn. We weren't even there when it happened. I'm left wondering if we did enough to make him part of the family. Maybe the fact I'm not absolutely crushed tells me I didn't...' Brogan picked at the gun mount. 'Somewhere right now his wife is going about her business, buying supper in the supermarket and all that. Her life is about to be wrenched apart. I don't feel like I have a right to the knowledge he's dead when she probably doesn't even know it yet. She's the one that cares most. I'm not deserving of it. Does that sound strange to you?'

Nick judged that Brogan was not finished; the question rhetorical. He was right.

'Then there's me fucking gutted about Jojo, and he's *alive*. It should be the other way round. But what's screwing with me most tonight sir, is it should have been *me* on that Vallon. He's my best friend and yet I shoved him to the front. All the lads know it and I can see them thinking it when they look at me. I was fucking soft to take a breather after my swim in that ditch. Jojo picked up my Vallon and now he's the one in a chair for the rest of his life while I jack-off up here. He might yet die and he's got a wife and boy for fuck's sake. And yet... I can't deny I'm not pleased to be in one piece. It's all twisting me up sir, I'm not ashamed to admit it. Corporal Milburn. Jojo. I hate myself tonight.'

Having talked a lot, Brogan swallowed saliva with a grimace. To Nick it seemed as if he was trying to ingest the bile somehow, to banish his words back to the vault where guilt and anguish are stored. The nuclear waste of killing.

'I hear you.' Nick uttered it almost at a whisper. Then a spiny monologue formed in his throat.

Don't I know it Pat. I lost my very best friend when I was barely ten years old. Andrew Alderson. Never 'Andy' or anything. Always 'Andrew'. We were frolicking in a canoe while everyone else enjoyed a siesta. He was in our care, on a family holiday with us, so I'd have a friend my own age to entertain me. My little brother was still a toddler. Andrew's death unpicked my parents' marriage. Shame and blame made a stronger couple than them. But it was Andrew and me who took the canoe out. We knew it was wrong. We were just boys, pissing about. It tipped over. Life jackets were all part of the thing we thought it would be fun to feel defiant of. To this day, nobody knows how I saved myself while he drowned. I made for the shore as fast as I could. I ran pointlessly for help. I can't even tell you exactly what happened to him. They said afterwards he'd hit his head. But also that he probably struggled in the weeds. What difference does it make? Guilt isn't fussy about what it eats.

But the words never revealed themselves. They escaped his lungs, as they always did, skulking inside a sigh. Nick's confession was no way to confront Brogan's pain. The man had really just needed a vent.

'How much longer are you on stag Pat?'

'About forty minutes more sir, then Mac is up.'

'Good. I'll stag-on with you. We'll crack this one together shall we?'

Nick dragged another tin over and settled himself onto it, resting his rifle against the parapet and reaching for the binoculars. 'Let's make best use of this fading daylight.'

Major JP Lockley
OC B Coy
FOB Bussaco
Op HERRICK
BFPO 639

Dearest Darling Lottie,

As usual I am writing to you from my desk in the operations room. I'm joining the late shift because we have some chaps on the ground tonight. Private Baker just came on duty to man the radios. I love the preparation he puts in beforehand – always a very carefully selected picnic of sweets and biscuits, plus one or two lads magazines. Unlike his oppo, Private Oldman, Baker is a most fastidious character. I've just watched him square off all the notepads and parade all the errant map pins into a straight line. He should have joined the Guards. Oldman and Baker do battle over the ops room like a couple of ill-suited flatmates. I thought we were the bickering fools! Bested I'm afraid.

Long before you read this, you will have heard about the setbacks we suffered yesterday. It doesn't feel like yesterday yet. But looking at the clock, I see that it is. I've just finished the first draft of our 'learning account'. What a typically military piece of jargon. It is a simple enough document really. We explain what happened so that others can learn from our mistakes. I won't talk any more about it here. I probably oughtn't to anyway.

The sadness is that our day was such a success otherwise. Amazingly, the locals turned out to help us build a new base in the next village, to our south. Who would have thought it? There are one or two characters down there that I really think we can work with. It would mean so much to all of us if we left this spring having moved things on a bit. I hate the thought of all this not meaning much at all.

We've left Jack Russell down there in the new place, with his Afghans.

I feel responsible for old Jack – especially after you told me that you saw him wandering around barracks during his R&R. He told me he was going to spend it with his father in Northampton. Anyway, Sergeant Langdon is down there with him too thankfully. Perhaps you remember him? He was the one that went to all that trouble finding you a taxi when you were pregnant with Lucy on Waterloo Day. He is such an old friend to me – as good as old Carl Barnet probably.

Would you believe that I just nodded off there? I'm absolutely shattered. I rather hoped that writing to you would keep me awake. It's nearly 24hrs since we got up for the op. It will be simply glorious to slink back to my cot eventually. In the meantime I'm going to stand up and see if Baker wants a strong coffee. It might tease out one of his best Queen's Park Rangers war stories.

I love you so much my butterfly. What I wouldn't give to slip into bed with you now. Please don't let the news worry you unnecessarily. As you know, I spend most of my time sitting in this bunker trumpeting orders down the radio like a Chateau General. Hopefully we will have spoken on the phone well before you read this. Give Lucy the Squidge an extra big squeeze for me. That little lock of hair you packed me off with has been, well, you can imagine. Missing you as much as ever. More in fact…

Your adoring, Jamie xx

Lunch with Sultan was becoming a pleasing habit. Back in the fort, Nick had been more focused on his relationship with Captain Kamran, the ANA company commander. They were civil to one another but had little in common. Kamran was much older than Nick – nearly fifty – and seemed essentially disinterested in his services.

Nick had to admit this aloofness was justifiable. The man had been at war his entire adult life and was not about to defer to 'Major Lockley's chai-boy',* as he had phrased it memorably during one heated exchange. Trained by the Soviets, he fought against the Mujahideen for the communist government before deserting to join the infamous Ahmad Shah Massoud's forces in the Panjshir Valley. Wounded during the bloody conflict that followed Soviet withdrawal, Kamran went into self-exile, returning again to fight the Taliban on behalf of the Northern Alliance opposition forces. Into his third year in Helmand with the ANA, Kamran was war weary

---

* **Chai-boy**, literally translated, it means 'tea boy'. But there are often darker, pejorative associations due to the well-known practice of adorning, preening and petting Chai-boys, with even pederasty a not uncommon occurrence.

and longed to retire. He hardly ever patrolled, preferring to watch 'Bollywood' movies in his bunker and dabble in a bit of recreational corruption with the local community – mostly by selling his supplies to them. In his eyes, Kamran had earned the privilege, exercised by a great many of his superiors.

By contrast, Sultan badly needed the counsel and supervision of a professional soldier. He emulated Kamran without enjoying his reserves of experience, assuming that casual disinterest must be the mark of tactical genius. Like many young ANA officers, Sultan was terrified of losing face. He avoided decisions in case they were wrong, bowing instead to Nick's judgement and buying back his self-respect with petty criticisms. Once divorced from Kamran's condescension, Sultan was coming to life. Although they knew that he had been commissioned less than a year, it surprised them to discover that Sultan was still only twenty-one. He seemed so much older than that.

'I am the eldest of all my brothers and sisters,' he had explained with pride. 'I have been in charge of someone else for as long as I can remember.'

Sultan stood waiting for Nick on the ANA side of the compound. The two groups of soldiers had already established an invisible territorial divide. There was no malice or exclusion in it, simply mankind's inclination to understand what is theirs, and what is not theirs. Language was the divide.

'Good a-fter-noon Mis-ter Nick,' Sultan said.

He greatly enjoyed exercising his English greetings, and always reserved a nod for Mohammad the interpreter. They all moved under a small cloister in the compound. Nick shook hands and settled down on an old piece of carpet against the wall outside the Afghans' accommodation. He propped his body armour and helmet upright alongside him. It resembled a disembodied knight standing guard in the hall of an old stately home. Everybody kept their weapon and equipment within arm's reach, even inside the little fort.

'Quiet day so far Sultan,' Nick opened. Mohammad settled into his fleeting exchanges.

'Yes. I see a good day for laundry.'

Brogan and McMaster were taking advantage of the midday sunshine to do some washing. They had teamed up to wring out a pair of trousers, twisting in opposite directions. The tightening material drew them closer together, as water spattered audibly on the baked earth.

'And for lunch,' Nick said. He acknowledged the large paper plate placed in front of him, piled high with oily rice and a pimpled piece of chicken perched atop the summit. Some bread followed, not like the locals made it – wide and thin as the head of a tennis racquet – but a stack of discs the size of side plates.

Sultan's appetite was betrayed by a palpable impatience. He eyed his own plate then pointed south. 'Let us hope we are not disturbed.'

There was, as always, a pause in conversation while they took lunch, and Nick reflected on Sultan's throwaway comment.

True to the major's expectations, concerted Taliban harassment was a daily feature. Private Stephens coined it 'the honeymoon period'. He explained his theory one morning while they were shaving from metal bowls on a trestle table. Nick was trying to compare the length of his sideboards in a mirror no bigger than a credit card.

'You know what they say about sex in the first year of marriage sir?'

'Go on Steveo…'

'Well, if you put a pound in a jar every time you shag your Missus during the first year and then take one out every time you shag thereafter, the jar is never emptied. It's probably bollocks, right, but I reckon it'll work with the Taliban. Every time they brass us up* here in the first month, we'll put an empty shell case into an ammo tin. Then after the first month, we'll take one out. I bet we don't empty the tin before the end of the tour.'

A reasonable theory, thought Nick at the time. And it got put to the test. Mostly it was speculative long-range fire – almost clockwork in the evenings – with more concerted attacks pressed home every couple of days. The major's ambush on their first night came to nought, possibly because it had been compromised by observant locals. Equally, the insurgents could have been exhausted after that succession of skirmishes on their first day. One never knew. With his modest force of sixteen, including Sultan's Afghans, Nick lacked the wherewithal to try anything similar since then.

Sometimes the fire was extremely accurate. Private Mailer leaned down to pick up his pen for the sentry's logbook one morning when a bullet thwacked into the wooden frame behind his head. If he had been sitting up, it probably would have killed him. Rifle grenades were another particular hazard, prompting Nick to ban his men from sleeping in the courtyard.

Being a tethered goat had some advantages for their way

---

* **Brass up**, army slang for shooting or being shot at; derived from the brass shell cases that accumulate.

of war. The Anchor kept busy with his mortars. 'It always rains in Shingazi,' he would sometimes say. Other times they were able to secure the services of drones and Apache attack helicopters operating in tandem. The Apaches loitered over the horizon while the high-flying drones scanned the countryside for insurgents getting into position. Two fighters with a rocket-propelled grenade launcher were killed this way on Nick's third day in Shingazi. One of them survived the missile strike and tried to press home his attack regardless, so the Apache sought him out with its chin-mounted cannon, the pilot giving a blow-by-blow account over the radio. Nick almost found himself rooting for this unseen, dogged character. But his men were not so generous with their spirit. As the cannon chattered away in the firmament, little Private McMaster kept repeating, 'fuckin' get some.'

There were no intrusions this lunchtime. Nick swept a piece of bread around his plate to soak up the oil and a few elusive grains of rice. Afghans ate with their hands, a skill that allowed Sultan to play the part of teacher. He and Mohammad could never conceal an impish glee when Nick tipped rice onto his chin. They communed in cultural ridicule. Bread served as Nick's face-saving measure: he adapted a technique using little strips of it as an edible scoop.

A young ANA soldier removed their plates and they took tea. Nick suffered a brief craving for fresh fruit – a succulent peach perhaps. Instead he produced sweets and raisins from the British ration packs. Sultan had a smoke. Their contented silence lasted a little while longer before Nick sat up and removed his notebook.

It was their habit after lunch to discuss something martial, using props or a piece of paper. Nick gave little lessons in how to construct a defensive position; the places most likely to encounter mines; husbandry of ammunition. On the first afternoon the lesson drew a few curious onlookers from Sultan's platoon but he shooed them away saying, 'this is officers' business.' Nick enjoyed imparting his knowledge and surprised himself with the detail he could remember from his own instruction, when often the entire class of officer cadets was physically exhausted.

'So Sultan, what would you like to cover today?'

Mohammad hardly needed to translate it.

'Sorry to say I am on patrol soon,' Sultan said. 'Perhaps you can tell me again what you told me yesterday?'

'My mistake. Of course you are,' Nick said.

The only bar to Sultan's informal military curriculum was the fact that they never patrolled together in Shingazi. Nick deemed it unwise to put both officers on the ground simultaneously. He was better placed in the patrol base with good radio contact back to the fort – their only source of assistance if they got out of their depth. When Nick took patrols into Shingazi, Sergeant Langdon stayed behind with Sultan. He was Sultan's shadow.

'Right then,' Nick said. 'This won't take long. Let's revise how to extract a casualty under fire. Remember it's a simple method: just the reverse of an attack, really.' Nick started nominating objects in the manner of a military bore regaling his exploits at the dinner table. 'So these sweets are the patrol, and the yellow one here is the wounded man. Being a man of faith, you must be the green one.'

He waited for Mohammad to translate and Sultan smiled.

'And you are crossing this ditch.' Nick placed a pencil on the ground. 'Now show me how you'd get your wounded man across the ditch.' He was mindful not to sound too much like his mother correcting comprehension at the kitchen table.

They were engrossed in this game when the ANA soldier manning their gate sangar hollered down to the courtyard excitedly. Sultan shouted something back. Nick could never tell whether or not it was an emergency. The Afghans only had one volume setting for communicating with their sangar.

'It is the man Gul Khan,' Sultan said.

'Excellent. We'll do this another time. Don't delay your patrol on his account. Never give the impression they can tie us down with visits.'

Nick shouted across the compound to Brogan, who had finished his laundry and was making improvements to the hessian screen around their latrine.

'Put the kettle on the stove, will you Pat. I've got a visitor.'

For days now Gul Khan had contrived to keep his distance from the fort. Surely wise. Shingazi's elders had met with the major two days after the battle and he stayed away. He had got carried away the day the foreigners arrived. Looking back on it, his enthusiasm felt rash. Gul Khan's opponents – both the long-sighted hawks in Haji Mansur's Movement and the cowardly sceptics like Haji Khan Mohammad inside the village – would profit from the perception that he was an agent, nothing more than the puppet of the foreign officers. Of course he would never convince his enemies. But enemies were not his audience. The shepherd and the wolf do battle over the flock: those with less wisdom but collectively a louder voice. They need to be convinced that the men making decisions do so with pure motives.

Lying awake at night, alone without Sanga, Gul Khan needed convincing too.

How endless the night can feel when a man is gripped by the jaws of quandary. Was this crusade of his simply a way to make sense of Mamur's death? Was he busy weaving moral principles to conceal the shameful reality that he had *sold* the services of his son to Haji Mansur? It seemed absurdly and cruelly ordinary to Gul Khan now – the material desire for something as simple as a solar-powered light. Janan had one and Gul Khan coveted the convenience of it, drawing power during the day and illuminating the hours before bed.

The decision seemed like the deed of another life: meeting Haji Mansur outside the mosque, the exchange of greasy tattered currency, the look of pride and exhilaration on Mamur's face when Gul Khan explained the task before him.

One night Gul Khan had thrown off his blanket and scrabbled for the money tin, pulling out the notes and striking his plastic lighter to burn them. But he had stopped. No, the money must survive, unspent, to remind him. Otherwise the righteousness of his stand against the Haji might paint over that memory of Mamur's sacrifice in beguiling colours, as if some noble stroke of fate.

Eventually, somehow, Gul Khan would fall asleep. And then dawn brought relief. Not answers, just renewal of purpose.

When Gul Khan was a child he once convinced himself that the shape in the corner of their room was a brooding beast, waiting for him to sleep before it pounced. Daylight revealed it as a chest with a cushion at one end. He supposed this adult world was similar: the fears always returned but every new day showed he had been wrong to fear the worst.

In the eight days since that battle, the soldiers had tried to visit him in his compound twice. Both times he had been in his fields, rectifying the neglect caused by all this turbulence. Gul Khan's father used to say that life had three messengers to tell a man when the march of time was leaving him behind: children, livestock and crops. With his family still in the city, Gul Khan leaned on Janan to help him with the spring weeding. It would chiefly have been Mamur's job, just as it was Gul Khan's when he was the same age, before leaving to fight the Russians. There had always been something therapeutic in working the little sickle up and down the rows of young crops. Now it was the direct opposite of his nocturnal anxieties – rooting him to his land, to belonging. His decision to step forward and lead the villagers could still be something virtuous and princely.

Nothing would bring Mamur back, nor atone for his short-sighted greed. That realisation should be a weapon, not a reason for spinelessness.

The regular thump and crackle as the Movement probed Shingazi's little fort reminded them all how fragile their hopes were. Those foreigners seemed determined though, and since their arrival, none of the Haji's men had set foot in the village – even the two brothers he had recruited from there. Now that most people were starting to accept that they might have to live with the fort and its occupants, Gul Khan judged it was time for the next step in his plan. He was already tainted by his associations on that momentous day. If he stayed away too long, it would look like he regretted it. He would appear weak.

Gul Khan shouted up to the Tajik skulking inside a sandbagged bunker on the roof of the fort. He exercised his weak Dari on the assumption that the youth probably spoke little Pashtu.

'Peace be upon you soldier! I am a friend. Gul Khan. I am here for British Sahib.'

The boy disappeared and there was a shrill exchange within the compound. A handful of village imps were hanging around the gates on the vague chance of some treats or entertainment. The ringleader knew who Gul Khan was and whispered something to a little girl. She took one pace forward and then changed her mind, spinning back around and tugging on the boy's filthy kameez. Gul Khan shooed them away.

'Not got anything better to do?' He knew perfectly well they didn't.

He surveyed the fort. It had transformed since that day he crossed the threshold in defiance. Two roof-top positions commanded the approaches. Strips of netting made it hard to espy who stood within, to make it hard for snipers. The Russians had done the same thing, he remembered. A few radio antennas reached above the walls, which were topped with a coil of very angry-looking barbed wire. In the Mujahideen, his group used to call it 'Karmal's kite string' in honour of the then Communist leader of Afghanistan. What would his comrades say if they could see him now? They had pounded little forts like these, rattling the walls with every type of ordnance they could carry. For all his costly efforts, he had never set foot inside one. Now he stood at an opening gate, hailing the Afghan 'traitors' as his supposed friends.

Even the greatest trees sway in a strong wind, remember.

A different Tajik beckoned him over, gesturing for the Kalashnikov slung over Gul Khan's shoulder. Because he was well known to the soldiers in Shingazi now, he never left home without it anymore. The habit was one part personal protection, two parts symbolism. The weapon had become a sort of talisman.

Having placed the rifle down, the soldier started lifting Gul Khan's shirt to reveal his bare chest. This haphazard search was cancelled by the British officer, striding over with a chopping motion across the front of his own throat and a stream of English that neither of them understood.

Gul Khan received a warm welcome from Nek. He seemed genuinely pleased at the opportunity to show some hospitality. The young Afghan Army officer was on his shoulder, earnest and uneasy. He shook hands with Gul Khan and greeted him formally. Then, taking his leave, strode towards a group of his soldiers gathering their equipment.

Gul Khan followed Nek to a shaded area under a camouflaged tarpaulin and they sat down on oblong green sleeping mats. A long strip of sticky tape dangled from one corner, covered in dead flies. Nek removed the heavy body armour he had put on to approach the main gate.

'Tea?'

Gul Khan nodded and Nek called to one of his soldiers, who then had a question. So Gul Khan made eye contact with the interpreter.

'Health and happiness. What is your name friend?'

'And to you Gul Khan. My name is Mohammad. We met on the day I arrived here.'

'Of course. I remember now. Was that your first battle?'

'It was not. I have been in Helmand for nearly a year. Before that I grew up in Kabul. I was a young boy during the civil war and the bombardments. Those were my first battles.'

Nek was finished and Gul Khan realised he might have

insulted his host by making conversation in his own tongue. In his bashfulness, he turned away and noticed a small wooden cross set against the compound wall opposite. There were some curious objects at the base.

Pointing, Gul Khan turned back to the interpreter. 'Mohammad, please ask Nek if that is a shrine to the Prophet Isa.' The question was passed.

After Nek explained, Mohammad started speaking. 'Not exactly Gul Khan. It is a shrine to the memory of our comrade who died here last week. They use the cross of Jesus to... show... his sacrifice. I think that is the right word. Christians believe Jesus died to save men but I am not sure of everything Nek just said.'

Sensing the confusion, Nek gave the interpreter a different, shorter, sentence. Gul Khan sat patiently, wallowing in the curious melody of this language.

'It is a shrine to the memory of our comrade and that shape is the symbol for all Christians.' Mohammad spoke quickly, with relief.

Gul Khan nodded his understanding. 'When I was a warrior, we moved all the time. Their memory was celebrated in our hearts.'

'Very true. In our religious book, Gul Khan, we have a saying.' Nek paused to choose his words for Mohammad. 'To die for your friends is the greatest love a man can have.'

'I will remember that holy wisdom. You are a young man Nek, in the prime of your life. As you grow older, you will find that these martyred friends – they remain young in your memory.'

Beaming with affinity, Nek leaned forward to him. 'This is one of the most famous sayings of our own warrior culture

Gul Khan.' He waited for Mohammad to catch up so that he would be sure to get the next bit right. 'They shall grow not old, as the people that are left grow old.' We read that when we gather on the same day each year to remember the dead in war.

A whimsical expression crossed Gul Khan's face. 'We have no such gathering. Most of my friends from that time are among those eternal young.'

'You could pick a day Gul Khan,' Nek suggested. 'A day all to yourself. When did the Russians leave? That might be the right day.'

'There is a holiday for that day already, I believe. But when the Russians left, that was simply the start of more war.'

On translation, Gul Khan could see that Nek was crestfallen, so he added quickly, 'but I like your idea. I will think of a day and do as you suggest.'

Their body language created a pause that a heavy-set British soldier leapt into. He had been hovering in the background with his equipment on. The Afghan officer stood behind him, wearing the beret and sunglasses that Gul Khan remembered from their first meeting.

The British soldier spoke to Nek with a deference that transcended the language barrier. Gul Khan also read a tinge of self-consciousness in the older man's manner, as if he was adopting extra formalities for the sake of appearances. In the background a group of a dozen or so soldiers – both Afghan and British – milled about smoking and chatting. It was obvious that they were heading out somewhere. Gul Khan surmised that the older man must be discussing some kind of patrol. Then he heard his own name. Gul Khan's ears pricked up. The rest of the words had been nothing more than music. Nek noticed this and suspended his conversation to explain.

'I have asked my sergeant to take his patrol close to your home Gul Khan. I am concerned for your security now that you have been seen helping us.'

'That is kind Nek. Please don't take trouble.'

The two British soldiers finished their discussion and immediately the waiting group gathered themselves, shouldering equipment and cocking their weapons. There was a relaxed mood in their actions. Gul Khan wondered if the afternoon sunshine made them forget where they were. Tea arrived: three paper cups balanced in a triangle between the hands and fingers of a skinny soldier with short, thick hair. Once the cups were distributed, the soldier reached into a baggy thigh pocket and pulled out a green foil packet.

Nek apologised. 'I am sorry for the delay Gul Khan. The kettle always seems to boil slowly when you are waiting for it. These biscuits taste good though.' He reverted to the matter in hand. 'It is no trouble to keep an eye on you. We acknowledge the risks you are taking. If I might ask a personal question, how is your family?'

'They are not here… for the time being.'

'That was prudent. But sincerely I hope you have the confidence to bring them home soon. Our goal here is to make life…' Nick searched for his words and Mohammad filled the silence with his soft translation. Then Nick finished, '…to make life more normal.'

'I understand your intention and I respect it Nek. But your words carry different meanings for us. I side with you to banish what has *been normal* Nek. We want something *not* normal, at least for us, in this valley.' Gul Khan canted his head, to convey the irony.

The words sunk in for Nek, who looked slightly chastened

to Gul Khan's eyes, and chose to keep their conversation practical.

'What do you think the elders want out of it?' Nek asked next.

Gul Khan chuckled. 'Just as I said... but they want it without tax! Nevertheless, they have resigned themselves to your presence here. Understand that it is not something welcomed. It is necessary. Such is the curse of the Afghan.' Gul Khan paused for Mohammad and resumed. 'The elders can be trusted as long as the wind blows favourably.'

'What of the men that helped us make the fort?'

'They were light-headed. We all were. Hope is like the pure, thin air of high passes. It can rob a man of his balance. Everyone will continue to follow you. We have little choice now. But this is not love. It is reason.'

'I understand Gul Khan.'

'I trust you do. The Mullah tells us that American people see love and loyalty differently to us. For example, your brides choose their men and there is no gift to the father. No price.'

Nek swallowed a laugh. 'There is some truth in that... but let me explain.' Mohammad frowned in dread of the complex thoughts he might have to convey. 'In the past our culture was more like yours in this respect. Some would say even quite recently. Choice can be an illusion. Some fathers still have a very strong hold over their daughters, and some men seek wives for the status they will bring to a marriage. Wealth has power wherever you go Gul Khan.'

'But the women can still choose.'

'Yes, the women can choose. Have a biscuit please – do not be shy.'

Gul Khan reached for one. It had little bits of dried raisin in it, softening in his mouth as he chewed. The tea was not sweet enough for his tastes. It was bitter. So the fruit helped him finish it, as his host had. Gul Khan was observing closely to make sure he did not offend the officer. Nek spoke some more.

'Whatever the realities, our culture celebrates the idea of marriage blooming from love.' There was a brief aside as Nek made sure that Mohammad knew what he meant by that. He was gesticulating to make himself clearer. 'It is central to our belief in the rights of individuals, the importance of individuals to express things for themselves. Sometimes the community suffers because of our personal freedoms, perhaps. I don't know. There are many, many opinions where I am from. But things are as they are.' Nick smiled at Mohammad as if to say *well done* and tried to push the dialogue on again. 'Do you not have love poetry in the Pashtun culture Gul Khan?'

'Of course Nek. It is very beautiful... but something magical, forbidden. They are mostly stories of the poor boy seeing the rich girl drawing water by a stream. And they mostly end in death!' Gul Khan giggled at his own comment and it felt odd waiting for Nek to catch up. 'Love is something that grows for us. First marriage, then love. You seem to try it the other way round.'

'Yes – and that too often ends badly!'

Gul Khan saw that Nek's laughter was dry as autumn leaves. He was desperate to ask whether the man had lain with these wild-sounding women, galloping with freedom. He wanted to hear Nek's own perspective on the matter. It all sounded so fantastic and dangerous. Surely there must be hideous violence if everyone was able to compete for love. But there seemed no way to delve into that without being rude. He opted for something totally conventional.

'Do you have a wife Nek?'

'No Gul Khan. Not yet. Sometimes I think I'm married to this.' He patted his rifle, smiling. 'She's very faithful you know. We look after one another.'

This tickled Gul Khan. 'That was my first wife too Nek. She still lives with us… unfulfilled, shall we say!'

'Until now Gul Khan.'

'Yes – until now.'

The time had come to do business. Whatever topics one chose to deconstruct barriers, brick by brick, one always arrived at the subtle point where the real agenda could be revealed. Perhaps 'revealed' was not the right word because in Gul Khan's experience, the agenda often sat there in plain sight.

'I fear my old rifle will not be enough when you are gone Nek. We need to give this village its own legs to stand on. Those Tajik soldiers will have no interest in this valley. The army was the same when the Russians left. They protected roads and cities and profit. We need our own militia here. Our own police. Not thieves.'

'I am sorry to say this is really a conversation to be had with my commander. I know there are many officers considering this problem. For what it is worth, here is my advice.'

'I am listening,' Gul Khan said.

'Help us here, in this little fort, in Shingazi. Show that you can be trusted.' Nick let Mohammad finish. 'Let us start with something small. You and the other men of Shingazi can be our eyes. Show us the mines you find. Tell us if strangers appear in the area. Offer to guide us into places where the Taliban sleep – where they feel safe.'

'I can do these things.'

'It will be an honour to stand beside you Gul Khan. But if the village has made the choices you describe, then *they* must embrace that risk as well. It is too much for you to do this alone.' Nek then turned the coin over. 'The west can be generous too. Very generous. This is not all about peril. It's also the language of opportunity.'

Gul Khan digested these terms. They were much as he expected. Nek drew his legs up to his chest as a signal that he was about to stand and end their meeting. 'We will speak again on this matter.' It was of no consequence that the meat of their discussion had been so small a share of it.

'Perhaps at my house next time,' Gul Khan offered. 'When my wife returns, she can prepare us some lunch. You must be tired of eating from packets.'

'I look forward to the honour.'

The three men stood. Nick hefted on his body armour to walk Gul Khan to the gate.

'Does that armour give you courage Nek, or does it remind you how fragile you are?'

The officer simply laughed.

When they reached the gate, the Afghan sentry returned Gul Khan's Kalashnikov. The magazine had been removed so he replaced it carefully and slung the weapon back onto his shoulder. As he did so, Nek extended his hand. Gul Khan took it and immediately Nek placed his other hand over the top.

'I have been meaning to say... how very sorry I am about your son.'

'Goodbye Nek.'

PB Shingazi c/o FOB Bussaco
Op HERRICK
BFPO 639

Dear Dad,

Sorry I haven't written in a while – and sorry that I always say that. I know you understand. Your last letter made me laugh. That is just the sort of thing I love to hear about. What on earth possessed you to go to a fancy dress party as Henry VIII? It must have cost you a fortune. You can't blame lonely women for thinking you were game with that costume, especially when people start serving margaritas. Didn't I meet the Wrights once at Robin Cottage?

Your take on the news coverage sounds about right. We don't see many journalists up here – it's one benefit of being in the middle of nowhere I guess. We did get a visit from the brigadier though. He stayed a full 24hrs. That tells you so much about him doesn't it? He insisted on going out on patrol. Tom says he even offered to carry a ladder. He's the kind of man who never raises his voice. Steely though. He gave us the impression he misses this sort of thing. Some people belong to it I guess.

The Skipper has moved me down to a new patrol base in a village called Shingazi. My letters will take even longer to reach you now. This one started its journey in the boot of a Jackal 4×4. They come down to pick them up about once a week. If you write again there's no need to change the address. It all goes via the FOB.

It was a long day getting this place established but since then it has felt good making progress and Langers keeps us out of trouble. Even he would agree all our efforts have something they can bite on at last, like there's traction. I haven't felt this useful in years. I do miss the others back in 'The Swamp'. But I've made friends with one of the locals here called Gul Khan. He's an extraordinary character. Langers and I can't work out whether he's amazing or just mad. Maybe it's both. He fought the Soviets last time. His boy was an insurgent and got killed by us. Now he's got it in for the Taliban instead, and he's on our side. Figure that one out. It's like something from a Kipling story. You wouldn't want to piss him off. His whole manner and expression is totally single-minded.

Our ANA are coming on well too. I've been working more with Sultan than Captain Kamran. He's really come out of his shell. Living so closely with the Afghans has created some amusing episodes. One of the older ones has taken a shining to little Mac. He's not exactly a chorister but we are a long way from home! "Any port in a stormy sea" – isn't that what they say? The ANA got bored of the volleyball net we bought them and have taken to a form of football / rugby / cage fighting that none of us can fathom. There's loads of feminine screams and then bone-crunching violence. But everyone finishes up mates. They asked us to play and I had to contrive a patrol to save face.

Please pass my news onto Mum. She wrote me another letter but I didn't know how to answer it.

It was asking too much. I can understand her instinct to tidy things up, with me being over here. But it's a big ask. We're really busy. Maybe you can say something. I couldn't face going to Dubai on my R&R like she asked, and seeing that pedant Roger. We only had twelve days as you know, and I just needed a dose of quiet. Running out of room. Drats. Enjoy your Vivaldi concert old man. Don't miss the train home this time! Hold on, I'm being stupid… You'll have seen it by now.

Love, Nick

A man should know when to show gratitude – and acknowledge the hand of Allah in his successes.

This was Haji Tor Amin's philosophy. He never surrendered to self-satisfaction. Though shrewd in his dealings with men and money, he would not have generated his wealth without the smile of providence. Profiting from other men's misfortune is the lowest form of advancement.

When his brother died childless, he inherited land to grow poppy and then acquired more when a neighbour fell into debt. This allowed him to purchase small roadside commercial properties in the city, which he rented to vendors. When the money poured into his lap, he first used it to undertake the Haj – holy pilgrimage to the sacred cities – giving thanks to God for his acquisitions. The money continued to flow so he built a modest mosque adjoining his new compound and recruited a Mullah to lead his village in worship, and teach their children.

Haji Tor Amin had never cultivated an interest in politics. It seemed arrogant to impose one's will on men who were not tied to you by blood or bondage. The Movement's rule had delved too far into the affairs of men. Though he found their methods intensely distasteful, one paid one's dues and looked the other way. Until they banned poppy at least, they had even been good for business. Then the Christian foreigners arrived, uninvited, spreading their corrupting beliefs. It was his religious duty to redress the violation and support those fighting for it. If politics and piety must be married, well then, he would bless the union.

Hence it came to pass that his compound was a regular way station for fighters moving up and down the Helmand River valley. Every few weeks Haji Tor Amin also played host to a meeting for commanders. They were careful not to convene too regularly, or indeed too often in the same place. There was a trick to be played, between varying the location of meetings and the number of compound owners the Movement could trust.

On this occasion, Haji Mansur and three of his men had been called north to discuss the recent British expansion into Shingazi.

Haji Mansur was nervous about it. The loss of Shingazi tasted of failure. Fortunately he would not be compelled to air the issue in front of all his peers. This was not a general meeting. But on the other hand, it did not bode well that effectively he had been summoned…

Gatherings of this nature were nocturnal, which allowed them to travel in daylight amid the throng of normal traffic up and down the valley. Haji Tor Amin always fed his guests well and set aside comfortable rooms for the purpose. He was a discreet man. He never sat in on their deliberations.

'The less I know of your affairs, the better I sleep,' he used to say, backing out with exaggerated gravity.

Haji Mansur was sure to turn up before the other delegation. He and Haji Tor Amin attended sunset worship in the private mosque. The neat little Mullah had a beautiful voice for the call to prayer, standing on the roof inside a six-foot covered pulpit that passed for the minaret. It sported a small battery-powered loud speaker that he checked with a demure cough before drawing breath for his recitations, his white turban turning pale orange as the sun dipped into the dusty horizon. Afterwards they drank tea together until the other Mullah arrived an hour or so after dark – Mullah Elam.

That was almost certainly not his real name. Elam was a mountain in the Swat Valley of Pakistan and the Mullah always claimed to have been born in the Afghan city of Kandahar. The extent of his theological credentials was also questionable. Anyone bold enough to ask when and where he had studied received the same dismissive answer. 'Pakistan.' But no one doubted his qualification to command the district, both as soldier and shadow governor. Mullah Elam had a prosthetic leg from wounds sustained during the civil war. In the recent conflict he had survived two direct attempts on his life. In one instance the missile struck the wrong vehicle; in the other he was blown off the back of a motorcycle when the missile impacted wide of the mark. Losing the prosthetic in the blast, Mullah Elam had the presence of mind to crawl into a nearby canal so he could negate his disability by swimming to safety. A badly broken nose from that escape gave him the look of henchman rather than a mastermind.

Now understandably cautious, Mullah Elam devised a complicated procedure for attending these meetings. He would arrive at a staging compound, wait for dark and then transfer to his destination by other means, some followers splitting off so that any drone would have to choose between at least two scattering vehicles.

As the meeting commenced, junior fighters – the escorts – languished around a fire in the courtyard, taking turns to patrol the environs beyond the gate. Their conversations had long assumed a nostalgic flavour, opening with a form of social rollcall.

'Where is Jandral? I have that bag of snuff I owe him.'

'Shahid brother.'

'What about that goofy Noorzai fellow with teeth like a donkey? I can't for the life of me remember his name. I like his jokes.'

'Najibullah? No idea. We assume he's Shahid as well. He went to lay a mine and we never saw him again.'

'All that is on earth will perish. But Allah will abide...'

Only two other men attended Haji Mansur's private audience with Mullah Elam: each permitted themselves one lieutenant. That way there would be a record of what was agreed in the event anyone was killed or captured later. Haji Mansur chose Sadiq. He was loyal and attentive. But first they honoured their host by eating supper. Haji Tor Amin selected one of his plumpest turkeys for the privilege of dining with Mullah Elam. His wife complemented it with potato and onion. Haji Mansur had no appetite and forced the food down out of politeness. He wished his foot would stop tapping and itching. Eventually, replete, their host took his leave.

'Mullah Sahib... Powenda Sahib...' He nodded to each in turn. 'I will see you later for night-time prayers. If you need more tea, simply send one of your men for it.'

The four fighters were left to talk. In different circumstances Haji Mansur might have opened the conversation, to assume the initiative. It did not seem appropriate here... Or was courage failing him? The opportunity passed.

'Do not be alarmed by this meeting Powenda,' Mullah Elam said. He used Haji Mansur's codename, just as Haji Tor Amin had. 'Your deeds on the battlefield have established a reputation that could resist many such setbacks. Now tell me what has gone wrong in Shingazi.'

It was an unconvincing opener. Mullah Elam did not break cover and risk his life for turkey and potatoes.

While Haji Mansur chose his words the lieutenant opposite wore a painfully condescending expression of concern. Why did these aides always presume to carry the authority of their masters?

Let's see how long you would last in my shoes.

'A tilted load never reaches its destination Mullah Sahib,' Haji Mansur replied. 'I will be as honest as possible. This has been a failure of intelligence. As you know better than any of us, we can only defeat the foreigners in places and times of our choosing.'

The Mullah nodded ruefully. Haji Mansur continued.

'There is a man in Shingazi. You won't know him. He's called Gul Khan. His eldest boy did some work for us and got martyred by a missile. This Gul Khan was paid well. But for some reason he has decided to hold us responsible. It is the only conceivable explanation for such a sudden and concerted love affair with the foreigners. The day his boy died I met with him to offer my condolences. I could see how he trembled with hate. I assumed it was something we could channel for our own ends. But instead he has persuaded the elders to invite the Tajiks and foreigners down there. They arrived incredibly quickly. They must have their own spies. We received no warning. They use a compound to the south of the village now, as a fort. My boys and I have attacked time and again but the soldiers control the road bridge now. We are forced to use crossings further south, which causes problems for our supplies and our wounded, not to mention tax—'

Mullah Elam interrupted. 'Let's stick to the man Powenda. One thing at a time. The practical consequences can wait.'

'As you wish Mullah Sahib.' Haji Mansur sat back. Only then did he notice how far he had been bent forward during his speech.

'What is Gul Khan's background?' the Mullah asked.

'We're still finding that out. Apparently he fought with the Mujahideen during the Communist time. But he's just a farmer now – and getting old.'

'I see this character has bruised your pride Powenda. That is no reason to dismiss him. You need not be concerned that I think less of you. We clarified that at the beginning.' Mullah Elam's flattened nose gave out a faint whistle when he was talking and breathing. 'Who is your source of information in Shingazi?'

'I'd rather not be specific Mullah Sahib. He's reliable. Up until now it has just been simple requirements. When and where foreign patrols have passed through, and that sort of thing. He failed me on this one. It is conceivable that they excluded him from meetings... but that's exactly what we pay him to solve.' Haji Mansur sighed. 'I have one or two other contacts... they are kids though.' It pained him to sound so impotent.

'How you repair or improve your network in Shingazi is your business Powenda. Regardless, we need to know more about our new friend. The weak link here is not the fort but Shingazi's acceptance of it. They must pay for the decision they have made. That is how we will dislodge the British. My advice... No, not advice. My *order* is to bring Gul Khan's story to an end. Make an example of him, preferably ugly and public. Much that is positive will flow from that.'

'It will be hard to get into the village. He never leaves it anymore.'

'Air your misgivings with your men, if that's your style Powenda... I'm not interested. You are a resourceful and cunning man. Think this one through. What I *will* do is give you some more boys and any of our... specials... you think you might need. Send word of your requirements. I'll also see what my own friends can find out about this Gul Khan. Our response must echo back up the valley just as loudly as the British arrived. Perceptions are fickle.'

The lieutenant pitched in. 'We can't afford any more of these... local awakenings.'

Haji Mansur felt the veil coming down. A cautionary hand touched the small of his back. Sadiq knew him so well. Fortunately Mullah Elam shot back on his behalf, without even looking at the lieutenant.

'I didn't hear Powenda asking for your opinion, Ali Jan.'

The Mullah scratched his beard, wondering if there was anything else to discuss. There was not.

'I am going to leave you to your evening prayer with Tor Amin. I will say mine when I get where I'm going.' The Mullah paused, to measure his words. 'Allah deliver you Powenda Jan. You honour our Movement with your exploits. I know we can rely on you to turn our problem around.'

His prosthetic creaked audibly as the men got to their feet. Out in the courtyard, the escorts all sprung up, only to stand around self-consciously while Haji Tor Amin and the rugged commander bid their formal farewells. Mullah Elam's party left on two motorcycles. As the gate swung open, weak yellow headlights picked out thin tree trunks, and the shadow of long rail-like ruts in the road.

After evening prayers, Haji Mansur insisted that his host retire to bed. This freed Haji Mansur to relax in the courtyard, drinking warm goat's milk around the fire with his men. They settled into the usual gossip. Sadiq hazarded a quip.

'Brothers, you should've seen how close the Mullah's

sidekick came to feeling a shoe across his backside! Cocky little bastard!'

It was a generous interpretation. Sadiq meant well. But Haji Mansur was needled at the reminder of all that tacit censure. He forced a thin smile.

One of the other fighters could not contain his curiosity.

'So what will we do next Haji Sahib? Did Mullah Elam have any suggestions?'

'All in good time,' Haji Mansur replied. 'I need to think.'

Sadiq caught his cue. 'Right brothers,' he said. 'Let's get to bed. Do you want a cigarette Haji Sahib? It is a good clear night. Moonless. The stars won't mind if you make a few clouds of your own.'

Haji Mansur smoked it slowly, losing himself in those bright little grottos between the logs of a fading fire.

First he sketched out his plan. Then he travelled home for a short spell, holding each member of his family in turn and finishing with his wife. He joined her under the covers, inhaling the fug of feminine warmth trapped within.

Part of him wished he could have fought the foreigners at the beginning, when he carried nothing more than the contents of his pockets. This kind of life comes more naturally to the young. Growing up, the Movement was never a calling he expected. The holy war had been and gone. But as the Movement gathered momentum across southern Afghanistan, his father saw that the family stood to gain much by establishing a presence within it. The young Mansur was chosen. While not the strongest of his two brothers, he was the most devout. In those days the Movement valued virtuousness: a man's piety counted for something. The young Mansur stood apart from the throng of volunteers who sought merely power and excitement. Once recruited, it was inspiring to be among so many dynamic and charismatic purists! They set to work cleaning out the stable: bandits and rapists fleeing before them like rats. Or, Allah willing, being strung up in front of their victims, as a carcass hangs outside the butcher's shop.

Their struggle was a different one now. It had become elevated. They were manning the ramparts against Christian aggressors who threatened believers all over the world. Those first, local grievances felt far away sometimes. Almost easy to forget. Haji Mansur's intense and fanatical teenage self would have no problem connecting the two agendas. But the intervening years had changed both Movement and man. As for the Movement… the blade was dulled. Power and privilege had built a wall around their garden and choked it with weeds. As for the man… Haji Mansur had married. He had roots. A future can be burdensome to the righteous.

The guest room was quiet when eventually Haji Mansur entered it. His companions were already slumbering, each form dim under the meagre glow of an oil lamp. Leaving his shoes at the door, he crept silently to where his bed had been prepared on the floor. Somebody always made the effort to do that, but none of the men ever took credit for it. It was as if they wanted their leader to know that the gesture was from all of them.

In the Movement, one got used to spending the night fully clothed. They always slept ready to fight, or escape, at a moment's notice. Raids by foreign commandos were common. Haji Mansur removed only his waistcoat and cap, folding them neatly and placing his short Kalashnikov on top of the pile, so it was out of the dust. Lifting one half of the blanket, he slipped deftly into the makeshift bed and closed his eyes.

His lips made silent words.

'Allah, I seek Your forgiveness and Your protection in this world and the next. Allah, I seek Your forgiveness and Your protection in my religion, in my worldly affairs, in my family and in my prosperity.

'Allah, conceal my secrets and preserve me from anguish. Allah, guard me from what is in front of me and behind me, from my left, and from my right, and from above me. I seek refuge in Your Greatness, from being struck down from beneath me.'

Haji Mansur drew the blanket up over his shoulders, turned onto his right side and placed his right hand under his cheek.

'Allah, with your name I die and live.'

He was asleep within minutes.

There was a scruffy handwritten diagram pinned up outside the door. It depicted where everybody slept. The torch beam paused briefly over infantile artwork while the searcher clarified what he already knew. The beam then swept its way across the mud-floored accommodation to pick a path. There was not much room for his feet between the silent prostrate figures, their weapons and possessions. Being unfurnished, everything either lay on the floor or hung on nails driven into the walls. His man was intentionally easy to find: far right-hand corner. Under normal circumstances they might have posted him close to the door but here that would make him vulnerable to assailants. There was always the risk of attack when sleeping in the same compound as others who were not their kin. The searcher knelt down carefully to avoid kicking the neighbouring occupant.

'Sir…' There was no response. His palm found the sleeping man's shoulder beneath the bedding and squeezed it. He hissed again. 'Sir…'

The sleeping bag shifted. 'Mmm?'

'It's Sergeant Langdon sir.'

'What…?'

'It's zero-four-hundred-hours. Your friends are going to be here in thirty minutes.'

'Right. Thanks…' Nick raised himself onto an elbow, the nylon sleeping bag whispering. 'Sorry. I was deep under.'

'Anywhere nice?'

Oblivion was a welcome side benefit of his fatigue. His hand snaked up from the depths of the bag and rubbed the inside corners of his eyes while he let out a weary sigh. Sergeant Langdon's question got answered with another.

'Is it cold out there?'

'No worse than when you came off stag at two sir. I've already got the brews on.'

'You'll make a fantastic wife one day Langers. Wake the other lads up will you.'

The Mullah's loudspeaker made a 'tock' sound as it sprung to life. Traditionally, the Morning Prayer was timed when the dawn shed sufficient light to discern the difference in colour between a black thread and a white one. These days he used a digital clock specifically programmed for the purpose. You simply set the date and selected whichever region of the planet you were in. They sold them in the city. This one was a gift from Haji Abdul Baki. Sometimes the Mullah would treat it like a time machine, fiddling with the controls to place himself in all the far-off exotic places Allah had created elsewhere on the globe. Places Allah had not yet willed him to see.

It came with a manual that contained a tiny map of the world, dissected into shaded bands to show what time it was compared to where he stood. Most often he imagined visiting islands. The Mullah had never set eyes on the ocean. From the one or two photographs he had seen in books, it resembled the desert south of Kandahar – miles and miles of flat, featureless space – but water instead of sand. How glorious it would be to stand on the shoreline and praise Allah in front of such a vast creation. The storms must be incredible whipping up the fluid landscape to create sweeping dunes of water.

When he first indulged this game, it filled him with panic that he might not be able to return the clock to his home time in Afghanistan, and Haji Abdul Baki would be insulted that the Mullah had broken it in childish play.

———

As the Mullah's classical Arabic suffused the fields around Shingazi, Janan felt a flutter of panic. He and Gul Khan had hoped to be safely clear by now, secure amid the faceless throng attending morning prayers. Instead the two men were leading a patrol that would soon be subject to the attentions of Haji Mansur's scouts. Gul Khan might be resigned to a public association with the British, but Janan was yet to dip his turban in that indelible dye. He had only joined the expedition out of solidarity – guilty that Gul Khan shouldered the whole burden of cooperation with the foreigners.

They had been punctual for their pre-dawn rendezvous but movement in darkness always took longer than normal, even with Janan and Gul Khan as guides. And the truth was, Gul Khan had got confused and led the column astray. By the time he corrected himself, daybreak was upon them.

Everybody now sensed the tug of time. Nek abandoned his scrutiny of a distant treeline and turned around to his Afghan companions. There was hardly any need for Mohammad's translation.

'You two should be getting back. We'll abandon this one.'

Janan nodded – relieved – and drew his shawl tighter across his shoulders, as a gesture that it was time to go.

'No Nek. I have a better idea,' Gul Khan said. He had that gleam in his eyes that worried Janan. 'I'll go and fetch the mines. You can find somewhere to wait for me.'

'That's out of the question. What if they're booby-trapped? That was the whole point of us coming with you. You show us the Haji's cache, and we make it safe with specialists.'

'They won't be booby-trapped,' Gul Khan scoffed. 'Anyway, we no longer have time for mine hunters' puzzle games. If we all cross those fields in daylight, there'll be a battle. If I go alone, it is just one farmer. I won't move anything that looks like rat bait.'

Nek grimaced towards the treeline again and sucked his teeth. Gul Khan laughed.

'Relax old woman.' Mohammad was embarrassed to translate these good-natured insults. 'Think about this,' Gul Khan said. 'Mir Hamza is certain where the mine cache is. Tomorrow it may be gone. I'll be back before you know it. Janan can stay here and sooth your nerves with a lullaby.'

Nek was enjoying the mockery but remained visibly unconvinced. Janan tried to sense where the other soldiers stood in this debate. Maybe they would have a vote. But even if they did have an opinion on the matter, impassive faces betrayed nothing of the soldiers' feelings. The encumbered youths just knelt there, watching the countryside with the patience of livestock.

Even the mine hunters themselves wore the expression of cattle. And their fate rested on such decisions. They carried enormous packs. There was all manner of strange things tucked into loops on the outside: metal hooks and coils of cord. He had heard about the little robot but he could not see it. Probably it slept inside one of the bags. Janan respected and pitied these curious, burdened characters in equal measure. What kind of person chooses to snake around on their belly tinkering with homemade mines? In their shoes he would be a nuisance to the commander, questioning the necessity of such folly. After all, mines are harmless once you know where they are.

Ever since the fort had been established, Haji Mansur's men sought to isolate it with dozens and dozens of mines. Out in the desert they planted twenty-kilo monsters designed to remove the front end of a military vehicle. If a Shingazi resident triggered one en route to market, in a normal car, so be it. Collaboration has its price. The monster mines would scatter a Toyota, and its occupants, to the heavens. On the west of the canal, among the fields sweeping across to the river, the Movement planted smaller mines to hit foot patrols and deter the foreigners from moving any further south. Here too, the risk to farmers and their families was considered a necessary consequence.

But the locals were attuned to these dangers. Whereas a well-camouflaged mine might elude the foreigners, the farmers knew every inch of their fields. The slightest change in texture or colour on their footpaths sang out. Once on less familiar terrain, they suffered the same predicament as the soldiers – only more so, because they lacked any machines to find the mines. Unfrequented fallow land and vacated properties held centre stage in parental worry. Shingazi's children were losing their right to roam. The presence of a mine spread faster among mothers around the water pumps than it did between men on the byways.

Gul Khan duly passed all this information onto Nek and they hatched schemes. Gul Khan would arrive at the fort an hour before dawn and lead the British to the exact spot. By sunrise Gul Khan was gone. The Haji's scouts would awake to find the soldiers already in place, as if they had found it themselves, and the mine would be destroyed. The ploy served mutual interests. It protected the local population from reprisal while reducing the risk of ambush for the mine hunters.

Janan's involvement made life easier for Gul Khan. If they did it in pairs or small groups there would be less fear of being singled out as the traitor – the same social stockade they had thrown up when building the fort that day. With small steps, confidence would grow. So far only one other man had taken part. Saifullah, Haji Khan Mohammad's challenger at the council meeting. He led Nek and the others to a large mine in the desert just east of Shingazi's road bridge. Its destruction created a tower of dust that could have brushed the belly of an eagle.

This time the prize was not mines but a cache of the bits and pieces necessary to build them. Not the explosive charges in their yellow cooking-oil containers but the batteries and wooden shoes you stood on, to set them off. Mir Hamza had seen the Haji's fighters placing a sackful under a pile of dried poppy stalks. Nek was excited by this prospect, because normally the mines had to be blown up one by one. He explained to Gul Khan that stealing a bag of the parts might yield information about the people who made them. Apparently like any craftsman, bomb makers have signatures.

Nek made a 'tutting' sound and sighed.

'I can't stop you Gul Khan. It's your decision. Let the sky hear me – I told you not to do it.' He waved at the southern extremity of Shingazi. 'We will be waiting over there. If there is any doubt, I urge you to walk away.'

Gul Khan proffered his Kalashnikov. 'Look after this for me Nek.' They shook hands and Gul Khan wagged a finger at him. 'Don't be getting any ideas. I want it back.'

'Well you'd better hurry then. They go for good money.'

Nek barked something at his men and everyone clambered to their feet. Gul Khan was already scurrying away, doubling back towards the canal. He gathered his shawl over the top of his head like a hood to copy the appearance of a labourer walking to work. It was a common sight in the early morning chill of the valley. Soon he was lost in the trees.

The patrol picked its way across the field and Janan led them through a treeline via the farmers' recognised safe route. Here Nek split his force in two. The mine hunters returned to the fort leaving a dozen or so men behind, including a small party of Tajik soldiers. They lay down on the edge of the field. Two men with mine detectors swept positions for a couple of sentries – one with a machine gun on skinny metal legs. Nek and Mohammad settled in behind the machine gunner and beckoned for Janan to join them.

Nek removed a glove. 'You can go if you like Janan. I don't need a lullaby. I'll bite my fingernails instead.'

Imagining what Gul Khan would think if his cousin abandoned the patrol, Janan shrugged with resignation.

At least he was hiding in the ditch. There was no need to speak.

Nek understood. 'Very well friend. I'll be grateful for the company.'

Consulting a map, Nek spoke into his radio and then spent a minute or two briefing the machine gunner. Eventually he turned back to Janan with some more small talk.

'Tell me Janan, what was Gul Khan like as a boy? He must've been in trouble all the time.'

'He has always been someone with a horizon further than most men. When we were boys Gul Khan would explore all the time. He challenged himself to go beyond the village, and then the canal. He always made friends – other boys or old men. He always seemed to know so much about other people. Sometimes we didn't believe him.'

'I was the opposite as a child. Timid.' Nek paused and spoke with Mohammad. Perhaps that word didn't exist in Pashtu. He spent a time explaining something with his hands, making angles and scoops.

Mohammad nodded patiently along and then beamed with recognition. 'Nek Sahib's mother used to try and persuade him to go on the metal towers they build for children to play on. You slide down a kind of chute. But he was afraid he would hurt himself.'

Janan could not believe it. 'You are a warrior Nek. That can't be true! If you had met Gul Khan when you were boys, he would probably have punched you until you climbed the tower.'

Nek nodded his head. 'Yes, probably. I had a friend like that. He always encouraged me.'

A curious cloud had crossed the man's face. 'Did you have a peaceful childhood in your country Nek?'

It took him time to respond. Janan expected the answer to be 'no'.

'Yes I did Janan. Peaceful, certainly. I suppose that's something we take for granted now in England. But my grandfathers had to fight the greatest war the world has ever witnessed. And their fathers too, before them. The way I see it, our peaceful childhoods were their gift.'

'That is one war that did not come to Afghanistan.'

'No. But you've had more than your fair share.'

'We have. But also I think of all the badness in between. Warlords and bandits getting fat on the blood of this country, like leeches. We are lucky in the valleys. Sometimes they are too lazy to come and bother us.'

Mohammad interjected – no longer the passive interlocutor. 'I agree with you Janan. I am from Kabul and that is one place they never bypass.' He then had the courtesy to tell Nek what he had just shared.

Janan could see that the exchange played on Nek's mind. Then the machine gunner asked him a question and the two men had a little conversation of their own that Janan could not understand. He decided it would be rude to ask Mohammad what they were talking about, even though he suspected it related to what had just been said.

Instead, in a low voice, he made his own inquiry of Mohammad's childhood.

'I am sorry Janan but I slipped earlier. I should only speak the words that flow through my ears. It makes the foreigners nervous when we interpreters journey into our own language with you.'

'I understand that. I will not be offended.'

A shot cracked in the distance, followed almost immediately by two more in quick succession. The soldiers all tensed as one, muscles contracting in the manner of a spooked mule. Mohammad rolled onto his front and squirmed into the soil. Nek garbled something into his radio and everyone strained to see what was going on. Now they could hear the buzz of motorcycles somewhere beyond view. Suddenly Nek flashed an arm out and said something that sounded like 'sheet'.

It was Gul Khan, haring into the field a couple of hundred paces away.

He ran awkwardly with one arm swinging across his front. The other was securing something on his back. Nek pursed his lips and let rip with a shrill whistle. Gul Khan heard it and froze. But he did not know where it had come from. Nek tried another. Giving up, Gul Khan set off again.

Nek sprung up and dashed a few yards into the field, shouting and waving his rifle. This time Gul Khan spotted him and raised a hand in greeting, as if he was out for a stroll.

As he made towards them, a motorcycle appeared on the track where Gul Khan had first emerged. There were two men on it. They spotted Gul Khan straightaway. Unable to drive across the field, they picked up a narrow footpath running parallel to the treeline and sped off to close the distance at an angle. The pillion passenger brandished a Kalashnikov.

Jumping into the ditch, Nek acknowledged the machine gunner's shouts with a curt nod and the boy settled back behind his long black instrument. There was a pause while he composed himself and then the gun exploded into life, gobbling at the brass belt voraciously. Janan's ears were ringing.

The first burst scythed wide off the mark, behind the

motorcycle. The rider swerved before kicking an extra jerk of speed out of it. Judging the risk to himself, Gul Khan dived face down in the field. But it was unnecessary. The motorcycle's angled progress increased the gunner's freedom. His second, longer burst was directed ahead of the bike in an attempt to ambush it.

Preparing to return fire, the passenger had raised his weapon by the time the rounds arrived. One may have struck the rifle because it flicked into the air like a toy as the man was knocked bodily off the motorcycle into the ditch by successive hits to his chest. His sudden departure overbalanced the rider, who struggled manfully for control. But the bike lolled to the left and lost the track, flipping up on end, with its engine screaming in protest. Flung forwards against a sapling, the rider dropped out of view.

Over to the right, on a different avenue, a second motorcycle appeared, nosing speculatively into the open. A Tajik soldier jostled forward with another machine gun, covered in belts of ammunition. It dwarfed him. The bold little man screamed something in Dari and then, brandishing the weapon from his hip, hosed an extravagantly protracted stream of bullets in their general direction.

Albeit skyward, the demonstration was sufficient to elicit a hasty U-turn from the second bike. Janan could hear the gears changing as it accelerated away.

Gul Khan was already up and running when the deposed rider limped into view again. He was trying to drag his dead comrade through the thicket of the treeline with his one good arm. The other hung useless. Instinctively, the machine gunner drew forward into the aim. Nek shouted, with a chopping motion left and right across his throat. The gunner relaxed.

For some reason Nek felt he needed to explain himself to Janan.

'We've done enough. We're not butchers,' he said.

The soldier did not seem happy about it. He fidgeted and tutted to himself. Janan thought he was right. War is war, surely?

Then Gul Khan arrived, panting.

'May the peace of Allah be upon you Nek! Have you enjoyed your picnic?'

He grinned ear to ear with phlegm in his beard and sweat beading across his brow. 'I've done the shopping,' he said. Gul Khan dumped a fertiliser bag at their feet and fished into it, flinging out short wooden planks, nine-volt batteries and coils of white electrical wire. 'Look.'

Nek beckoned him to stop. 'Gul Khan, Gul Khan, be careful with the evidence. We don't want your fingerprints on it.' Mohammad translated it twice.

'What?' Gul Khan's wide eyes darted up.

'Come here friend. Get your breath back.' Nek placed a hand on his shoulder. 'Tell us what happened.'

'Hey Janan! Still here cousin? I thought you might have nipped home by now. I lost my hat back there. Had to go back for it. That hat and I are old comrades. You never abandon a comrade.'

Everybody let him jabber away.

'The boy was bang on. Who'd have believed it from an imbecile? He should be your spy Nek – reliable as a sunset and nobody will suspect him. I just had a spot of bad timing, that's all. One of the Haji's hawks clocked me putting the poppy stalks back. I suppose it was obvious what I was up to.'

Janan noticed Mohammad was struggling to keep up with Gul Khan's speed of delivery.

'I tried to hold my nerve and walk away, cool as a landlord, but it was a mistake. I should've got a head start. The hawk used his radio and some muscle turned up. I'm not as fast as I used to be. I owe you one Nek.' Gul Khan looked down at the machine gunner. 'You too. Good shooting boy.'

Mohammad passed on the compliment and the soldier patted the top of his weapon, like the skull of a dog.

Nek ended their excitable conference. 'We need to get moving. Hang around here much longer and there'll be follow-up.' He spoke into his radio, nodding along with the conversation as if the distant messenger could see him. All the soldiers gathered themselves to move, servants of a perpetual nomadic routine. Kneeling down to put his spoils back in the fertiliser bag, Nek addressed the two cousins.

'You two had better put some distance between us. It's been a profitable morning. Lie low for a bit.'

Gul Khan wiped his beard and scratched at it. 'That would be nice Nek but Janan and I have got some farming to do. Health and happiness. God willing we meet again soon.'

Nek returned the Kalashnikov to Gul Khan with exaggerated solemnity. 'Maybe you should take this with you next time.' He shook hands with each of them in turn.

The cousins strode away, leaving the soldiers to their painstaking serpentine progress, and headed back towards Gul Khan's compound for tea. After a few minutes an acquaintance came the other way with his sons.

'May the peace of Allah be upon you Gul Khan. Has the battle ended?' He shot them a knowing look.

'And also with you Baz Mohammad. It has. There is a

patrol just beyond those trees. Give them a wide berth if you're worried.'

When they were alone again, Janan had to say something. Part of him was proud of Gul Khan but the sense of dismay prevailed.

'Was that stunt wise today cousin? You are becoming rash.'

'Almost certainly unwise Janan... but it felt good tugging the Haji's tail. Look around you. He hasn't bothered the fort for days now. You never see his men in Shingazi anymore. We are finding his mines almost as fast as he lays them. The British major says that the district governor is planning to pay for a local police force in this area. I think the Movement is running out of ideas. Dogs barking long after the caravan has moved on.'

Janan could never hear a proverb without remembering how his father would always pause after using one, raise a finger and follow it with his favourite: '...and remember there is no proverb which is not true.' Then came the smug, wheezing chuckle. The only person unconvinced of this act was Janan's mother. If in earshot, she – with equal predictability – would click her tongue and say 'and he who marries for wealth sells his liberty. So go and fix the gate...' or whatever job she'd been nagging him to complete that week.

Janan's mirth owed something to that memory. 'I hope you are right,' he said.

Still irrepressibly ebullient, Gul Khan chased the moment, like a storyteller riding peals of laughter. 'Hope?! That's what I do with the weather old friend. At least this business I have some control over.' Gul Khan brandished his Kalashnikov theatrically.

They enjoyed the escape for a few more paces.

Gul Khan delved for a memory. 'Hey cousin, do you remember that Eid when we were Mamur's age?' The loss of his son did not seem to intrude on the recollection.

'Who could forget it?! Haji Karim Karimi, shaking his fist!'

It was a matchless piece of mischief. Aching with hunger and fatigue from daily fasting through the Holy Month of Ramadan, the two young adolescents had longed for the Eid feast: the arrival of a new moon, the return to routines. It was always up to the Mullah to declare precisely when this would be. Gul Khan could not wait. Egged on by Janan, he stole into the mosque, scampered up the narrow staircase and, at the top of his voice, impersonated the Mullah. The arrival of Eid was duly declared.

Taking flight, they sought refuge with Gul Khan's father, panting and giggling as the gates clanged shut behind them. They knew they would be beaten. Yet the victory tasted so sweet.

A bull-like elder called Haji Karim Karimi led the remonstrations. Standing in the alleyway outside their compound, his rage carried over the walls. 'Boy! If it's not Eid tomorrow, I *will* fuck you!'

They felt alive then, just as they felt alive now. Sometimes life revealed moments of unqualified optimism. Mirages. Janan always embraced them.

When Gul Khan spoke again, he had recovered some of his usual circumspection. 'I'm going to send for Sanga. She should be enjoying the taste of these changes with us. Maybe she will stop me behaving like a reckless youth again.'

Islamic Republic of Afghanistan
Islamic Movement of Taliban

General commission of intelligence administration

This is to inform all the people of Shingazi, North Central Helmand District, that their affiliation with the Christian aggressors is illegal and immoral.

We are also very well informed about the activities of Gul Khan, resident of Shingazi, spying on his Mujahideen brothers and working to stop Taliban activities.

You have no obligation to shelter him or the foreigners. We strongly warn you that if you do not evict Gul Khan from your village in a very short period of time, you will be responsible for all the consequences and for all the destruction that takes place as a result.

Once victorious in removing the Christian aggressors, we will attack your homes and we will kill you and all of your family members. Not even your animals will be spared.

We are always merciful to those that follow the light and reform their behaviour.

This letter belongs to the Islamic Republic of Afghanistan

Private Stephens reached up under the rim of his helmet to scratch a stubborn itch in his matted hair. But it was right at the top, beneath the padding. He tried pressing down on the helmet to rub it against his scalp, eyes screwed shut to focus his efforts.

'Jesus Steveo, will you stop fucking fidgeting. It's driving me up the wall.' Brogan knelt against a compound on the other side of the alleyway.

'Well, you go an' see what's taking the boss so fucking long then. I swear if I had a pound for every hour spent on stag in this bastard village I'd retire to Magaluf.' He picked up a pebble and tossed it in protest.

'You got up on the wrong side of bed this morning Steveo.'

Stephens giggled. 'Actually worse than that Pat... I had a wet dream in my gonk bag.'*

'You didn't! I wondered why you were scratching around in there this morning. I thought you had a dose of sweat rot.'

Corporal Lennon walked up the alley. 'Who's got sweat rot?'

'No one corporal. Steveo—'

Stephens cut him off. 'Don't you fucking dare.'

'Fine,' said Corporal Lennon. 'You teens keep your diary secrets. But if anyone's going down with anything, I need to know. Get your lunch in – one at a time.' He wandered off again.

Brogan checked that he was out of earshot. 'I don't know what's wrong with Beatle. His sense of humour fucked off on R&R at some point. You eat first Steveo.'

---

* **Gonk bag,** army slang for a sleeping bag; see also 'doss bag', 'fart sack' and 'scratcher'.

'Cheers. Can you fish it out of my daysack for me? Rear right pouch, on the outside.'

Stephens leaned forward and Brogan fussed about. First he tried doing it one handed, then rested his weapon against the wall and dug around in the pouch. 'Noodles?'

'Yeah – and there should be one of those fruit gels in there too.'

Brogan placed the two packets down next to Stephens, closed the pouch carefully and picked up his weapon.

'Can I sort you out Pat?'

'No thanks. Mine's in my thigh pocket.'

Stephens sat down against the wall and laid his rifle across his knees. Then he dropped his chin and tugged a brown plastic spoon from one of the pouches on the front of his body armour. Slapping the green foil packet against his knee to settle the contents, he ripped a strip off the top and poked about to cut the tepid, oily pre-cooked noodles into spoon-sized mouthfuls.

The whole point of staggering their feeding was that Brogan provided security. But his own hunger created an involuntary fascination with Stephens' fussy procedure. His mouth even watered. Forcing himself to look away, Brogan made conversation.

'Have you heard from Little Miss Chocolate recently?' He could hear Stephens swallow before he answered. His girlfriend worked in a shopping mall chain confectioner, so this was the name they had given her.

'I got a letter last week. She sprayed some perfume on it. I swear I got a hard-on. You should read some of the stuff she says.'

'Fucking pest. No wonder you let one go last night.'

'That's the thing. There's nowhere to abuse yer'self in the PB.'

'Not when you're up on stag?'

'Not here Pat. Not with the shit they throw at us.' Stephens paused for thought and then chuckled. 'Can you imagine getting into a serious brass-up right at the point of no return? The lads all stand-to* and you're there clutching your fella. That would be about as bad as it gets.'

'The worst.' Brogan went quiet for a moment while a memory formed itself. 'Did I tell you about the first time Celina's folks came over from Poland? Now that was embarrassing.'

Stephens had heard the story but he let Brogan continue. They had nothing better to do. Brogan drove on.

'They're dead traditional, so we decided to meet them in the pub right? We didn't want them to know that we were virtually fucking married. Are you sure I haven't told you this one?'

'You might've, but keep going.'

'I'd been out with some of the Mortar Platoon lads in the centre of town, that "Rat's Keller" place where they brew their own lager like monks. Celina had no idea. We were all hammered. That stuff creeps up on you. It was a schoolboy error.'

An old man shuffled towards them. His shalwar were particularly short, revealing thin, leathery ankles like chicken's feet. Brogan suspended his anecdote to acknowledge the

---

* **Stand-to**, the army's equivalent of 'all hands on deck': a high state of alert when the entire garrison is manning defensive positions.

pedestrian. Their cheery greetings provoked a babble of Pashtu: half inquiry, half entreaty. Nonplussed, the two soldiers shook their heads. The greybeard threw up his hands in frustration and stalked off, as if it was intransigence or stupidity that had stolen their tongues.

Brogan could still hear him remonstrating as he passed Corporal Lennon and the others at the next junction.

'We have those in Ireland too...' he mused. Then he turned back to Stephens.

'Anyway, as I was saying. I'd spent way too long in the Rat's Keller. I realised I'd have to go straight to the place I was meeting Celina and her folks. The fresh air hit me and I thought, "This is OK Pat, you can walk this off." I got to the bar a little early and I ordered a beer, playing it cool. I really thought I'd got away with it.'

Stephens interrupted him. 'You can have your scoff now Pat.'

'Cheers.' He dug into his pocket and pulled out a foil pack similar to Stephens'. In the joy of his reverie, Brogan had nearly forgotten his hunger pangs.

'So Celina arrives with her folks – first time I've ever set eyes on them.'

'I bet she was looking gorgeous mate.'

'Beautiful. I can see her right now, in her favourite black skirt. So I step forward and it's all kind of awkward. I kiss Celina on each cheek and she's saying "this is my mother, Iwona." Now, we'd talked about this – it's tradition in Poland to kiss a woman on her hand. So I take her hand and kiss it like in a film. She's all flattered and shy, and I'm getting a bit carried away in the moment. You know the drill – a mixture of nerves and drunkenness. And then her old man steps forward and he's got this really happy round face with a kind of comb-over thing going on, and you'll never guess.' Brogan was already giggling. 'He went to shake my hand and I went and fucking kissed it.'

Stephens did his best to recapture some of the hilarity on first hearing Brogan's favourite story. It didn't matter. Brogan was having fun all by himself.

'The look on his face Steveo! I've no idea why the fuck I did it. You think he would've snatched his hand away but he didn't. So I held onto it, all limp like. I heard myself blurting out that I was drunk. Celina and her mum were laughing so hard that it took her time to translate it. When the old man got the gist, he roared like a bear and patted me on the back.'

Corporal Lennon bellowed at them down the alleyway. 'Oi! Clowns! What the fuck d'you think this is?'

Brogan raised an arm in surrender. 'My fault, Corporal. Sorry. We're on it.' Chastened, he returned to the story in lowered tones. 'Ever since then he's treated me as an excuse to get out of the house and find trouble. I'm almost dreading the wedding. They kill you with kindness.'

Laughter reached Gul Khan from the alleyway. It had an almost adolescent abandon, and reminded him of his boys ragging in the compound. When they slaughtered a goat Mamur used to chase Imran around with its head, shrieking that he'd found him a wife, and why wouldn't Imran kiss her. If Imran shared those memories at this moment, he did not betray it. The boy was hovering above their little lunch party dutifully, replenishing glasses and waiting to remove plates.

The sharp remonstration from some unseen authority figure provoked an apology from Nek, who was a little more guarded than usual in the presence of his commander.

'Please forgive my soldiers Gul Khan. I fear they are not being as well entertained as us.'

'Perhaps I have kept you too long Nek. It is easy to forget that we are not at peace here quite yet. One day it would be good to take our time without such considerations.'

'If that day comes, it will be time for us to leave,' Nek said.

The major nodded in agreement with him. Then he gestured towards Imran. 'When this is nothing but a memory, God willing, your boy will build a huge family and delight his own grandchildren with tales about serving tea to the foreign soldiers.'

Gul Khan gave a wry smile as he listened to the translation. 'I admire your optimism commander Sahib. It assumes that there will be no more foreign soldiers after you. That would be something truly exceptional for us.'

'We live in hope Gul Khan. One certain, exceptional thing is your generosity.' The major gesticulated across the remnants of their meal.

That signalled the end of a meal that Sanga had prepared with the best ingredients they could afford for the time of year. They killed a chicken. She had found some small red peppers and salad leaves to serve alongside the flatbreads. But first there had been a confused discussion over what to serve the two British officers. Sanga was the more thoughtful.

'How do you know they'll like our food?' she had posed. 'Surely they would prefer the tastes of their home. They must miss that.'

'I don't have a clue what they eat on the other side of the

world. All I know is that they like biscuits with dried grapes in them.'

'We can't give them biscuits and dried grapes. A good host would find these things out before inviting people for lunch. It won't be my fault if they gag on it.'

'It's never your fault Sanga, as well we know.'

It disappointed Gul Khan how quickly they resumed their habitual bickering when Sanga and Imran got back. He had missed them so much. The first day reunited was all hugs and laughter. Even her observations about the state of their home had been nothing more than good-natured teasing. Gul Khan had not noticed half the things his wife rectified as she bustled about rearranging the bedding chest and cooking utensils. Imran and his father shared a few knowing looks. *Back to normal then*.

Janan's wife came over to help with the cooking. Evidently Sanga had shared the menu debate because Zarmina was clucking about sweets.

'Have you got candies?' she said. 'Janan assures me that the British like their candies.'

How on earth did he know? This was ridiculous. Gul Khan understood that Nek was an honourable man. The food was of no consequence compared to the gesture.

They spread out their finest rug and cushions for the guests, in shade under the cloistered section outside their principal mud rooms. Sanga laid thin cloths for the dishes to go on. As she did so, bird droppings spattered one corner. Tutting with exasperation at such inopportune timing, she shooed Imran off to fetch a wet rag and turned on Gul Khan.

'I told you to remove that birds' nest from the arches.'

He had no recollection of this. 'They kept me company when you were away Sanga. It would feel disloyal to turn them out now.'

Once the guests arrived she would have to retreat indoors. Only Imran could emerge to wait upon them. That was a relief.

But Sanga still had more to give. 'Try and make sure they don't rest their oily guns on our cushions. I know they won't take their boots off. We may as well invite cattle for lunch.'

'Please be patient Sanga. This is important to me.'

'Yes. I'm getting used to that Gul Khan.'

She had not called him that to his face for years.

Sanga was strong and gracious enough not to voice her pain at returning home to a house without Mamur. When she left it was still sharp – urgent. In those first days moving around the city she had tried to find him, as if Mamur was a runaway. Once she even spotted him, fleetingly. Feeling detached and blinkered under the net face veil of her burka, she tried to throw it off, to be free to run after him as fast as she had ever run. Gul Khan's brother-in-law had been forced to restrain her. Sanga knew she had been seeing things, willing things. But Mamur's death felt so unreal, so like a nightmare, it was hard to face the waking world. Eventually those weeks away, waiting and worrying, put the upheaval into a colder perspective. Her sense of faith and duty kept her upright. It was Allah's will. Sanga's place was alongside her husband. The pain no longer stabbed. It ached, unrelenting, like a rotten tooth.

Then the Movement's letter arrived in the village. Sanga could not read. But it took no time for the contents to be spread by ear. Naturally, Gul Khan tried to dismiss it.

'They're desperate Sanga. This is just words designed to scare us. If they meant it, they'd have done this by now.'

Maybe that was true. But it dawned on her there would be no tomorrow without shadows. For as long as the Movement had breath, every joy – every hope – was tainted. Submission to fate and to God had helped her come to terms with her stillborn son, the death of her daughter and now Mamur. The manner of his passing was less important than the fact of it. If it was Mamur's time, so be it. There were many ways to die. The letter changed this way of making sense of things. She could see Gul Khan's hand in all of it now, clearer than the squiggles and shapes of the printing. Where does fate and Allah's design meet human choice? It confused Sanga.

Clear though were her thoughts when she saw Imran, her last remaining child, her only mark on the world.

'I knew I was right,' she had sighed. 'This is your crusade and you've brought it upon the rest of us.'

Sanga understood honour. She was raised to believe in it. But it had been a long journey from her birthplace in Kunar. Try as she might, her love could not conceal the unremitting weariness Gul Khan's decisions had invited into her life. It was almost pointless blaming him. He was a product. Men created so much needless suffering with their childish preoccupations.

Later that afternoon, when the two officers had left and Imran was tending the animals, Gul Khan tried to buoy her spirits. He was wise enough to recognise that most people gambling for high stakes are prone to exaggerate their chances of success. In the old days Gul Khan had seen many friends perish in ignominy, often with an expression of surprise and disbelief at their fate. It is a human-enough tendency, he reflected, perhaps encouraged by the Pashtun diet of legends about great daring, guile and improbable victory. After all, nobody went to the Hujra* to hear stories about prudent decisions or inglorious failures.

He knew he was guilty of projecting his own determination onto Sanga. But that's what a strong husband should do. It was simpler when he had been left alone with this challenge. The return of his family replaced one sort of loneliness with another. Sometimes he wished the Mullah was a better, wiser man. Someone he could confide in.

For all that, lunch had lifted Gul Khan and he was sure Sanga could feel the same way. The officers had been even more dismissive of the letter than he was.

'Why wouldn't the Movement deliver "night letters"?' they had said.

It was a trusted method of intimidation. The major had explained patiently that it was always wiser to judge the Movement by their actions, not their words. Their propaganda lay in the line 'once victorious in removing the Christian aggressors...' Singularly they had 'failed to achieve that,' the major explained, and the foreign mission in Afghanistan had 'years to run,' he said, not to mention international support to Afghanistan's security forces 'long after withdrawal.' It was not the same as the Soviet times, when money dried up because their empire collapsed. The United States was a rich and powerful nation.

'You see Sanga, they agree with me,' Gul Khan said.

'How do the affairs of great nations affect us in Shingazi

---

* **Hujra,** a Pashtun gathering place – private or public – to socialise and hear bards or elders regale entertaining stories in the oral tradition.

my love? You are a farmer. The Movement does not have to be victorious in Afghanistan to have a victory over our family, and our village.'

'They explained that too, Sanga. As we speak, Haji Mansur is being hunted by spies and planes. Apparently such men rarely survive a year in Helmand once the foreigners turn their attentions on them. The major told me about other influential commanders in the Movement, further afield, that recognise the folly of their struggle. The foreigners have extended the offer of dialogue.'

'His friends can still find us.'

'Please Sanga. Things have changed in this village while you were away. I would not have brought you back until I believed that. Soon we will have our own police force, to serve alongside the foreign soldiers, who have kept the Haji's men out of this village for weeks. Other men have already come forward.'

'So why has this supposed police force not arrived yet?' Her logic was relentless as always. Gul Khan started to resent it. The blows were denting his armour.

'Because these things take time. It is not a simple thing to provide us with weapons and uniforms. The politicians in Kabul are wary of raising militias in the countryside.'

Sanga gave out a squawk of derisory despair. 'So you are placing your faith in thieves now!'

Gul Khan flushed. 'Not those oafs. The British. They have influence over such things. I trust them.'

'Why do you trust the British warriors? The commander doesn't know us and you tell me Nek isn't even married. That's not a good sign at his age. Where are his morals? Where is his standing?'

Her manner needled him. He had grown fond of Nek. They were friends. 'Now you are being silly Sanga. They have a very different culture…'

'An immoral one I tell you.'

Finally he raised his voice. 'These men have crossed the world to fight for us woman! I watched one die here in our village. They want for nothing but our help. That's enough now. I simply ask you to trust *me*.' He prodded himself in the chest. 'Not them. *Me*.'

Sanga retreated. She knew that Gul Khan was every bit as stubborn as her. It was impossible to undo what had already been done. Hopeless as she felt, there was precious little to be gained by argument. Eventually he would simply hit her. She put her arms out.

'Come here my love. Hold me.'

It took him a few seconds to climb down. Then tenderly he pushed back her cotton scarf and gathered her head in the crook of his shoulder.

'Have I told you that I missed you when you were gone my Sanga?'

Her voice was muffled by his waistcoat. 'I did wonder if you meant it.'

'Of course I did.' He kissed her hair and she looked up at him. His beard tickled her face.

'Just promise me that this isn't vanity. You are no longer the young man with strong arms that came to Kunar and carried me away.'

'I have the same heart. And every day I have *lived* since that war has been a gift from Allah. Duty cares nothing for our lives, only for what we leave behind. If there is vanity in honour, so be it.'

She exhaled audibly through her nose. There was nothing more to be said.

'Look Sanga, I have some things to show you. Nek gave them to me.' Gul Khan broke the embrace and walked over to a recess in the wall of their room. First he held out a green rubber tablet with a sort of metal pen attached to one side. 'They are signal flares. He told me that if we are ever alarmed, we must fire one of these into the air and he will come as soon as possible.'

She handled the alien object, weighing it in her palm because she was not sure what else to do. He took it back and passed her a thin, tarnished metal tin. On more confident ground now, she snapped it open to reveal a neat row of filtered cigarettes on one side and a note tucked into the other.

'They're English cigarettes Sanga. Good ones. I haven't smoked any yet. They look too perfect to disturb. Nek carried this tin fighting in Iraq. He said it would bring me luck.'

'What does the note say?'

Gul Khan unfolded it. The top half was written in English, the bottom in Pashtu.

'Apparently it reads the same thing in both languages,' he said. With undisguised pride, Gul Khan read slowly and deliberately, at the limits of his literacy.

'*To Gul Khan, the bravest man I have ever met. Please, no more gallant acts. Smoke these instead. From your brother in arms, Nek.*'

Sanga was puzzled. 'What gallant acts?'

Imran called from the compound. 'Baba, I think one of the goats is lame!' Gul Khan placed the note back in the tin and snapped it shut. 'I'm coming Imran!'

Sanga followed him out of the room and stood in the doorway to the courtyard, angry again. 'Don't ignore me! What gallant acts?'

CF2/B/SITREPS/EXCP/16

CO CF2

SHINGAZI

1. Summary. Following our TELCON last night, I can report that progress in Shingazi is highly satisfactory. Insurgent harassment has proved ineffective and they are now reliant on intimidation. But the situation remains balanced. We must demonstrate an enduring commitment.

Patrol Base

2. BRITFOR. Capt Russell has done a superlative job of establishing the PB. As you know, I had my reservations about his robustness to assume the command. He had taken a few knocks on this tour already and sometimes doubts himself. He has proved me wrong. Much of what has been achieved — in short order — is down to his drive and charisma. There is a British garrison of eight pax, seven drawn from call-sign Advisor 42 plus one Mortar Fire Controller. We await replacements for two of the casualties sustained in his multiple.

3. ANA. Their contribution has been public throughout. Lt Sultan Mazari commands an ANA garrison of twelve (fluctuating). They rotate on a weekly basis but Lt Sultan remains in place. Capt Russell reports that he is developing well. However, the Tolay commander in FOB Bussaco (Capt Kamran Badakhshi) is adamant that ANA will withdraw from PB Shingazi when coalition forces do. This fits the general expectation for isolated bases in CF2 but awaits corroboration at higher level.

Insurgent activity

4. PB Shingazi was harassed most during the investment phase (D-Day to D+10) with 32 contacts logged (excluding single-shot engagements). This harassment tailed thereafter with only 18 contacts reported since, mostly in the period D+10 to D+21. No attempts have yet been made to close with and assault PB Shingazi. Predictably, IED activity has increased in proportion to the reduction in contacts. This includes devices targeting local nationals. One night letter has since been delivered (see INTSUM 11/014). Some direct intimidation has also reportedly occurred in the city bazaar. Objective STOCKTAKE is assessed to be orchestrating the intimidation campaign.

Local nationals

5. Gul Khan remains pivotal to Shingazi's security (see INTSUM 11/011). We assess him to be highly reliable as both a conduit for low-level information and the lynchpin for maintaining local support. He continues to refuse all my offers of financial compensation for the death of his son. Insurgent intimidation is now being directed at him personally. We do not assess that the village will evict him: elders are supportive of our presence in Shingazi and the village council has signed consent forms for an Afghan Local Police (ALP) detachment. However, confidence is assessed to be fragile. Gul Khan remains one of only three local nationals that have assisted us publicly since the D-Day 'cooperation'.

6. Elders are voicing impatience at delays in clearances for the ALP. They are beginning to think we do not trust them. Having signed the consent forms, they have now climbed off the fence and are understandably anxious for security they can guarantee for themselves. Rumours of

our withdrawal spread freely. It is increasingly difficult to mollify these concerns. They have also made repeated requests for assistance with urgent repairs to their road bridge. We have made no promises on that front. But the policy of limiting low-level projects (water pumps etc.) in order to prevent wage inflation is now looking like neglect. We are in danger of failing to deliver on 'the offer'.

Conclusion

7. The wider ramifications of an ALP detachment in Shingazi are well understood; as is the reluctance of the District Governor to invest finite political and financial capital in an area so far removed from his core support base. Shingazi is not a priority for anyone, except the insurgents. We will continue to buy time and space but cannot do so indefinitely.

JP LOCKLEY
Major
OC B Coy

The four Mehsuds squatted off to one side, talking quietly among themselves. They shared a packet of snuff and started leaning out of the little clique one by one to spit green juice into the sand. Behind them was a wheelbarrow containing their automatic grenade launcher – the size and weight of a small motorcycle engine. The long belt of grenades was gathered on top of a fertiliser bag, ready to be fed into a tin drum-like magazine.

The youngest Mehsud had earlier arranged the grenade belt to clean with a paint brush, resembling a cross-legged onion vendor on the city road. Without looking up from his labours, he explained the habit to Haji Mansur's inquisitive fighters.

'If this thing jams, the show is over. It has a very delicate appetite.'

The Mehsuds had arrived in a dusty white Toyota saloon, creaking and squeaking on its rear axle. Three of them were crammed along the back seat and the launcher sat in the boot under a stained dust sheet. It was a long, stressful and uncomfortable road from their village in Pakistan. The leader opened the front passenger door and stretched himself like a dog waking up. After a customary formal greeting, Haji Mansur had inquired after his journey.

'That car was the smooth leg,' their commander grouched. 'We crossed the border in the mountains with the launcher on a donkey. The Punjabi soldiers have put more posts in recently. We had to move at night. Attaullah there – he got shoved off the ridge when the dumb animal spooked.'

The tall fighter threw his head back with a wry laugh.

'I thought it was my time!'

Two thick tresses of shoulder-length hair flowed astride his narrow bearded face, cut by a centre-parting. This was the distinctive mark of a Mehsud tribesman from South Waziristan – perhaps the most fiercely independent of all Pashtuns, and bane of the British Empire. Even today, successive incursions by the Pakistan Army failed to pacify them. To a man, the four travellers exuded this pride and truculence.

Mullah Elam had been good to his word: extra manpower and 'a special'. The Mullah's courier had informed him of their arrival.

'These boys have a reputation. They don't come cheap, so use them wisely Haji Sahib.'

Their leader had cut his hair to appear more like an Afghan. This was the penalty of being a wanted man in both countries. He leaned back into the car and was curt with the driver.

'Unload it and park on the covered side.' Taking in his surroundings, he then said simply, 'tea.'

Haji Mansur felt mildly provincial in their presence. All afternoon, the Mehsuds had reclined under a tree in the compound and shunned attempts at conversation by the talkative Sarbaz. One of the men, Tawooz, took offence.

'Who do these hairy mountain goats think we are? Virgins?' he said.

Sadiq, as always, placated the mood humorously. 'I suspect

that you are, in fact, a virgin Tawooz! Don't let it cut you. It's for their own protection. We'll probably never see them again anyway. Let's just get this done and be grateful they're here to help.'

Eventually, Haji Mansur closed the divide by calling the two groups together to rehearse their plan. For half an hour he had busied himself creating a diagram in the dirt. It demanded lengthy explanation. But first he delivered an invocation.

'Allah is benign to whom He pleases. He is the Knowing, the Wise.'

A dozen voices murmured their assent.

'Let us welcome our Mujahideen brothers from the Student Movement of Pakistan and give thanks for their safe arrival. As you have seen, they bring with them "the Mother Hen". For all of us who have been on the receiving end of British versions, it will be an honour to throw eggs back at the same rate.' One or two sycophants triggered a ripple of chuckles.

'For the benefit of our guests, let me explain our problem, and my plan to solve it.' Haji Mansur's stubby index finger meandered around above a seemingly random collection of rocks, corn husks and scratches that he had arranged everyone around. Turning to the Mehsud commander he apologised.

'I am no calligrapher but hopefully you can picture it now.'

The lead Mehsud acknowledged Haji Mansur's concession with so much grace that some in the Haji's camp suspected it was sarcastic.

'Your artistry is worthy of the Blue Mosque in Mazar-i-Sharif, Haji Sahib. Please continue.'

A trace of sarcasm was not lost on Haji Mansur either. There was no question that the Mehsuds increased their odds. They were determined veterans, of proven courage. But a large part of Haji Mansur wished he was embarking on this foray with his own men, and nobody else. The inclusion of Mullah Elam's friends – accompanied by a whiff of some ambiguous mercenary dimension – only served to reinforce his own sense of failure. And if they pulled it off then the credit would be attributed to the Mehsuds, even though the bulk of Haji Mansur's raiding force came from within. It vexed him. But if he resented their presence so much, then why had he not attempted something like this before?

He silenced his inner voice. Now was not the time for such reflections. The job demanded focus, and his men deserved it. They had assented to his scheme unquestioningly, loyal as always.

As the night's activities were played out in prospect, over the rocks and corn husks, there was more discussion and suggestion than Haji Mansur had envisaged when he rehearsed it all in his mind. The plan was better for it. He had to admit the Mehsuds were cunning and resourceful. Belief started to flow into all their extremities. *This could work.*

Eventually, Haji Mansur reached his conclusion. 'Tonight will be dangerous brothers. We are grabbing the foreigners by the belt and bringing them so close they'll be able to taste what we had for dinner.' He paused for effect.

Unfortunately, a nearby goat kept bleating. It prevented him from casting a spell exactly, but his men were nervous enough by now to give him their full attention.

'The foreigners normally have the advantage in darkness. But we have surprise and guile. Thanks to our Waziristan connections, some of you will have the green night glasses. As I have just explained, much will hinge on what our brothers can achieve with the Mother Hen. One of my friends has paced

the exact distance from the British fort to your firing position.'
Haji Mansur addressed his key lieutenants in turn.

'Sadiq...' He caught his comrade's eye. '...Your mines should give us the edge when it gets personal.'

'You can trust me Haji Sahib.'

'I know old comrade. Sarbaz: you and I will take two of our Mehsud brothers and place the jewel in the virgin's navel. Let me remind everybody that all the other activities serve this single objective. Is that understood?'

The irksome goat was first to answer.

'Good. If I am graced to be a Shahid then look to Sadiq. He will be best placed to judge what is wise in the overall scheme of things.'

This status was a surprise to the lieutenant. He betrayed his pride by trying too hard to look seasoned and impassive. A hand came from behind and patted Sadiq affectionately on the shoulder.

Haji Mansur brought the meeting to an end.

'Our cause is just and we go in Allah's name alone. We will close as I started.' He raised his palms and shut his eyes. 'O beloved! Have you not seen how your Lord dealt with the men of the Elephant? Did He not cause their device to be ruined? And He sent against them flocks of birds, striking them against stones of baked clay. And thus made them like broken straw, eaten up.'

They dined early. Haji Mansur knew these moments all too well. He had warned his host not to prepare much food. Bred and raised to be a generous host, the compound owner ignored this advice. Much was left untouched. There was more enthusiasm for the preparation of weapons, and other distractions. Haji Mansur led them in prayer at sunset and watched its retreating fire with some melancholy. He might never see it rise again, at least not from the mortal domain.

When the time came to file out of the compound into the deepening countryside, Haji Mansur was not the only one among them to look at the talkative goat with a tinge of envy. It chewed and shat its way through life as a neutral spirit, unburdened. It knew only instinctive reactive fear, not the grip of anticipation twisting in the Haji's belly.

The neighbour's children lingered in the alleyway below the sangar, vying for Pat's attention. 'Chokallat Pat!'

'You's ought to fuck off home. It's getting late. Go on. Shoo!'

They ignored him. He lifted the camouflage net and flicked a couple of pebbles at them. It brought only renewed shrieks and less than a second's respite.

A warm evening breeze found the band of sweat just under the rim of Pat's helmet and cooled him. Shingazi was sleepy. A few cooking fires, some distant chatter. Two flies were flirting around the muzzle of his weapon. He checked his watch. Only twenty more minutes and he could take his equipment off. It would feel good cleansing his scalp with a wet rag. Nice cup of tea and a 'boil-in-the-bag' lamb curry. 'Dancer', as Steveo would say.

Dancer... Celina flitted into his mind, light on her feet, lithe. Yes... a see-through summer dress and her hair up, somewhere sunny, at peace, Mediterranean even, net curtains shifting in a breeze, everything white. He snared her as she flashed past, spinning her into his arms and resting both hands on her buttocks. 'Pat!' she said in mock indignation, stepping deftly to place his thigh between her legs. A little pressure... a tongue in his ear...

The radio emitted two staccato 'tfffts' of white noise to herald the distant company second-in-command. Once acknowledged, the captain's clipped delivery gave a simple command.

'Fetch your sunray,* over.'

Pat longed to say 'fetch him yourself, fucker.' There was something vindictive about the radio that never seemed to respect where a man was in his thoughts and reveries. Nor did anyone ever appreciate that, come the evening, the radio in PB Shingazi was kept in the sangar. Pat would have to crawl backwards across the compound roof, shout down and crawl back. Inevitably the netting would catch something on his helmet and give his neck a good yank, or he would knock one of the sandbags and make yet another hole.

Captain Russell's cheery 'yo' reached him from below.

'It's the ops room sir. I don't know what they want.' Pat crawled back into position, his boots and knees rasping over the baked mud surface. His head thumped on a wooden support, sending dust down the sweaty nape of his neck.

Shortly the officer appeared, grunting and fussing his way into the narrow space. Pat stopped him.

'You can hold it there sir. I'll pass you the handset. No use exposing yourself up front.'

'Thanks Pat. How is it out there?'

'The usual sir. Kids and flies.'

The officer nodded and keyed the handset, reclining on his

---

* **Sunray,** army codeword for 'commander'.

side and resting on one elbow: a playboy ringing one of his girlfriends from the double king-size. Pat could only hear one side of the conversation. Always faintly irritating.

'Roger. I read back: one AGS-17 grenade machine gun with up to six out-of-area fighters, possibly Pakistani, over.'

Then some unintelligible garble from the radio.

'Well that bit's no good to me. Why are they only telling us now, over?'

A pause and more garble.

Captain Russell sighed. 'How reliable is this stuff, over?' It sounded like a one word answer. 'Roger. Couldn't you ask them to expand? Over.'

The response this time was longer.

'I'm sorry. I just need to know what you advise, over.'

More garble, separated by a pause.

'Roger. That makes sense. But keep us updated. It's a pain for the lads if it runs on and on, over.'

One last 'tfft' came from the radio.

'Roger out.'

Captain Russell tapped the handset on a post, as if to knock his irritation out of it. 'Here Pat. Thanks.' He passed it back to Pat. 'How much of that did you get?'

'The general idea sir. Piss and wind?'

'Let's hope so. We're going to upgrade our dress states[*] until further notice. No movement outside buildings without helmet and body armour.'

'Even after dark?'

---

[*] **Dress States,** military parlance for the amount of personal protective equipment that must be worn, e.g. helmet, body armour, gloves, goggles etc.

'Especially after dark. Apparently they're making trouble with an AGS-17. Some cats have been brought in that know how to handle one. From a "reliable" source, we're told.'

'Fucking great. I'll be sure to savour the next quarter of an hour.'

The officer matched his dryness. 'The gift that keeps on giving Pat.' He moved to crawl away and then checked himself. 'Remember the grenades travel fairly slowly so you'll probably hear it firing before the drama arrives. I'm going to brief the others.'

When Pat was alone again, he double-checked the mechanism on his own grenade machine gun, set his helmet a shade lower over his safety glasses and consulted his watch yet again.

The major savoured a moment of rare solitude. The middle of the helicopter landing pad was his favourite spot in the fort after supper. Its open space amplified a cool stillness. With the moon yet to rise he ranged through the stars, wishing he knew more about the constellations, and their colourful names. Smoke from a stale cigar dried his throat. In the quiet night air the tobacco crackled with each draw.

Unusual not to hear a jet somewhere.

He tried to empty his mind at this hour, to displace the myriad swirling anxieties and uncertainties. It was in near constant motion, sifting through the regrets and providences of yesterday to find wisdom and purpose for tomorrow.

Perspective... Now there's a challenge, he reflected. Normally he could rely on time for that. But it did strange things there. 'Long days, short weeks' they all said. That had a ring of truth for him. The passage of time in this valley created no vantage point for the major. He did not feel he was resident long enough for perspective to do its work – creating fresh angles. But for him the real poverty was space. That was the heart of it, he decided. They had their nose to everything, constantly. No latitude. No way to gain height or distance from all the damned decisions; the constant press of discussions. Some days his jaw physically ached from them. Locals formed actual queues outside the gate. Then there was the military beast to feed. It always concluded that a perfectly productive conversation must be regurgitated into a keyboard afterwards, 'for the record'.

The best conversations were with the people under his command. They at least were comradely. But those interactions were still a drain on the mind, even as they fed his soul.

With all that talk, and prejudice for action, where was the space to stand back? What counted for durable wisdom in all this?

Yet, the major wondered where genuine perspective would really take him. He tapped a crown of cigar ash into the stones. Maybe it was best not to scrutinise the backdrop too hard. It might reveal the true limits of the stage for this tragic comedy. The major grunted at his own observation, and drew more of the strong-flavoured smoke into his mouth.

Two years before, when the system had told them they were bound for this war, joining the spreadsheet with its coloured blocks and acronyms, the major paraded the company. After a predictable ripple had subsided, he had seized the moment.

'Don't expect this to mean anything' he said. 'Don't expect history to be kind to us. We will go together. Most of us will return together. And, likely as not, soon enough we will be forgotten together. From here on in, the only thing that matters is the "we" part.'

Maybe those words would ring true in the long run. But right now all he could feel was the glare of spotlights on their stage, with the stalls invisible behind a blinding bright wall. There could be spectators there, in all manner of attitudes – the rapt, the indifferent, the slumbering. But their presence was almost irrelevant. The ones that counted were the unseen, future versions of himself and his soldiers, waiting to pass judgement after the fact.

The major's solitude lost its allure suddenly. Fortunately, some footsteps crunched on the hard-core and the shape of a man strode towards him, his profile backlit by strip lights outside the ops room.

They had all spent long enough together to know men by their gait and silhouette. The intelligence officer was an easy one. His shoulders rolled.

'Evening Ed,' the major said.

'I thought I'd find you here Skipper.'

'How can I help?' The major had long learned that if you always give people time when they need it, they tended to need it less. 'Do you want a smoke?' He went to open his breast pocket.

'No thanks Skipper. It's that HUMINT* report. The lads and I have been discussing it in the int cell. We reckon they're going to have a go at Shingazi. It makes the most sense for a team like that.'

---

* **HUMINT** (pronounced HUME-INT), 'Human Intelligence': insight gathered from agents.

'I agree. It makes perfect sense. What do you propose they do about it, down there in the PB?'

'Not sure. We don't have a time, a place, a method or an axis. It's just our hunch I guess.'

'My point exactly. We've already warned Jack. There's nothing more they can do. Add another message, singling them out, and they'll only get more stressed. You and I can do the worrying for them.'

The intelligence officer ran a self-conscious hand through his hair. 'Sorry to bother you Skipper.'

'You didn't Ed. Tell me, who's on standby tonight?'

'Tom's lot.'

'Make sure you have the same conversation with him. And you'll know you've done a good night's work.'

'Got it Skipper.'

My doss bag, Shingazi, Helmand

Darling Rosie,

I've just had my scoff and settled the lads in so I thought I'd drop you a quick line. It's turning into a nice cool evening here. The weather has been starting to warm up a bit during the day. Not as bad as Iraq or when we got here last autumn. But still cooking. No more freezing fingers on the dawn patrol. You know how I love to stick cold hands under your sweater! LOL. Just as well you're not here. It's been nice and quiet as usual. Old Terry Taliban keeps his opinions to himself and we're happy about it. There's some flap on tonight but it's probably someone making mischeef as usual. How are you getting on babe? Thanks for the parcel. I shared out the ginger nuts and gave one packet to the Afghans. They're mad for them. My boy Sultan the young officer I told you about who cuts about like those geezers in Miami Vice, he's going to bring us back some of his mum's biscuits from R&R. We could start some kind of biscuit club here, with its own fanzine. Teatime is even bigger here than it was in my roofing days. Any more news on that pitch you were telling me about with the crisps people? It would be blinding if you won the contract. We'd be drowning in freebies or do they have rules about that sort of thing these days? One of the officers here got a massive box of teabags so it must be possible. I've been thinking more about what your boss said. It's not on. I'm sorry it's such lousy timing with me being away but we'll be home soon enough to talk about it. Touch wood and all that. Your old man speaks a lot of sense. The important thing is not to be hasty. Things are going well for you there and it's a big enough company to create some space if you have to. Maybe just as well I'm stuck in Afghan. I'd only make things worse dishing out some slaps ☺ You know I wouldn't really! Now to the important matter of our holiday. I was thinking about Greece. One

> of the lads has that film on his hard drive, the one about the officer with a mandolin who falls in love with the shepherd girl. It looked beautiful. We always go to Italy. Time for a change. What do you reckon babe? Oozo and bright blue w

Nick heard a shrill cry of 'incoming' from Stephens up in the sangar just as flat percussive hammering reached his own ears. Sergeant Langdon's head torch flicked up from the letter he was writing. *So the intelligence boys were on the money after all*. Everyone winced.

The compound rang with the crash of exploding grenades, thickening the air. A pall of dust and smoke boiled through the door of their room, picking out shafts of light from the few torches already on. Men in sleeping bags fought to extricate themselves, cursing and colliding with those throwing on body armour. A cup of tea was kicked noisily across the floor, its steam merging with the dust haze.

Sergeant Langdon had dropped the pen and leapt to his feet, swinging his body armour up over his head. Forgetting about the head torch in his haste, he then got embroiled in a tangle.

'I'm on it Langers!' Nick shouted. 'Stay in cover. Account for the lads.'

A second burst arrived. Instinctively everyone dropped to the floor, hunched, even though most of the projectiles seemed to impact beyond the walls – in the alley and neighbouring compound. Sergeant Langdon barked over the commotion.

'Roger sir!'

He had slapped his helmet on. In the cold white torchlight, Nick could see Sergeant Langdon's thick fingers trying to fasten the chin strap.

Having only just returned from a check on the sangar, Nick was already geared up. He paused at the door, nose filled with the sooty tang of low-quality explosive. The commotion over on the ANA side could easily have been mistaken for a fight. Nick bellowed up to Stephens in the sangar.

'Steveo! Can you see the firing point?'

If there was an answer, it was drowned out by the snapping of gunfire. Green tracer whipped across the sky above him, too high to be much of a threat, but it augmented the theatre of disarray. Nick half expected to see an instructor with a clipboard and high-visibility jacket. This was just the kind of night attack thrown at them constantly during training, often with a real machine gun set to fire harmlessly above the range.

But one thing Nick had learned since then was the difference between the forced uniform scream of an actor and the plaintive agonies of a genuinely wounded man.

It was coming from the latrine. He turned back into their room and called blindly. 'Casualty! Get me the medic.' Without waiting for a reply, he sprinted out into the yard, crouching in expectation of more grenade fire.

The ANA sangar sentry had started pumping bullets in all directions, notably back into the village.

'Tell that fucker to cease fire!' Nick shouted.

It was the most pointless order he had ever given. Nobody could hear him, let alone comprehend. But his surfeit of adrenaline was in the driving seat.

A third salvo of grenades impacted just as he reached the latrine. In his periphery Nick caught a bright succession of white flashes, like massive Chinese firecrackers. He threw himself to the ground and felt a sharp crack across the top of his helmet, as if someone had struck it with the end of a broom handle. Scrabbling forwards on hands and knees, he reached the latrine, resting his redundant rifle to free up both hands.

Of all people to be wounded, it was the medic. Private Mailer was gathered in a foetal position, having collapsed the hessian screen to one side of the latrine. His trousers and underpants were around his ankles. Nick's nose betrayed the presence of fresh faeces in an open shit bag somewhere. His torch picked out deep bleeding flecks in Mailer's pale thighs and backside. The back of the thin wooden box-privy was similarly lacerated. Fortunately, it appeared to have borne the brunt of the blast. Mailer had also been rewarded for the discipline of shitting with his body armour and helmet on: his left arm was bleeding but that was the extent of it.

Mailer acknowledged Nick's arrival with a gasping apology. 'I'm sorry sir. I'm man down.'

'Don't be daft Doc. I'm going to get you out of here.'

Bending over, Nick grabbed the carry straps on the shoulders of Mailer's armour. He tried spinning the medic over to drag him on his front but abandoned the idea: the next salvo was already overdue. Nick started dragging him back to the cover of their accommodation, Mailer cupping his exposed genitals. The wounded man cried out as grit bit into his injuries. Another pair of hands appeared and the speed of their evacuation doubled. Irish profanities betrayed the assistant's identity as Pat. Having bumped straight through the door of their room, grenade concussions flashed and danced around the battered, abandoned latrine.

'Fucking hell sir, that was close,' Pat said.

Nick ignored the comment. 'Right lads, let's get him sorted. Use his med kit. It's over by his bed space.'

Brogan lost no time in rolling Mailer onto his front and

squeezing long draughts of bottled water over the man's grimy, bloodied rump. The plastic bottle made crackling sounds as it re-expanded. Black humour flowed as readily.

'Jesus Doc! Go easy on the chilli sauce next time yeah?'

Nick shouted for Sergeant Langdon.

'Here sir!' he replied.

'I'm going up to the sangar. Maybe check on Sultan.'

'Roger.'

'Where's the Anchor?'

Ebullient as ever, the mortar man sprang into view with a sharp 'I'm 'ere sir!'

'Be ready to replace Steveo up in the sangar once I'm up there. We're going to need illume.'[*]

Nick paused again at the doorway and realised suddenly that he'd left his rifle by the latrine. He burned with indignant self-censure. Even given the urgency, there was no excuse. Misplacing one's weapon was the stuff of ridicule.

'Oi! Sir!' It was Sergeant Langdon again, almost cheek-to-cheek. 'Don't even think about it.' He held out Mailer's rifle. 'Doc didn't take it with him to the dunny.' He smiled his forgiving, avuncular smile. 'Keep low out there.'

The distant insurgent had slowed his rate of fire. They were probably low on ammunition, the grenades being expensive. Nick was up the ladder like a seasoned mariner and squeezed himself into the sangar space. He found Steveo in blasé form, hunkered as low as possible behind the sandbagged parapet.

'Alright sir?'

---

[*] **Illume,** short for 'illumination': large parachute flares fired from mortars or artillery that each provides half a minute of soft orange light across the area of a football pitch.

'What've you got for me Steveo?'

'Well, he's found a nice angle to hit the PB and I can't really reach him from this sangar.'

'You'll have to speak up. My ears are fucked.'

Stephens was a silhouette in the darkness. A low yellow moon failed to cast its light through the sangar netting. 'I said: he's got a nice angle to hit the PB and I can't reach him. You can just see his muzzle flashes in that treeline. The ANA sangar could probably hit him but they're just brassing off.'

'What about the small arms?'

'That feller's been nipping up and down but not really adding much value. It's the fucker with the AGS that's impressing me. I've no idea how he got our range so well in the dark.'

'And no follow-up?'

'Nothing yet sir. I guess they could still be working their way round.'

Nick reached for the radio handset. It hung on a post next to a shielded chemical light. 'I've already sent the contact report sir.' Stephens almost sounded defensive.

'I assumed you would Steveo. You're a safe pair of hands. Doc's been wounded in the arse. I'm going to swap you out with the Anchor in a minute.'

Nick hailed the ops room before Stephens could reply. After one or two attempts he rapped the handset against its post.

'I can't hear a fucking thing out of this,' he said, and put it back to his buzzing ear.

'Don't worry yourself Sanga,' Gul Khan said. 'This hasn't happened for a week or two now. They're using the darkness to make it safer for themselves. Nek and his men will handle it. We'll stay indoors and sit it out.'

Sanga had gathered Imran to her breast and now sat up on their bedding with blankets drawn around her shoulders. The boy's wide, fearful eyes stared at Gul Khan trustingly. Mother and son flinched in concert as stray bullets snapped close to the compound. As soon as the battle started, Imran had scampered into their bed, reverting to the toddler afraid of thunderstorms. He had slept close to them every night since returning from the city. The space once shared with Mamur was cold and lonely now.

Gul Khan walked over to check there was enough oil in the lamp. It was a pretext. He slipped the green rubber tablet into the pocket of his kameez as surreptitiously as he could. Sanga's voice cut into him.

'I saw that.'

'Can I have some quiet in here please? He's struggling to hear me.'

The captain leaned back into the desk and put one finger into his left ear in the manner of someone trying to use their mobile telephone in a nightclub. The low-ceilinged ops room had filled up rapidly as the situation in Shingazi became apparent. Tidy duty staff contrasted with the handful of men roused from sleep – yawning, bleary faces framed by tousled hair and down jackets thrown over a T-shirt. Bulked up by his fighting equipment, Tom, the standby-team commander, crowded out one corner awkwardly like the tourist ferrying luggage during rush hour.

The captain enunciated his words clearly. 'Say all again, over.'

Nick's reply came over the loudspeaker for all to hear. Small-arms fire chattered in the background.

'Zero, this is Four-Two Alpha. No audio. I'm sending blind. We have one category B casualty[*]; zap number, Mike-Alpha-Five-Seven-Two-Eight. Shrapnel in the buttocks. Stable. Caz-ee-vac request to follow. We request immediate illume and top-cover, over.'

Without being asked, a young signaller scrutinised the noticeboard in front of him. 'That's Private Mailer sir, the medic.'

The captain nodded and keyed the handset. 'Roger. Wait, out.' He turned to one of the sleepy cohort. 'Can you fix the illume Sergeant Marsh? Drop it to the south-east.'

'Leave it to me sir. I expect the Anchor will come up on my means any minute.' He picked up a field telephone and opened a sidebar conversation, peppered with even more jargon than usual.

The captain turned to another of his attendants, this one wearing gym clothes. He was still sweating from his interrupted late-night training session. 'What about the top-cover Corporal Wilkes? Is there an Apache in the air already?'

'Not available sir. The Special Forces are already in a scrap down south. They're giving us the stand-by bird but it's still

---

[*] **Category B casualty**, military classification for a wound that requires evacuation in a 3–4 hour timeframe. Category A is immediate (life-threatening) and Category C is routine (24hr timeframe).

on the tarmac. You're looking at thirty minutes, maybe twenty best case.'

'Roger.' He turned to the major, who was standing off to one side with his arms folded. 'Happy so far Skipper?'

'Good work. I don't see the ANA in here yet.' The major pointed to the standby commander. 'Get that fixed Tom.' To nobody in particular he added, 'Kamran's bound to be up watching a Bollywood classic.' Then he returned to the room. 'We need to keep an eye on the casualty. If he deteriorates then it will change priorities. On the assumption he stays stable, I want the Apache to focus on finding that AGS. It's a prestige asset. That means they're up to something.'

The sweaty headset nodded and signalled with a thumbs-up. Their commander finished his direction with a comment.

'I'm surprised there's no follow-up assault yet. It fits the situation.'

Nick had not heard the grenade launcher fire for a minute or two now. That could mean it was on the move, jockeying to a fresh firing point or maybe extracting altogether. Only a trickle of ineffectual small-arms fire remained. If the attackers were planning to close in and assault the patrol base, they must be nearby now.

Nick found the handset again and raised the ops room. They took a minute to reply.

'I'm blind here. These guys could be on us imminently. Any word on our top-cover?'

'It's inbound... any minute, over.'

Nick slapped an upright post in frustration. 'For fuck's

sake.' He took a breath and keyed the handset. 'You said that ten minutes ago. The Taliban could be at the back gate for all I know.'

The patient captain – a friend of his after all – gave a rather hollow 'Roger…' and then 'over', almost as an afterthought.

Nick issued a resigned 'roger out' and started to think. Maybe they would be better off outside the walls of their makeshift outpost. Less predictable.

He called down to the accommodation for Sergeant Langdon. The least they could do was be ready to move. Corporal Lennon appeared instead. 'Langers is over with Sultan sir.' Of course he was. Nick remembered his suggestion.

'Get the lads ready to move Beatle. And the Afghans. I think we might need to hustle. Get on the front foot. Make our numbers count.'

There was a slight hesitation. 'Langers didn't mention that sir.'

'I know,' Nick said. 'It only just came to me.'

'Sir.' Corporal Lennon ducked away.

Nick turned to the Anchor. He had replaced Stephens in the cramped sangar and had been busily conversing on his mortar radio net.

'Are you happy with the claymores, Anchor? They could be close.'

'Sure sir. No worries.'

'Great,' Nick said. 'I'll get Steveo back up here with you. Give me a shout if that thing pops off again.'

He descended the ladder and called for Private Stephens. 'Get up there with the Anchor again Steveo. Don't hesitate to clack-off the claymores. They could be right on us for all I know.'

There was still no sign of Langers. Sultan was Nick's next stop anyway. Corporal Lennon stood alone under the cloister. Nick beckoned him over.

'All set?'

'The lads are sir, yes.'

Something was amiss. Nick tried to size him up.

'What do you mean Beatle?'

The man shifted from one foot to another, avoiding Nick's eyes. Sharp shadow from the illumination flares exaggerated his drawn features, washing his face in monochrome as if he had stepped out of a graphic novel. 'I'm staying here if we go out sir. Someone has to take care of Mailer. It's going to be me. I'm the next most experienced at cannulation if he deteriorates.'

Perhaps it was the air of finality that needled Nick – something more than the simple fact of having his decisions pre-judged. He was reminded of being ripped off by a mechanic: the assumption of his passivity; too much shifty detail. With firm voice, he countered.

'Sergeant Langdon stays here when we go out. You know that Corporal Lennon.' Nick dispensed with nicknames to emphasise that this was a hard stop. 'He's more than capable of handling Mailer. You'll deploy onto the ground with your boys.'

Then Nick added, pointedly, 'Where you belong.'

Corporal Lennon's front collapsed at first pressure. He had no fall-back position. Literally, he wavered, looking for somewhere to sit down. Finding none, the man dropped to one knee and rested his helmeted head on the muzzle of his upturned rifle, as a leaning post. His right hand reached down and, for a darkly surreal instant, Nick thought he might be about to shoot himself. But Lennon only used his hand to steady his posture.

Immediately Nick regretted his tone. If only this had happened another time, less dramatic, it would have been wiser to come in soft and subtle. He knelt down beside Corporal Lennon and placed a conciliatory hand on his shoulder.

'Eh… eh… talk to me Beatle.'

Nick heard him clear snot from his nose. The man's response cracked with perplexed self-pity.

'I'm fucked sir. I just can't do it. I can't go out there tonight.'

He was shaking his head from side to side.

'I thought I was OK now. It's been quiet lately. But I reached my limit weeks ago. This place is going to get me. I know it. I'm going to bleed out like the other lads, blinking at the sky. I see them in my sleep, their stumps twitching. Every step here… every step is hell. Don't make me do it. Please.'

He looked up, his face a rictus of stress, fighting back tears. Then he slipped his feet into a negotiation.

'I'm begging you sir. Not tonight, not into the darkness with those fuckers out there waiting for us. If I can stay here… I'll be alright tomorrow. I won't let you down again.'

'Jesus Beatle… Why didn't you mention this to me before?'

'I thought I had it under control sir.'

Nick looked about to see if anyone was watching them. In the doorway Brogan was pretending not to notice. But he knew well enough what was being discussed. There were no secrets in their tiny human village. Brogan lit two cigarettes at once and then gave one to an unseen figure behind him.

'Listen Beatle.' Nick jabbed him on the upper arm. 'Look at me! You've no idea. Don't you understand? Decisions like this… They never leave you. *Never*. Believe me.'

The man just shook his head, still staring at the ground. Thin strands of snot dragged audibly in his nose as he breathed.

Nick thought of playing the strongest card in his hand – to leverage Corporal Lennon's loyalty to the junior soldiers. But he could not afford to gamble on the man outside their sanctuary. There was no time for this. Not tonight. Nick sighed.

'Fine Beatle. Stay here in command and look after Mailer. We'll sort this out in the morning.'

Nick patted him on the shoulder again and stood up, deliberately not giving Corporal Lennon a chance to respond. Any expression of gratitude would only add yet another blow to the man's self-esteem. It pained Nick to recall the brash, tattooed young leader in his prime: dragging stragglers along on route marches, pulling the pin on a grenade, raising a pint of beer to his lips midway through a bawdy tale at the bar. That man was probably gone forever now – as sure as if he had trodden on the mine he so feared.

Sergeant Langdon jogged across the compound with Sultan and Mohammad in tow. Nick met them a discreet distance from Corporal Lennon.

'I've got the lads good to go, Langers, but Beatle's out the game.'

The older man simply nodded. Maybe he knew already. Maybe it was something in Nick's voice that articulated the whole story. Maybe it was the bigger problem he then revealed.

'Well he's not alone sir. Kamran ain't letting Sultan deploy with his ANA after dark. Whatever it was you had cooking, we're stuck here anyway.'

The party paused at a junction. It had been agreed not to use radios. Surprise was vital and they assumed the foreigners would be eavesdropping. Haji Mansur just had to trust that Sadiq's party were in position. The two Mehsuds with Mother Hen had operated absolutely according to plan. The thud and crackle of their exploits covered any sound made by the infiltration.

Shingazi's dogs were already disturbed, and voicing their alarm in a different direction.

In fact, the only hitch so far had been a brief scare on the outskirts of the village when neither he nor Sarbaz could remember exactly where their mine had been laid near the footbridge. They had splashed through the stream to be safe. He could see the elder Mehsud was unimpressed. The water was cold, and now wet sand oozed between Haji Mansur's toes. They were all too preoccupied to think of removing their shoes beforehand. He had been lucky not to lose them in the sucking silt of the stream-bed. Trying to escape barefoot at night would make a fool of a man.

One thing at a time, he chided himself, tightening the grip on his Kalashnikov.

All four fighters crouched down while Sarbaz directed the lead Mehsud. Haji Mansur's original plan was for Sarbaz to wear the night glasses because he already knew the way. But he had only lasted a few paces before wrenching them off in a characteristic huff of hoarse whispers.

'They make me feel sick Haji Sahib. It's sorcery! I'm afraid I'll see ghosts. Let the Pakistani brother wear them if he wants.'

Now the Mehsud was their scout. They had timed the attack to coincide with a waning three-quarter moon, rising just as they approached Shingazi. So now there was enough ambient light for them to follow the village layout without the glasses. Haji Mansur reasoned that this moon would reduce the night-fighting advantages enjoyed by the British whilst still providing some deep shadow to hide in if they encountered locals.

Content of their bearings, the party moved off again. Sarbaz insisted this alleyway would deliver them right to the target.

They had it on good authority.

Gul Khan was starting to feel caged in his room with Sanga and Imran. Their fear fed off itself under the blankets. He sat on a cushion fiddling with the tiny floor fire. For a few minutes she had been humming the same old lullaby repeatedly and it was not really helping. Rather than let it get on his nerves, Gul Khan introduced some banalities to calm them.

'Tell me Imran... are you due for a new shalwar kameez? I've noticed the sleeves are getting too short.'

The boy tried to be brave and meet his father's intentions. 'I don't know Baba. Soon I think. My cap is old. Perhaps we can find a new one when the harvest is sold.'

'Never mind the cap! I look forward to the day when I buy you a Pakol like mine. The older they get, the more character they have. Like a gate.'

They were interrupted by a pop overhead, followed by a strange soft 'whooping' sound that some colourful bird of paradise might attract a mate with. Sanga looked up, even though all she could see was the ceiling.

'What is that?' she asked, drawing Imran tighter still until he complained quietly, with affection and understanding.

'You're hurting me Adi.' He seemed torn between his maternal past and masculine future.

Gul Khan reassured them. 'I think it's a flare fired from an artillery gun. The Russians were fond of them. We used to say they were afraid of the dark!' He caught Imran's eye. 'Imagine a sky filled with small suns, floating down to earth.'

'Can I see Baba?'

'No my boy. You must stay here and take care of your mother.'

Gul Khan's mind stepped through a door into the past, back to night assaults against hilltop perimeters, flares streaking overhead, starting as shrieking meteors, then bursting into a cascade of swinging lanterns when their parachutes opened. The dancing shadows of a copper landscape. He had never forgotten the beguiling harmlessness of tracer bullets, seemingly drifting towards you at first and then zipping past with a sudden terrifying malice. Long speculative streams would reach into clefts of rock where the Russians thought the 'ghosts' had gone to ground, the ricochets scattering in all directions, tracer bullets lazy again, making looping arcs. The shattered faces of his Shahid brothers resembled ghouls in that shifting, sour light...

'I'm going outside for a smoke,' he declared.

'If you must,' replied Sanga with forbearance.

'Don't worry. I won't stray beyond the cloister.' Gul Khan picked up his Kalashnikov and shut the wooden door gently behind him. There it was – the old, eerie orange wash on everything. True to his word, Gul Khan did not venture into the open. Flares were carried inside hollow shells. It was these heavy vacant vessels that 'whooped' their way to earth.

The battle had started to ease off. 'Perhaps it was just a

hit-and-run attack?' he wondered to himself, sitting down on the rope bed they kept outside for the summer. He rested his rifle on the grid of knotted cords and lit a cigarette, pausing to tug at his beard. As always at night, the dog was roaming free in the compound. It had got bored of barking and wandered over for company, still growling in trepidation at the manmade thunderstorm and suspicious of the odd, premature dawn.

'Health and happiness, you grumpy old warrior,' Gul Khan said.

The dog regarded him uncomprehendingly.

'You don't have to say it. I know what you're thinking. "That makes two of us..."' Gul Khan gave a low chuckle and returned the cigarette to his lips.

There was a sharp bashing on the metal gates.

Gul Khan jumped so violently that the cigarette fell into his lap, sparking as the tip fell off. The dog – even more startled than he was – spun around full circle and let rip with a relentless throaty bark. His other animals jostled one another in bemused disquiet.

'Open up cousin! It's me, Janan.'

An icy serpent darted down Gul Khan's neck and coiled itself deep in his belly. He knew his cousin. That voice was not his.

Immediately Gul Khan knew what he should have done when the attack started. Unalterable situations always delivered him such redundant insight. He should have taken his family and hidden in the graveyard under the protection of his father and God, or headed into the desert and invoked the hospitality of nomads. *Proud fool.*

The gates banged again. 'Hurry cousin. Wake up!'

Gul Khan suffered the paralysis of nightmares. His heart

had doubled in size and now it surged at his ribcage, filling his throat. *Think Gul Khan, think. Now is not the time to freeze.* He grabbed his rifle. *Do I cock it? Do I answer him?* The indecision feasted on his dwindling time.

There was muttering and shuffling from beyond the gates. Again they banged.

A soft entreaty – anxious – came from behind the bedroom door. It opened ajar. This galvanised Gul Khan. He sprang up and closed the distance in two strides, blocking the door with his body.

'Sshh Sanga! Stay inside. It's nothing.' He was panicking.

Eager fingers met his on the door-frame and squeezed them. 'Please don't open the gates my love, whatever you do,' Sanga said.

Another flare carrier whooped down. The whole scene felt fantastical: Sanga's wide-eyed face in the door frame as if squeezed into a wooden vice, the syrupy light, this peculiar deception at the gates, a half-hearted battle in the distance, sifting around for other men's fates. Where was the dawn when you wanted it? He yearned to see their compound restored to brilliance, birdsong, domesticity...

Someone kicked the gate this time. 'You always were idle cousin! Must you keep me waiting?'

The bad actor's absurd masquerade had run its course. Surely soon they would attempt a break-in. Then it would be time to fight.

He cursed the blank sweep of his western wall. No back door: a frugality of his father's, seemingly so inconsequential all those years ago. The compound was too small to warrant such a luxury – 'a monument to idleness' as the old man might have said. That decision had laid dormant, patient, like some kind of cancer. And now it would most likely kill him.

Gul Khan turned and raised his Kalashnikov to cock it. The gun knocked against something in his pocket. Nick's rubber tablet.

'Say again, over.' Nick had heard the first time but asked the captain to repeat it anyway – the way people often do when surprised or disappointed by something.

'I'm afraid they've called a second priority down south. You've lost your Apache.'

'But we're still in contact. What about my casualty?'

'He's a category B and you're a base location. These guys are out on the ground with two category As. There's a serious punch-up ongoing down there. They're going to spin up another one for you but we're back to square one. There are guys getting crashed out of bed to help.'

Nick drew breath to send a sarcastic acknowledgement, some unfair remark about pilots getting their beauty sleep.

But he never keyed the handset. A red signal flare arced into the night sky. Nick's stomach dropped.

'Shit.'

'What is it sir?' The Anchor reacted to the oath. The flare had risen behind him.

'Gul Khan's place. Shit. He's just popped an SOS.'

'What are we going to do?'

Nick did not answer. *Fuck*. So that was the follow-up. Not their base at all. The grenade bombardment as a diversion. A simple-enough plan, painfully obvious suddenly.

But maybe the insurgents had mistimed their run. No grenade fire anymore. Gul Khan was still in the fight.

I can do it this time. I've been given time to think. I can do what I should have done before, for Alex, that summer. Nick had a vivid sense of the cool green vegetation on his wet flesh again; the burn in his sinuses; his chest rising and falling, rising and falling...

The decision acted like a starting pistol. 'Right.' He seemed to be addressing himself. Grabbing a beam for support, he leaned over into the courtyard.

'On your feet lads! Gul Khan's in the shit!'

Sergeant Langdon appeared and was about to shout something back but checked himself and climbed the ladder instead. When he was close to Nick, he spoke in lowered tones.

'Sir, I like to think we've been through enough together so's I can be frank with you.'

Nick knew what was coming. 'Sure Langers.'

'Mailer's wounded, Beatle's on the bench and we're going to need to leave the Anchor up in the sangar. Plus the ANA aren't playing and we've got no top-cover. What the fuck do you propose we do with only five of us and an unarmed interpreter? We haven't a clue how many bods are on the enemy team sheet tonight. Have you even cleared it with the ops room?'

'I'm not asking you to come with me.'

It was a crass remark – a punishment for inflicting awkward truths. Sergeant Langdon's chinstrap shifted as his jaw came forward. Nick had never seen the famously good-natured man so close to hitting anybody. He felt small for uttering it.

'I take that back Langers. I'm sorry. It was a fucking stupid thing to say. You're right. You're always right. But this time I can swim back. I can do the right thing.'

'Swimming? What the fuck are you talking about sir?'

'I can't leave that guy to die. Otherwise what's it all for?'

'I get that. So do the lads. But that's no reason to bin your judgement.'

'What the fuck is the point of these people risking everything if we just sit here?'

'You've done us proud here sir. Everyone can see that you've created something special. But you piss with the cock you've got. Tonight that's five blokes and a 'terp. Fine if we were going to creep around on a recce. But not enough for a smash-up. We'd be on our own out there.'

'So is Gul Khan.'

From across the village a sharp clatter of automatic fire seized their attention. Then another burst followed, chasing the first as it reverberated through the night air beyond.

The signal flare had cracked like a pistol shot as it left the pen discharger, Gul Khan's trembling fingers barely dextrous enough to have screwed the cartridge onto the end. It startled the dog, which had now approached the gates, and the scent that lay beyond them. As Gul Khan loaded a second flare, it was clear the assailants judged a timer had just started running. They dropped their pretence at last.

'Your friends are occupied Gul Khan. Let us all stop being cowards. It's me, Haji Mansur, as you probably already suspect. Have the honour to open this gate and meet your fate as a man. If we have to force our way in, I will not spare your family. Think on that for a moment.'

It was an artful piece of manipulation. Up until now Gul Khan had harboured no expectation that Sanga would be left out of it. Imran was on the cusp of manhood. He might just be afforded the status of an innocent. Even though Gul Khan did not trust Haji Mansur, the offer burrowed away.

Die fighting and Sanga would definitely join him. Die on his knees and she would probably join him. Probably or possibly? How does a man balance honour against the lives of his family? Is it more honourable to try and save her or more honourable to battle his enemies? There was not much poetry in this finish.

Not yet. Gul Khan might sometimes have savoured the hope of a peaceful ending but he never truly believed he would survive his stand. Faced now with the reality – the mask removed – he felt a renewed faith in the resolve of those first days after Mamur's death, when vengeance and honour had written his script. He clicked off the safety catch on his Kalashnikov.

Then Sanga spoke quietly from the doorway behind him, strangely icy and neutral.

'There's another choice my love. Climb onto the roof and drop off the back wall. Maybe they haven't surrounded us. There's time for you to do it while I distract them. Without you, Imran and I have no value as corpses. It would be a crime. Maybe they will kidnap us and your friends can help. Nek will have British gold. Whatever happens, you get to fight on, to lead this village.'

He turned to her. 'I can't do that Sanga. There is only shame down that path. It works much better the other way. You go.'

The gates rang and shuddered under the blow of a sledgehammer, fixating Gul Khan's dog. The gates were old and would eventually yield. Haji Mansur's man knew where the weak spot was – a thin bolt on the offside set only an inch or two into the dirt. Every set of gates in this valley had more or less the same design.

Gul Khan turned to Sanga and hissed. 'Go! Lower Imran down by his hands.' Without waiting for a reply, he raised his Kalashnikov and fired a short burst into the gates from an oblique angle. They sparked under the impact, all sound merging into one terrific, hammering crash within the compound walls. The dog spun and retreated. Blinded by his own muzzle flash, Gul Khan fumbled for the safety catch. In his haste and indecision, he had put the weapon on automatic – the first position on the lever – rather than single shots. Already he had squandered a third of his ammunition. The defiance won him only about three seconds before the snout of someone's weapon pushed between the widening breach in his gates. The entranceway lit up as if in a thunderstorm: bright instantaneous snapshots echoed by the skip and a dance of bullets struck the wall opposite. The dog, skittering and bounding around opposite the gates, dropped with an abrupt yelp.

Such was his focus, Gul Khan hardly registered it. The dog was never going to be the difference between death and survival. If he was to prevent his assailants from gaining entry, he would have to find a more direct angle for his rifle, which of course risked exposure to their blind bursts. Better, he thought, to get into a position of ambush to cut them down whenever they plunged through the gap. He ducked into the most cluttered corner of the compound, seeking some kind of cover. Gul Khan could not see Sanga and Imran anymore. They must already have flitted up the rickety wooden ladder that led onto their roof. Time alters its stride in the throes of battle.

Calm befell him finally, lulled by the measured rhythm of hammer blows. His family was, Allah willing, away into the night, making haste to the sanctuary of Janan's compound. Gul Khan had a hand in his own fate now – a chance to shape the way he would be remembered. If he took one or two fighters with him, even the bitter old Haji Khan Mohammad might spare a grudging tribute.

Gul Khan pictured Imran one day, muscular and bearded, regaling his wide-eyed young bride proudly with the tale. 'Yes, my father died many years ago Little Dove. He avenged my elder brother under falling stars, tumbling from the heavens to to cast a light on his honour…'

The pounding of the sledgehammer ceased abruptly. From his position, crouched behind Sanga's tandoor, Gul Khan saw one gate flap inwards under the final blow. He inhaled deeply, index finger stroking the narrow trigger of his trusted Kalashnikov.

Our very last tune.

Not like the ailing picker busking for a pittance on his tired Rubab,* never quite sure when death will silence its strings.

No! A fine, soaring climax.

---

* **Rubab,** a Pashtun musical instrument similar to a lute or banjo but with the addition of drone strings, like a sitar.

'Wait sir! We should number off before we go, in case we have to rally in the darkness.'

Sergeant Langdon stood at the back of the line – pitifully small given the uncertainties lying beyond their fort. Everyone was carrying the minimum amount of equipment, dispensing with the cumbersome packs and ladders they were accustomed to. Instead they were as heavily armed as possible, having stuffed extra grenades and belts of ammunition into satchels, and slung slender bazookas over their shoulders. Mohammad was given the spare telescopic metal detector and a clutch of hand-held illumination rockets, which he gathered awkwardly under one arm like scrolls. He resembled some kind of bookish shipping surveyor, co-opted by pirates to value what they were about to privateer.

Nick started the chain by barking 'one!' But Mohammad, who was standing next to him, did not grasp what was required. Brogan got things moving by uttering a curt 'three' and then leant towards Mohammad.

'You're number "two" mate. If the boss shouts "number off" out there, we all shout our number in turn. That way he knows if anyone is missing.'

Mohammad assented by saying 'two!' and nodding his head with anxious animation. It was not just the weak light causing his pallor.

A final confident 'six' from Sergeant Langdon signalled that it was time to go. He had taken possession of Nick's decision. Anyone arriving on the scene would be forgiven for believing that the entire enterprise had been Sergeant Langdon's idea. Nick could find no hint of their brief altercation evident anywhere in his voice or demeanour.

Nick read it as loyalty. What Sergeant Langdon had seen

were the men. No sooner had Nick alerted them to Gul Khan's predicament, they were grabbing the extra weaponry and psyching each other up with declarations of solidarity for the Afghan. The distant gunfire only served to fuel this unanimity and impatience. Sometimes their world was more democratic than it appeared.

As they strode towards the gate, Sultan intercepted them at a jog trot. He brandished a rifle and, unusually for him, wore a helmet. Apparently addressing them all, he called out and Mohammad translated.

'He says that he is coming with you. The night is not so dark in the company of friends.'

Someone behind Nick gave a little cheer. In another setting it might have sounded ironic, like the cry that goes up in a pub when the barman smashes a glass. Because both Nick and Sultan were carrying weapons in their right hands, they shook with their left in the attitude of two arm wrestlers. Nick acknowledged him in his best pidgin Dari.

'A very good evening to you Sultan Sahib.'

Other hands reached out to cuff the Tajik officer as he joined the little column.

Sergeant Langdon beckoned Sultan to slot into the middle near Mohammad. It messed his numbering but there was no time for that now. As the last man he turned around as they moved off – that instinctive final sweep of someone vacating temporary accommodation. His eye caught a silent hand being raised in farewell: Corporal Lennon stood in the doorway to their accommodation, watching them depart.

Nick led them through the gate manned by one of Sultan's soldiers, transmitting as he did so the dreaded radio message he had spent the past few minutes postponing.

'Hello Zero, this is Four-Two Alpha. Gul Khan's compound is now under attack. I am on foot to his location with five UK personnel, one interpreter and one ANA, Sultan. All other pax remain in PB Shingazi.' Nick almost winced as he added, 'Over.' With no preliminary message of explanation, seeking permission, this was quite obviously a fait accompli he presented.

As if to emphasise this air of finality, the gates shut behind them and they were into the village, moving at a slow run down the alley. Benighted by a break in the overhead illumination, they all flicked down their night sights, elongating their faces to resemble an urgent procession of masked plague doctors.

The response to his message was clearly buying time while the operations room debated his bombshell. All that came back was a terse 'Wait, out.'

Waiting was the last thing on Nick's mind. Dispensing with the metal detector on the basis that the village had long been clear of buried mines, he tried to calculate how long it would take them to reach Gul Khan, and at what point it would be wise to halt and split the party for the final hazardous approach to the stricken compound.

His mind kept reaching for images of what they would find if this frantic, undermanned sortie was too late. Among them, bright and incongruous, was the upturned yellow canoe.

Sadiq sat cross-legged with his back to a compound wall. It bordered one of Shingazi's crossroads. The small vacant derelict structure had been used in the recent past by a migrant labourer. Sadiq's perch was decorated with a light scattering of household refuse.

This was Sadiq's first nocturnal battle and it made him feel claustrophobic. The dark malodorous corner closed him in. His sense of confinement pressed further by the weight of the night sky. Tonight the stars appeared to Sadiq as a crowd of prying onlookers, winking to one another in mutual fascination at his predicament.

Haji Mansur's plan sounded so simple in prospect – the commander's certainty and optimism repressing some of the probing questions Sadiq now felt he should have asked. His ears had been flattered by the Haji's public expression of belief in him. Damn those ears. They had not wanted the moment to be sullied by any misgivings his mouth might have voiced about the mechanics of this scheme. Rueing that moment of diffidence, Sadiq became nostalgic for his wife and her subtle scowls. But she too always favoured the moment over the future. It was one reason he now found himself sat in the sand, among the refuse, with a rifle by his side. Money... Never enough of it.

One of his two lookouts fidgeted on the roof of the compound's only building. The lookout was lying on his front, peering through a small hole used for rain drainage. His signal would trigger the ambush if the foreigners approached that way. But what guaranteed they would? Sadiq was distracted and intimidated by the possibility the enemy might take a totally different route, bypassing him completely. He had heard gunfire coming from Gul Khan's compound already – that seemed to be good news. Yet if the foreigners did not come past soon, and more fire came from there, how would he know whether or not to abandon his ambush and move to the

Haji's rescue? If he used the radio, the Haji might be furious with him...

In truth, the promotion he had been given constrained him. It piled on a burden of expectation, raising the price of failure somehow, and reducing his freedom to seek clarifications. Sadiq prayed that Allah would deliver the non-believers into his trap and dispel the fog of uncertainty with a divine breeze.

He drew the motorcycle battery closer to his groin and checked, for the umpteenth time, that the ends of his two wires were bared, and clean.

The younger Mehsud gave a grunt of satisfaction as one last strike flung the gate from its moorings. His elder companion had been firing through the gap and was now hurriedly changing magazine. The empty one dropped to the ground as he fumbled with them. The fighter got caught in a moment of indecision, stooping to pick it up and then changing his mind to focus on the yawning, perilous opening his comrade had just created.

Sarbaz had worked his way around the back of the compound to ensure there was no bolthole. Now an unspoken tension descended on the three men remaining astride Gul Khan's gate. There was a determined foe lurking beyond it, armed and desperate. Someone had to be first inside. Above them, the last of the falling flares was snuffed out, as if by the fingers of a puppeteer crafting this unfolding drama on a tabletop theatre. The scene reacquainted itself with moonlight. Haji Mansur was just about to shoulder his way forward – this was his feud after all – when the younger Mehsud threw down the sledgehammer, whipped his Kalashnikov off his back and darted forwards.

A sharp repetition of single shots did not so much hit the Mehsud as appear to trip him up. There was just enough sentience left in him to perceive the impact of his fall, which he tried to break with his arms, his rifle clattering to the ground as he flung it aside. But as soon as he was prostrate, more shots plucked at his crumpled form and he became lifeless, his long hair flicked forward over his face to conceal any expression.

The firing had come from their right – it was the way the youth's head had turned too – and so the surviving Mehsud stuck the muzzle of his own weapon around the gateway and hosed off a long, blind burst. They were fortunate that the gate swung left.

Haji Mansur took that as his cue to make an entrance. God willing, the Mehsud's fire would have kept Gul Khan's head down or, better still, struck him. In prospect of such situations, Haji Mansur imagined he might utter some rousing or intimidating war cry. Instead he discovered he was always too clenched – too tight with anticipation. There was more gunfire but had no sense of where it was directed, or by whom. In no time, he found himself at the far corner of the compound under a cloister. Spinning around to face where Gul Khan might be, he caught a brushstroke of pale clothing and, guided by instinct, squeezed the trigger at it. The muzzle flash from his stubby weapon obliterated all further detail – burning in his retina even after he released his index finger.

Somewhere far away, through the electrified ring in his ears, he heard the Mehsud baying.

'You've got him! You've hit him!'

Pacing forwards with the exaggerated care of a thief robbing someone in their sleep, Haji Mansur approached his quarry. Eyes fixed on Gul Khan, he shouted over to the Mehsud with an indicative cant of the head.

'Your friend is Shahid. Check these rooms.'

The column halted briefly while Nick confirmed his bearings. This was the time to split. Sweat gathered in his eyebrows. As he leaned forwards, the top of his body armour exhaled tiny hot, humid draughts with the rise and fall of his chest.

They had heard more firing moments ago, hastening their stride. But now Shingazi was still. Just the dogs. *Fuck*. Nick's gut sagged with dread. Failure bore down on him yet again. He could hear it breathing behind him, like a faster, stronger opponent on the sports field. Another chest rising and falling, rising and falling…

Gul Khan had trusted him. Those strong handshakes… The smiles.

Nick was grateful to be the only one with a radio. But there had been no row with the major. His greatest concern seemed to be the continued absence of any Apache helicopter to provide top-cover. Hence he had deployed the company's small standby force. Currently they were looping in via the desert road in support, their progress hampered only by the residual risk of mines. The major had added the experience of Company Sergeant Major Barnet to the team. Nick could hear his regular, frustrated progress reports being tugged and jerked by the uneven road surface.

The major did not give up hope of a helicopter either. 'Now that we've told them what you're up to, they are lighting a fire under it,' he said. 'But the QRF* are making best speed too.'

His only judgement on Nick's decision was simple and terse.

'This is on you now Jack.'

As if guilty at the finality of that statement, he had added, after a pause: 'go well.'

The major had agreed to hold off on the illumination flares while Nick closed with Gul Khan's compound. There was just enough moonlight for Nick to wonder whether his night monocular was worth it. A few of them had been flicking the devices up and down in perpetual experimentation.

Nick passed the message back down the halted column for Sergeant Langdon to come forward. The proximity of his bulk was a comfort. Body odour mingled with the sweetness of fresh sweat joining the stale, dusty infusion that clung to their equipment permanently. The confab was brief, clipped and breathless.

'Right Langers. Take Steveo and Pat. Push beyond this junction and get around to Gul Khan's from the north.' Nick caught his breath with a swallow, then two clear breaths. 'The four of us will hold here for a few seconds and then turn left, to come at the compound directly.' Another breath. 'I won't make that final approach until you report that you hold the north corner. Go. Run.'

Sergeant Langdon gave Nick's helmet an affectionate pat as he stood up. In a stage whisper he said simply, 'Steveo, Pat.

---

* **QRF**, acronym for Quick Reaction Force. The military jargon for a standby element, held in reserve.

With me,' and then set off up the road bent forwards slightly, his weapon in both hands.

By the time he hit the junction, Sergeant Langdon was a few paces ahead of Stephens. He paused for an instant at the corner to check left and right, like a pedestrian. He peered back over his shoulder to confirm he was being followed by the other two, and plunged forward anew.

A hand tensed at the end of the sentry's outstretched arm. Sadiq's heart reached full gallop.

The hand flapped up and down like the wing of a bird. Sadiq closed the circuit.

It was as if the gates of heaven opened for Sergeant Langdon right there in Shingazi's grubby streets. Before hearing anything, Nick watched his friend disappear into a brilliant, incandescent wall of white.

If only that had been the extent of it.

A wave broke. Nick recoiled along the compound wall, his helmet smacking Mohammad hard on the jaw. The interpreter bit off the tip of his tongue. Both men flailed and grunted. Neither man's senses were yet ready to process anything other than the mass of noise and pressure that had just cannoned down the alleyway.

Eventually, while rolling onto his side, trying to gather his wits, an inhuman scream reached through Nick's liquid deafness. He could see nothing. The moon had ducked behind a thick curtain of dust. His mouth had been invaded by grit. Other oaths and profanities filtered through. Sultan was talking to himself in Dari. A firm hand found Nick's shoulder.

'Sir! Sir, it's Mac. You OK?'

Nick now recalled that Mac had been at the rear.

'Yeah… I'm just a bit winded… wait.' Weakly, Nick fumbled for his radio and transmitted. 'Zero… this is Four-Two Alpha… contact. Contact IED, over.'

The screaming seized their attention. Mac was first forward into the steadily thinning dust cloud, wraithlike. Nick turned to Mohammad, who was spitting a thick black glob of blood from his mouth, congealed with dirt.

'Tell Sultan to watch our backs.' There was no response. 'Mohammad!' Nick poked him with a fist and pointed. 'Sultan. You and Sultan. Watch that way.' Without waiting for acknowledgement he followed Mac, urgency marshalling his faculties.

They reached Brogan first, sitting against the wall in the attitude of a beggar or a drunk. He was not the source of the agonised entreaties.

'I think I've got some crap in my leg sir… But… Get to Steveo. I'm fine.'

Stephens lay a few yards further on, writhing on his back, trying to squirm away from the pain in his shattered leg. Nick dropped to his knees.

'Find Langers Mac,' he said.

Nick put a hand to Stephens' face to gain his attention.

'Steveo! You're OK mate, it's Captain Russell. Try and take it. Fight it.'

He removed the soldier's ballistic glasses and stuck one of the ear bars into his mouth.

'Bite on that Steveo. I'll sort you with morphine. Just hang on.'

Nick did not really know where to start. Morphine was almost certainly not wise. Stephens' entire right side was a mess. His neck bled profusely. His right arm was limp and pulpy. There was a dark stain in his armpit above the body armour. When Nick's hands reached Stephens' right leg, he saw that there was only bone going into the boot. In the darkness, Stephens' trousers, thigh and the sandy road all merged into one. Blood flowed over the back of Nick's glove and he felt its warm wetness on his wrist. He could smell it, thick and human. Stephens' other leg twitched and kicked – bleeding but at least still recognisable.

'Please.' It was all Stephens could muster between gasps, lisping through the hard bite on plastic.

Unzipping Stephens' medical pouch, Nick pulled out a tourniquet and two field dressings.

'Mac! What about Langers?' Nick yearned for the sergeant's grip. For his answers. The soldier failed to respond so Nick looked up. Mac was standing over a body so inert and dusty that it could have been there for days.

'It doesn't look like Langers sir. Perhaps he's Taliban...'

Nick did not know how to respond. The anguish lunged up and barbed in his throat. He had to resist a howl. Never in his life had he wanted more to be somewhere else – anywhere else. Every single day lived so far, the blissful to the painful, even that impossibly burdensome childhood summer he had carried so long, fused into one warm image. It became a single, soft focus of memory, and declared itself preferable to this moment, this street, this night.

And then, somehow, through Stephens' strident agonies and his own turmoil, Nick felt something heavy dropping to the ground off to his right-hand side, like an apple in an orchard.

His self-pity was barged out of the way: a flying tackle of martial instinct. Suddenly, inside a millisecond, Nick read their situation perfectly, from the last chapter to the first. He had indeed failed. The assault on Gul Khan was a 'come-on'. This mine blast was an ambush. And now the inevitable effort to save their friend was being punished by the fighters lying in wait.

The apple was a grenade.

Nick had already lunged – unthinkingly – to protect Stephens with his body and heard himself screaming a hoarse 'grenade!' at the top of his breaking voice. He caught a glimpse of Mac diving away, just as the grenade detonated with a slamming, bass 'hhhhhunk'. Strangely it was his proximity to the blast that saved Nick. The shrapnel flew up and over him.

Then there was the banging of rifle fire, close and sharp, coming from behind. Twisting around, Nick saw it was Brogan, leaning around the corner where Sultan and Mohammad were.

'Pat! Pat!' Nick shouted. 'Get a grenade into it! They're in that compound!'

Nick was back in full plane. Up onto his knees, he directed cracked screams at Mac. 'Mac! Help me with Steveo!' His own voice reached him from inside his body; his ears singing a single ringing tone.

Grabbing the shoulder straps of Stephens' body armour, Nick commenced a laboured drag back towards the corner; rump first, in the posture of labourers pulling heavy sacks off the flatbed of a goods vehicle. When Mac joined him, Nick was able to release one arm and started firing blindly and haphazardly at the roof. Stephens left a dark wake in the alley.

As they passed the corner, Nick saw Brogan standing in the junction, his arm drawn back to throw.

'Grenade!' He screamed more with venom than caution. Brogan grunted as it left his arm, like a tennis player serving in the final set. Resisting the temptation to admire his handiwork, Brogan brought his rifle back up and loosed-off two parting shots before turning to take cover. Numbed by adrenaline, he had forgotten the injuries to his leg. But now the wounds asserted themselves. The damaged leg buckled under the extra weight placed upon it as Brogan spun around. He faltered.

Nick was already around the corner when the flashes of incoming fire flickered. A tracer round zipped away into the night, wildly free of the catastrophe unfolding on this nondescript junction.

But one of its companions found Brogan.

He flopped into the road in front of Nick at the same time as his defiant grenade went off with a crash in the compound beyond.

Brogan crawled for a yard or so into cover before losing all energy. He pulled his head back towards Nick and declared, in the most emotionless, matter-of-fact way, 'I'm hit.'

There was almost a lull until Sultan appeared alongside, discharging an entire magazine from his rifle without any pause.

The bright muzzle blasts lit up his grimacing countenance in freeze-frame animation. Mac laboured with Stephens, trying to fit a tourniquet, while Nick sprang forward to check on Brogan.

'Where Pat? Where are you hit?'

Nick lifted Brogan's head. It lolled, heavy and unsupported, like an infant's. His eyes were open: fixed and unblinking.

'Pat! Come back.'

Wherever Brogan had gone, he had taken Stephens with him.

'Sir…' It was Mac. He seemed hesitant to break the news, as if that would make it real – irrevocable.

'Steveo's…' He searched in vain for an appropriate euphemism. Never the most articulate of soldiers, Mac was the type that inserted 'fucking' where most people would use 'um'. Eventually he fell back on what the institution provisioned for such situations.

'Steveo's KIA.'

Nick looked about. Sultan held the corner, punctuating the silence with snapped, vindictive single shots. Mac knelt over Stephens with his palms open – weary and supplicant as an exhausted pilgrim.

'How are you Mac?' Nick asked.

'I copped some of that grenade sir, in my arm. But I'm good to go.' The bravest of lies.

Mohammad's mouth continued to bleed heavily. If he could speak he was choosing not to.

It was finished.

'Sarbaz! Sarbaz the Vigilant! Are you back there?'

The answer sounded closer than Haji Mansur expected. 'As ever Haji Sahib.'

'Well come around and guard the gate. We have our prize.'

Gul Khan lay on his side, facing away from Haji Mansur. His breath came in sickly wheezes. It was impossible to tell where he was hit. He wore a dark waistcoat over his pale shalwaz. But by the sound of it, Haji Mansur knew he must have put at least one bullet through Gul Khan's chest. Haji Mansur kept his weapon trained on Gul Khan's back while he stooped to pick up the Kalashnikov that lay close by. Dangling it by the sling, he swung the rifle round to a safe distance.

'Brother. Did you not know it would come to this?'

Extending a foot more gingerly than the confidence of his tone suggested, Haji Mansur rolled Gul Khan onto his back. The unbuttoned waistcoat revealed a dark stain. Even in the moonlight it was possible to discern the shallow rise and fall of his ribcage, accompanied by crackling rasps. Haji Mansur continued his rhetorical admonishment, relishing the opportunity for theatre.

'What was all that for Gul Khan? Where was your loyalty? Loyalty to your kin... To your faith... How much, I wonder, were they paying you?'

Finally, Gul Khan managed to speak, in a pained whisper.

'You... You are the only... one... who ever... had... to pay me.'

Haji Mansur drew breath but was interrupted by a shriek and commotion coming from the rooms behind him. The Mehsud emerged triumphant, full of spite with a woman and child. The long-haired fighter let out a haughty cry.

'Look! Livestock!'

Gul Khan squeezed his eyes shut and Haji Mansur pitied his infantile escapism. The woman stared straight ahead, humming some kind of lullaby. The boy whimpered and sniffled at the sight of his mortally wounded father. Haji Mansur could see this colliding with a deluge of terrifying imaginings about what might come next. But now was not the time for empathy. It was the time for a hard heart.

'I gave you an offer Gul Khan, and you refused it. There is no greater sin than Pride.'

Finding his stride in the role he ascribed himself, Haji Mansur happened on a piece of pure, perfect malice. Slinging his own weapon, he picked up Gul Khan's.

'She dies with your own rifle brother. That way you know it was your hand – your choices – that brought it upon her.'

There was no ceremony and no pause. Judging his cue, the Mehsud shoved the woman forwards and kicked the back of her legs so that she dropped onto her knees.

'I couldn't leave you my love,' the woman said, calm and clear. 'I was scared.'

She was handsome, though the darkness was no doubt being kind to her years. Haji Mansur realised suddenly how few women he had actually seen in the flesh like this. His own wife appeared before him, her hair of similar length. *Stop thinking man. Just do. The woman is complicit.*

As he raised Gul Khan's weapon to the back of her head the boy started screaming, 'Adi, Adi!'

Softly she uttered, very quickly, 'We will touch again in paradise my love.'

Haji Mansur wondered whether she was talking to Gul Khan, her son or both.

A powerful thud rocked the compound and Haji Mansur flinched. From the direction of the gate he heard Sarbaz yelp with glee and call out. 'That'll be Sadiq, Haji Sahib!'

'Your friends Gul Khan. Delayed now I think,' Haji Mansur said.

He tingled with the satisfaction of victory. Mullah Elam was right to show faith in him, just as Haji Mansur was right to have faith in Allah's will.

Using this moment of elation to distract himself, he pulled the trigger.

The boy's shock lasted for perhaps a second before his screaming started afresh, more intense than before. Gul Khan was trying to call out, to speak. His hand pawed towards where the woman lay, still. Whatever it was Gul Khan said, the boy drowned him out.

'Right Haji Sahib. One more, and we're done.' The Mehsud pushed the boy down into the same position his mother had adopted. A skinny arm reached for her hem. This gesture – the desperate snatch for some vestige of maternal contact – cracked Haji Mansur.

'Not the boy. He's too young.' He turned to the anguished child. 'Listen to me. You're to go to your cousins. Do you hear? Now say goodbye to your father.'

There was muscular disagreement from the Mehsud, who placed his rifle across the boy's chest as a symbolic block. 'With respect Haji Sahib, the boy is old enough. Mullah Elam's instructions to me were clear. Besides, he will grow and take revenge, on you, on us. That is my cousin lying over there. A man I will be forced to leave here, without the honour of burying. Let us finish this thing properly and be on our way before the planes arrive with their missiles.'

There was the crump of a grenade and then firing, closer than they had appreciated before. Sarbaz voiced shrill encouragement from his vigil at the gates.

The Mehsud continued. 'You see. We don't have time for this.'

'Do you really think either of us will be alive…' Haji Mansur gesticulated towards the fighting. '…When this boy becomes a man? I won't let you do it. Only I answer to Mullah Elam in this valley.'

'And I have my instructions. These people must know the price of collaboration.'

Another grenade crumped.

Haji Mansur weighed up the stakes. He could kill the thug and nobody in the Movement would be any the wiser. Sarbaz was loyal. The Mehsud might be thinking the very same thing right now. But he would have to tackle Sarbaz as well. Haji Mansur had the upper hand.

'I've made my decision. Harm that boy and I'll send you to Allah.'

He could see the Mehsud tensed with indignation, trying to balance emotion with reason. These mountain people were dangerously proud. Suddenly Haji Mansur remembered that he was holding Gul Khan's weapon. How many bullets were left? At least one but… Might he be punished for his earlier malice? *So soon?* How a man must be wary of exceeding Allah's guidance – of taking what he knows to be right, and stretching it to fit his own whims and designs.

The impasse yawned.

Then Sarbaz hailed someone. 'You! Stay there! You have no business here!'

Both men switched their attentions. The sentry's edgy

challenge forced the shift. It cannot have been foreigners or they would be in a sharp fight already. Haji Mansur was reminded that this was taking far too long. Sadiq may already be on the move back to their rendezvous. His firing had slackened off.

Another voice reached them from over the wall, pensive and speculative. 'It's Janan! Gul Khan's cousin.'

Sarbaz relaxed. 'You've played your part. Come back when we're gone.'

'I just wanted to... I thought...'

'Well we're still here aren't we? There will be plenty of time for digging later.'

Haji Mansur seized on the confusion, wrenching the boy free of the Mehsud and kicking him away. 'Go! I won't tell you again.' He shouted over the wall. 'Janan! The boy is coming out.'

The Mehsud clawed for the last word. 'Mullah Elam will hear of this Haji Sahib.'

'So be it brother. Whatever you feel you must do.'

A profound weariness spread into Haji Mansur's bones, turning the marrow to lead. He saw how shallow his earlier jubilance had been, how pointless. What sort of victory had he secured here tonight, when a boy watches his mother's brains propelled out the front of her face?

He noticed for the first time that Gul Khan had died all this while. The boy was shaking him, trying to mine some kind of farewell, precious enough to carry for the rest of his life.

Haji Mansur's theatre seemed even more arrogant to him suddenly: his desire for a form of justice that would grow with the telling, spreading fear. His only tool was retribution. Perhaps a necessary form of order, so every wrong is avenged on earth. But it was for Allah to make the *real* judgements, the divine judgements. The man lying at his feet was a corpse. Mute. Haji Mansur would never know whether Gul Khan had felt resignation, regret, contrition or even defiance with his final pathetic breaths. Nobody would ever know. Only Allah.

Yes, he thought, *I must trust in Allah*. If he places his hand on my heart, as he did tonight, I will always listen. It is right to interpret his will when one can. But always bend to it when one feels lost, however momentarily.

He placed Gul Khan's rifle down and removed the Pakol from under his heavy head. Inside it was still warm.

'Here boy. Feel that. It's your father's life. Not much, but something. Now go to Janan.'

Abruptly, Haji Mansur stood to his full height and set off at a run, beckoning the Mehsud to follow.

'Are you seeing those weapons Corporal Wilkes? It's so easy to mislead yourself with these bloody heat signatures.'

The major leaned closer to the monitor and traced the small white figures with his finger. Three men had linked up with another four in some kind of orchard and then broken off into two groups again, though not necessarily in the same compositions as they arrived. There was no sign of the AGS. That must have been extracted much earlier. With only the one helicopter on station they were forced to choose between the two groups. It made sense to favour the larger one, especially since they seemed more encumbered.

'I see them sir. Look!' The controller picked the second man in the striding column and sketched around him with the tip of a propelling pencil. 'He's got a long-barrelled weapon, in the trail. You can spot the curve of the magazine when it swings forward... there.'

In one sense it could be whatever you wanted it to be. But the major agreed. People seldom carried a shovel that way either. The farmers generally put them on their shoulder, like labourers the world over.

Everybody else in the operations room was silent and it weighed on the major – the pressure for payback, to level the scoreboard. They all wanted this to be the team that hit Captain Russell.

On hearing that three of his men had been killed, the major had swallowed – literally swallowed – the emotion that tried to force its way up his gullet, into his eyes and nose. Only through two gulps and a curt clearing of the throat had he managed to maintain his external poise. With all eyes on him, it felt like being afflicted with a dry, tickly cough during the slow movement of a concert. The loss of Sergeant Langdon reached deepest. Langers was a private in the major's very first command, as a young lieutenant. Fifteen years they had soldiered together. You know a man after that. You have watched him eat, sleep, bathe, shit, rage, laugh. Maybe even cry.

But he had to be sure. This was no time for blind punches.

The white group stopped. Their leader was looking for something. 'It must be a cache of some description,' offered Corporal Wilkes.

He was right. The camera shifted angle as the unseen drone changed course. Now the leader was stooped over what looked like a trapdoor. More weapons came out. 'Perhaps they are re-arming to hit us again?' It was the second-in-command this time. The major knew what his deputy was doing. If that was the case it would enhance their justification to strike.

'This is enough for me.' The major stood back from the screen. 'You have my authority Corporal Wilkes. Vector and hand this off to the Apache crew. My initials Juliet, Papa, Lima. Let's be quick about it.'

He turned to the throng in the ops room, scanning for anyone who had no concrete business there. These things were not a form of entertainment. The suggestion of vengeance tonight made that doubly relevant.

Corporal Wilkes conversed with the pilot inside his headset. They could only hear one side of the conversation. 'Roger. I read back "weapons hot, engaging with cannon", over.'

The major watched these four bleached figures living their last few seconds on planet earth. There was something arresting about the heat sources – their individual metabolisms, each a miracle of nature, host to their souls. Right this second they were still digesting food, growing hair, creating thoughts… Each source of warmth, its own complex little universe.

There was no sound, only images. The cannon fire arrived as sparking showers, like fireworks. Their targets tried to disperse. Two were visibly only chunks of meat now, spread around the orchard. The crew put another burst in and caught the man trying to sprint directly away from the incoming fire. He was shredded apart. Laconically, Corporal Wilkes gave some advice to the pilot over the radio.

'That's three. The fourth was hit I think. Shift your sights… wait… east and you'll see him.'

There is something feral in the way wounded men try and grovel to refuge. It always reminded the major of an unclean shot into a deer – on their knees so unexpectedly, their brains transmitting the signal to flee, but the body failing. The cannon shells were oblivious to this fighter's limping resolve. His primal determination won him another five seconds. Then he too was scattered across their image.

Did the person who made those shells ever wonder which ones would travel to the other side of the world and rip a man limb from limb? This was the price of such cold forms of killing. It either made you think too much or, in the case of others the major knew, not enough.

Time to move on.

'OK Corporal Wilkes. Good work. See if they have enough fuel to sweep back and look for the other group.'

Nick was relieved to have Company Sergeant Major Barnct travelling with the reaction force. He would know what to do with Langers and the others. His paternal voice had come through Nick's earpiece again, measured and confident, establishing the stricken party's precise whereabouts.

The four survivors left their friends in the places they lay, and concentrated on securing the shabby street corner where their fortunes had culminated. Despite the difficulties in finding one, salvation arrived first in the shape of an Apache. It spotted the enemy fighters withdrawing. That was the priority. There was no time to sweep Gul Khan's compound. Nick switched on a 'Firefly' – an infrared strobe beacon – to be sure they were not mistaken for Taliban. They heard the chatter of the helicopter's cannon, preaching the power and invulnerability of everything it represented.

There was not long to wait after that. The street being too

narrow for vehicles, their relief arrived on foot, brisk but not panicked.

His comrades seemed foreign to Nick, clean and unblemished, almost naive. Irrespective of how much they all had in common, there was now an impossible gulf between them: those who had been in Shingazi that night, and those that had not. This was a nuance of their unique dialect.

The company sergeant major knelt down next to Nick.

'Rough night eh Captain Russell?'

'It's good to see you.'

'I had nothing else planned.' He reached out and put his hand on Nick's shoulder. 'Listen sir. I want you to know, I'd have done the same thing. We all would've.'

'Can you do me a favour, Sergeant Major? Take me up there now. Let me see him.'

'Langers?'

'No. I don't want that. I want his memory to be the whiteness.'

'I'm not sure I follow you sir.' The patience felt like two men lifting Nick's arms in support.

'Gul Khan. Take me there. It's only a hundred yards up that way.' Nick pointed vaguely towards the moon.

'I'm sorry sir. There'll be time for that tomorrow. Best you come with us now.'

Afterword

In the quiet hours, then as now, I have pondered how to relate such a stark reality as warfare. For a witness, returning diminished to places of relative peace and plenty, it seems the most human and constructive thing you can do.

I have chosen to use fiction because it allows for an intimacy and honesty which a memoir of my time in Afghanistan would have lacked. Reading my thin 'bluey' acrogrammes all these years later – very like the ones replicated in this book – I can see the deliberate gaps clearly. It is the sort of content I would redact just as carefully now, to shield myself and others. Conversely, fiction creates freedoms. By focusing on a few single events, it encapsulates. It has allowed me to describe specific thoughts, behaviours, and suffering that I would not feel comfortable attributing to the living, or the dead.

But fiction's most important freedom was to see through the eyes of Afghans. For all the commentary from that long conflict, their perspective has not enjoyed balance. Yet I passed as much time communing and working with Afghans as I did with people of my own provenance. I met members of the Taliban too – mostly unknowingly, for they lived among us. But also, in some instances, explicitly. They were moments rich in insight. I could never relate the war in those villages faithfully without Afghan pain, conflictions and contradictions joining our own. Doubtless my attempts to voice their viewpoints will be distorted to some degree. But I am indebted to the Pashtun interpreters who read those passages, and put their seal of approval on them.

All soldiers have a lot in common too, and the British ones on these pages speak from a deep reserve of personal experience. If there's one abiding feature of life in the infantry, it is physical proximity. The years I spent in that world created friendships and confidences that could never have existed otherwise; at least not in that form. The infantry has given me the best and worst days of my life, often in the same waking period. The major sums it up well, as he chokes on the loss of Sergeant Langdon. I too have swallowed those moments. Many of us bear the so-called 'invisible bag', and will do for as long as we draw breath.

Hence I am choosing to stay anonymous. My own reckoning with those years lodges in a shuttered room. Nor do I want people who knew me seeking themselves or others in this book. Nonetheless, my hope is that anyone who experienced some of these things first-hand will recognise many of the characters' reactions and reflections. In this, perhaps they now feel less alone. For those who have not experienced such things, I trust it has opened a window onto our otherwise unapproachable world.

It is, of course, still just a story: a piece of drama, with all the inherent limitations that brings. But I have tried to make its authenticity my most important consideration. None of it happened; yet in other ways and guises it did. It is the closest, fairest testimony I can muster. The landscape is real and the people are faithful to their – our – very human nature. That is, ultimately, what war expresses.

Edward King (not his real name) saw extensive service in Afghanistan. All royalties from this book will be split between military mental health and Afghan aid charities.